OUT OF
THE DARK

OUT OF THE DARK

Heidi Amsinck

MUSWELL
PRESS

First published by Muswell Press in 2025
Copyright © Heidi Amsinck 2025 by agreement with Grand Agency

Typeset in Bembo by M Rules
Printed by CPI Group (UK) Ltd, Croydon CR0 4YY

A CIP record for this book is available from the British Library

ISBN: 9781068684418
eISBN: 9781068684425

Muswell Press, London N6 5HQ
www.muswell-press.co.uk

Our authorised representative in the EU for product safety is
Easy Access System Europe, Mustamäe tee 50, 10621 Tallinn, Estonia
gpsr.requests@easproject.com

To Nick

December

Day One

1

Detective Inspector Henrik Jungersen counted to three, flung open his car door and sprinted for the wrought-iron gates at the entrance to Ørstedsparken.

At least the rain kept the ghouls away, he thought as he nodded at the unlucky cop on guard duty and slipped inside the park.

The TV news crews were staying in their vans, watching from behind steamed-up windows.

Good.

He had no answers anyway.

One question had been gnawing at his brain all morning: how was it possible to abduct a child in the middle of Copenhagen, barely a couple of hundred yards from a busy metro station, shops and fast-food restaurants, without anyone noticing?

Nine-year-old Matilde Clausen had been missing for seventeen hours.

The playground, dug into the slope between the street and the large, vaguely boomerang-shaped lake in the middle of the park, was now a crime scene. As Henrik descended into the sandy hollow surrounded by trees and shrubbery, Detective Sergeant Mark Søndergreen came rushing towards him with an umbrella.

His face mirrored Henrik's strong sense that something was horribly wrong.

Every parent's worst nightmare.

'They haven't found anything, Boss,' said Mark, gesturing at the technicians working in among the trees.

Henrik wasn't surprised. Trampled on by dozens of kids and parents and soaked in overnight rain, the ground was unlikely to yield anything useful. But they had to try. 'At this stage, nothing is irrelevant,' he had told his team of investigators at the morning briefing.

The mobile phone Matilde had been given for her ninth birthday despite her mother's protests was switched off, last detected inside the park a few minutes after she went missing. If they found it, they might be able to determine if she had been in touch with anyone of potential interest.

'Give me a moment,' said Henrik as he sheltered under Mark's umbrella with the rain hammering on the canopy.

His jeans and boots were soaked, and water was trickling inside the collar of his shirt and down his back. He welcomed the icy sensation; he needed to stay awake, alert.

The past few months were a blur, a blank nothingness of training, shifts and paperwork.

Little daylight penetrated the thick cloud. The opposite end of Ørstedsparken, a sunken oasis of tranquillity close to Nørreport Station, was lost in the misty gloom.

You could almost feel it, the northern hemisphere hurtling towards the point furthest from the sun. The Christmas lights that had sprung up all over the city made a flimsy defence against the enveloping darkness.

Henrik tried to imagine what the playground would have been like yesterday afternoon, with screaming children crawling on the timber frame and being pushed on the swings by adults chatting and warming their hands on takeaway coffees.

It had been brighter then, a brief respite from the perpetual winter rain, but bitterly cold. The park would have looked beautiful, the light from the setting sun glinting off the surface of the lake, the old roofs and spires of the city just visible beyond the tree-lined perimeter.

'Talk to me,' he said finally, turning to Mark who had been waiting patiently, knowing better than to interrupt his boss when he was getting his bearings.

Good old Mark. Younger and fitter than him, energetic, loyal and hardworking. Did as he was told, a forgotten virtue in society at large, Henrik had always felt.

Mark had been a godsend after the turbulent events of the summer, quietly holding him up whenever he felt his knees buckling under him.

Above all, Mark knew when to keep his mouth shut and when to speak.

'Stine Clausen . . . she's the mother . . . was sitting over there, with Matilde's half-brother asleep in the pram,' said Mark.

He pointed to a wooden picnic table decorated with graffiti and Henrik was reminded that Ørstedsparken was open twenty-four hours. It was also widely known in Copenhagen as a gay cruising spot. Had been for more than 150 years. In his time, Henrik had dealt with rapes here, and a few stabbings, but never a missing child. Usually, such cases were solved before they reached his desk.

'And where was Matilde?' he said.

'In there apparently.' Mark gestured at the area of trees and bushes close to the picnic table, a mixture of evergreens and naked branches with a few yellow leaves clinging on for dear life.

Henrik had read in the notes that Matilde was a shy child, slight for her age. He frowned. 'What was she doing in there?'

Mark shrugged.

'And Stine?' said Henrik.

'On her phone, apparently. She would check now and again for Matilde, looking for her red coat, but then the baby began to cry, and she got busy settling him. When she looked up again, she couldn't see her daughter.'

For how long had she been preoccupied? Henrik wondered. Phones made people deaf and blind; they got sucked in, forgot their surroundings.

('You should know,' said his wife in his head.)

He kept meaning to put his phone away, to stop scrolling, but it had been like a compulsion in him lately, a shield against his thoughts and, God forbid, having to talk.

There had been other people in the park yesterday, lots of potential witnesses, and no one had reported seeing a little girl dragged off against her will. Someone Matilde knew then?

The distance from the playground to the nearest road made it hard to see how it could have been an opportunist move. It must have been planned meticulously, rehearsed even.

He rubbed his hand over the rough skin of his scalp and face. 'And then what?'

'Stine wasn't too worried at first,' said Mark. 'Only when Matilde didn't respond to her calls did she begin to panic. Other parents joined the search. They ran all over the park, and after about fifteen minutes, Stine called the police. It was almost completely dark by then.'

Henrik didn't have to imagine that part. He could feel the primal fear of it, hear the increasingly desperate cries for Matilde echoing between the trees, the scene transformed from serenity to terror in a heartbeat.

'The first uniforms were here in eight minutes and more arrived after that,' Mark said. 'They sealed off the playground and closed the park. The rest you know.'

Yeah, thought Henrik. *The rest is a big fat zero.*

The overnight response by operational command at Bellahøj police station had been textbook; he couldn't fault it. The trouble was that none of it had worked.

Henrik looked at the lake, wondering if they would have to get the divers out.

Mark read his mind. 'Matilde had been told not to go near the water under any circumstances.'

Since when did kids do as they're told? Henrik thought.

But he didn't truly believe the girl had drowned in the lake. It was more likely that she had left by the nearest exit to the playground, on the corner of Ahlefeldtsgade and Nørre Farimagsgade.

Alone or with someone.

Voluntarily or by force.

Most of the people who had been in the park when Matilde disappeared would have left by the time the police arrived. They needed those potential witnesses to come forward.

He looked at his phone, seeing missed calls from several crime reporters.

Jensen was a crime reporter, and knew his number, but she hadn't called.

7

For months now, they had managed to avoid each other.

In the summer, when Jensen's attempt to build a life with a new boyfriend had ended in disaster, he had been glad, hoping things could now go back to normal between them.

Until she had told him that she was pregnant and keeping the baby.

Jensen as a mother? It was unthinkable.

And it had changed everything.

Dreaming that he and Jensen might one day be together had made his marriage tolerable, like the possibility of escape, however remote, keeping a prisoner from abandoning all hope.

Now, the dream was dead. There would always be a child between him and Jensen.

Another man's child.

The child of a psychopath.

He hadn't known what else to do but throw himself into work – the more work the better.

He sighed, considering whether to return the reporters' calls. The media would spread the word faster, encouraging witnesses to come forward, and he needed that, but was loath to get drawn into speculation about what might or might not have happened.

Seeing everyone in one go would save time.

And Jensen might come.

Her baby was due soon, but if he knew her at all, she would be working until she went into labour, possibly beyond it. The thought made him smile, despite himself.

'Get the press department to call a doorstep,' he said to Mark. 'As soon as possible.'

Mark shuffled his feet, too polite to remind Henrik

that his boss, Superintendent Jens Wiese, was wary of him addressing the press.

Wiese was wary of him full stop.

If it were up to Wiese, he would only see daylight, muzzled and on a tight leash, when strictly necessary.

'You weren't my first choice,' Wiese had said that morning when he had assigned Henrik as lead investigator on the Matilde case.

Wiese needed good statistics but held his nose when it came to the grime and chaos of real-life police work.

Henrik knew it wasn't always pretty.

'I need this one handled sensitively,' Wiese had said. 'A missing child this close to Christmas is bound to cause a lot of fear. Her parents are beside themselves with worry. I don't want you crashing about in your size tens causing chaos.'

Henrik had blinked at him innocently. 'Why do you assume I'm going to?'

'I've been watching you, Jungersen,' Wiese replied. 'You're stressed, erratic, on edge. When did you last take leave?'

'I don't remember,' he said. 'But as you pointed out yourself, we're busy, so what are you going to do, send me home?'

Wiese had scowled at him, but Henrik knew he had no choice. There were just three lead investigators in Copenhagen's violent crime unit, and Jonas and Lotte, his peers, were both up to their necks in cases.

He turned to Mark. 'Just do it. I can handle the media.'

Just as well Jensen wasn't here to hear him say that. He could see her face now, hands on hips, dark-blue eyes flashing at him angrily.

Those eyes.

Stop it, Jungersen.

He shook his head again, and began to walk towards the nearest exit, with Mark hot on his heels.

'Get back to work, everyone,' he shouted gruffly. 'Let's find Matilde.'

2

The chatter around *Dagbladet*'s meeting table died instantly when Margrethe stepped through the door, tall and broad, dressed in a navy-blue blazer with a silver brooch.

For all the joy she spread in the room, she might as well have worn a black cloak and carried a scythe.

Someone had brought in an advent candle stuck in clay and decorated with fir branches and spray-on snow. The work of a nursery child, Jensen guessed.

It seemed inappropriate now, a pathetic gesture in the face of *Dagbladet*'s existential crisis.

After its takeover by a Swedish venture capital fund, the paper had seemed to turn a corner, but the positive momentum hadn't lasted. Rumours had been circulating for weeks that the Swedes had lost patience and were looking for further cut-backs.

The production of the print edition had already been outsourced to an agency, only a few subs remained, and repeated rounds of redundancies had reduced the editorial staff to a skeleton crew.

The pressure told on the faces of the journalists assembled

around the beaten-up boardroom table. What was going to happen next? For how much longer could they carry on?

'We're going all out on the Matilde Clausen story,' said Margrethe, her figure casting a shadow across the print copies scattered in front of her.

Jensen's article about the missing nine-year-old had made it onto the front page minutes before deadline last night but in the bottom corner, below a story about flooding caused by weeks of heavy rain.

By now, Matilde was the *only* story. Her smiling face, adult front teeth just poking through the gums, stared out from every digital front page in the land. She looked younger than her years, her white-blonde hair scraped back with a plastic tiara.

'What do we know?' said Margrethe.

Jensen felt her colleagues turn to stare at her. Her hair was still wet after the bike ride from Margrethe's flat in Østerbro, her sweatshirt soaked through where her coat would no longer do up.

'Very little,' she said. 'The police have just called a press conference.'

'Does that mean they've found her?' said Margrethe.

'More likely the opposite,' said Jensen. 'They'll be appealing to the public for help.'

'So, what's the plan?' said Margrethe.

'Find out if they have any theories about what happened, try to speak to Matilde's family, her school, neighbours, friends,' said Jensen.

All of it seemed inadequate.

'I want regular updates throughout the day. Give it everything you've got,' said Margrethe.

Jensen nodded, refreshing the feed on her phone for the hundredth time.

Still no news.

The baby kicked, startling her. She looked at her bump, watching as it shifted and moved under her jumper. It still felt unreal, like her body belonged to someone else.

She had been seven weeks gone by the time she found out she was pregnant. Not too late to have an abortion, as the doctor had pointed out when Jensen had told her that the father was no longer around.

The fact that he was a murderer awaiting trial was something she had kept to herself.

She hadn't so much decided to keep the baby, as drifted past the twelve-week point of no return without deciding. How could she, knowing that it might be her only chance to have a child?

Margrethe had taken her in when she had lost her home back in the summer. It was supposed to have been for a few weeks, but Jensen hadn't managed to find a flat within a reasonable cycling distance of the newspaper. At least, not one she could afford on her single income.

No matter which way she looked at it, her situation was dire. No home of her own, no partner, and a baby arriving in a couple of months.

Her year in Copenhagen was starting to look like a failed experiment.

She could go back to London, lose herself in the anonymity of a city with almost twice the population of Denmark. The container with her belongings was already there; she had returned it just a few months after first arriving in Copenhagen, convinced she wouldn't be staying. It had felt right to keep things temporary, to be able to leave quickly if a time came when it all got too much.

Such as now.

She spent the rest of the editorial meeting scrolling

through the Danish news sites, quickly concluding that no one had any more information than she did on Matilde Clausen's disappearance.

The TV news channels were all showing the same looped footage of officers moving in the rain behind the taped-off entry to Ørstedsparken.

When Margrethe slammed shut the black spiral notebook in which she orchestrated the news of the day, people quickly scrambled to their feet, relieved to have made it through another meeting without some grim announcement.

Margrethe cleared her throat loudly. 'Wait,' she shouted. 'There's more.'

The room fell silent, a collective suspension of breath. Outside, across the square with the giant Christmas tree, the bells in the City Hall tower began to strike the hour.

'As you know,' Margrethe began, 'we've cut our overheads significantly in the past year, but I'm afraid we must tighten our belts further.'

Were more people about to be sacked? Or would the rumours that the Swedes were dropping *Dagbladet*'s print edition finally turn out to be true?

'Hear me out,' Margrethe said, raising her voice above the anxious mumbling. 'As there are fewer of us now, we must shrink our footprint. Come the New Year, we'll be renting out the top floor of this building.'

A sigh of relief went round the table; everyone had imagined something far worse.

Everyone but Jensen.

She stared at Margrethe in disbelief. Her private room in the warren of corridors under the eaves where journalists had once been milling in and out of each other's smoke-filled offices to the tap-tap sound of typewriters had been her sanctuary, a safe space where she could ease her way into newspaper life after years of solitude as a foreign correspondent.

'To whom?' she said.

'A technology start-up. I forget the name,' said Margrethe, with a dismissive wave.

That figured. *Dagbladet* was yielding ground, literally, to the digital juggernaut that was threatening to obliterate it.

Margrethe pushed out her chin. 'The few of you still up there will need to be out by Christmas for the refurbishment to start.'

'But what about Henning?' said Jensen, clutching at straws. 'What's he going to say when he comes back and finds some baby-faced coder in his office?' The former editor who had come out of retirement to become *Dagbladet*'s obituary writer was still off work after a stroke in the summer. His office was across the hall from Jensen's.

'Henning won't be *coming* back,' said Margrethe. 'As you'd know if you'd seen him lately.'

Jensen bit her lip. She had visited the old man a few times in the concrete towers at Riget, the national hospital in the middle of the city, but not for a while now. She had assumed that he was recovering, that she would hear his slow, shuffling footsteps in the corridor any day now.

'We're also going to be doubling down on our digital strategy,' said Margrethe. 'We'll be stepping up video production, in addition to our podcasting. I'd like you to meet Jannik Fogh, who's joining us today in a new role of video editor,' said Margrethe with a sweeping motion of her left hand.

A muscular, red-bearded man in his thirties, wearing a black Copenhell festival T-shirt and combat trousers, stood up from where he had been resting on a windowsill, behind a pillar, and took a bow. Jensen hadn't noticed him before.

'We're going after a younger readership, and Jannik will be working closely with our social media team to make sure we reach them,' said Margrethe.

People around the table were nodding and smiling, and Jannik was beaming at them in return.

Jensen was frozen to her chair. Until a few months ago, Margrethe's teenage nephew, Gustav, had been creating *Dagbladet*'s videos, working as Jensen's unpaid journalist trainee after getting expelled from school.

She had been reluctant at first, but they had made a good team, notching up a handful of scoops between them.

The office had fallen quiet after he had returned to high school. She missed him terribly: his big mouth, his crazy ideas, even his incessant vaping.

'Oh, and Jensen,' said Margrethe as she gathered her papers, notebook and phone and rose to her feet, 'Jannik will be joining you in covering the Matilde case.'

Across the room, where he was busy shaking the hands of his new colleagues who had got out of their seats to welcome him, Jannik met Jensen's eye and winked.

3

The door to the second-floor flat in Kleinsgade was ajar. Low voices came from inside, mixed with the kind of anguished sobbing that Henrik had heard too many times in his life.

Mark knocked politely on the door. 'Hello?' he said.

Henrik pushed past him, following the voices as he picked his way through the jumble of boots and bags in the hallway, sidestepping the pram that took up most of the space.

The living room fell quiet when he entered, everyone looking up at him anxiously. He raised his hands, wanting to get the disappointment out of the way quickly. 'We don't have Matilde yet, I'm afraid.'

There was an audible exhalation.

The room was dominated by a giant TV, the sleek modern interior fighting a losing battle with baby paraphernalia and a set of hefty dumbbells in the corner.

In the centre of the sofa, a slight woman with thickly drawn eyebrows and dark hair tied into a ponytail was slumped over, crying miserably. She was clutching a soft toy, a blue rabbit. By her side, holding her hand, sat who Henrik assumed to be the owner of the weight-lifting equipment: a tall, red-faced, muscular man with crew-cut blond hair and a stubbly beard. Both his arms were covered in Viking tattoos.

An older woman, the grandmother perhaps, stood by the window trying to settle a whimpering baby. She was surrounded by a handful of people: friends, neighbours or perhaps relatives, all with worried expressions on their faces.

Henrik addressed himself to the couple on the sofa. 'You must be Stine and Simon,' he said, holding up his warrant card. 'I'm Detective Inspector Jungersen from Copenhagen Police, and I believe you've already met Detective Sergeant Mark Søndergreen.'

The moment passed when they might have shaken hands.

He gestured at the group on the other side of the room. 'Could we talk in private for a while?'

The visitors shuffled out, the baby screeching as it reached for Stine. She turned her face away. 'I can't,' she sobbed, leaning into her husband's chest.

'I want you to know that we're doing everything we can to find Matilde,' said Henrik.

'Oh yeah? What are you doing here then?' said Simon, flashing him an angry look.

'We've a big team working on this case with no let-up, I promise you,' said Henrik, pointing to an armchair. 'May I?' He sat down without waiting for an answer, keeping to the edge to prevent his wet jeans from staining the seat. 'I know this is difficult. I'll try to be as quick as I can. While we talk, do you think Mark here could have a look in your daughter's room?'

'What for?' said Simon, scowling.

His wife was holding onto his jumper, white-knuckled, as though fearful of slipping onto the floor. Her whole body was trembling as she cried.

'It's routine. We're looking for clues, any clues, as to what might have happened,' said Henrik, nodding at Mark, who quickly made himself scarce.

'Stine,' Henrik began. 'I need you to think for me. You told us you got to the playground around a quarter to three in the afternoon yesterday. On your way there, did Matilde say anything to you?'

'No,' she sobbed. 'I was exhausted, so I wanted to stay at home, but she persuaded me to go. She was skipping along the pavement.'

'Did she say why she was so keen?'

'She loves it there.'

Henrik passed her a tissue. 'What did you talk about on the way?'

'I don't remember,' she said, blowing her nose.

'That's all right. And what about earlier in the day?'

'She played in her room, I made her pasta for lunch and then we walked to the park, like always.'

'Always?' said Henrik.

'Every Sunday, unless it's raining, or I've been up all night with Daniel.'

That made sense, Henrik thought. Plenty of time for someone to watch and plan, picking off the little girl who preferred to play by herself, befriending her, ensuring that she would come away freely.

'We shouldn't have gone,' Stine cried. 'If only we'd stayed at home, Matilde would be here now.'

'Don't torture yourself,' Henrik said. He gave her a moment. 'I understand that she was playing alone in the shrubbery. Why was that?'

19

'It's quiet in there. She finds the other kids too noisy and boisterous.'

'So, it's a regular thing?'

'Pretty much.'

'And you were on your phone when it happened?'

'Yes.'

'Talking to someone?'

'No, just scrolling.'

The answers were robotic, toneless. Simon, on the other hand, seemed to be getting more and more agitated, his nostrils flaring as he breathed.

Henrik ignored him. 'Have you ever seen Matilde talk to anyone?'

'Sometimes we meet one of her friends from school.'

'I mean an adult, a stranger.'

'No,' Stine said, raising her voice. 'I'd never let her do that.'

'I understand,' said Henrik. 'What about having a feeling that you were being watched while in the park? Or recognising people from previous visits?'

'I don't ...' Stine turned to Simon, uncertain. 'What is he saying?'

'Look,' Simon said, his face the colour of a ripe tomato. 'She's told you nothing happened. She didn't see anyone, and she and Matilde didn't talk about anything.'

'No arguments? No telling off?' said Henrik, keeping his gaze on Stine.

'What difference does that make?' Simon snapped.

Stine lifted her tearstained face and looked at Henrik. 'Do you have kids?'

'Three,' he said, trying to convey with his eyes that he understood her pain.

All of it.

Simon got up. 'I've had enough of this,' he said. 'Our friends are out there looking right now, same as you ought to be.'

Henrik took a deep breath. He couldn't blame the man for kicking off, would probably have done the same in his place. Still, Simon was starting to get on his nerves. 'Last night was confusing,' he said to Stine. 'You might have forgotten something that will turn out to be important. People out of place. Unusual sounds. A conflict with Matilde earlier in the day, even if it felt insignificant at the time.'

Simon frowned. 'Matilde wouldn't have run off because she'd had an argument with Stine. It would be completely out of character.'

'We're keeping an open mind, not ruling anything in or out,' said Henrik, looking at him. 'Tell me, where were *you* yesterday afternoon?'

Predictably, Simon's face went from red to almost purple. 'What the hell has that got to do with anything?'

'Just tell them,' Stine said.

'I was at the gym,' said Simon. 'Satisfied?'

'We'll need the details,' said Henrik. 'To verify the information.'

'You don't have a clue, do you?' Simon spat. 'That's why you're sitting here worrying about where I was yesterday, instead of doing your job. If you're so determined to speak to someone, why don't you talk to Stine's ex?'

Stine pulled at his sleeve. 'No, Simon, don't start. You promised me.'

He jerked his arm away. 'They need to know what the creep is like. If you won't tell them, then I will.'

'Do you mean Matilde's biological father?' said Henrik, leaning forward. According to the officers who had spoken to him last night, Rasmus Nordby had been upset at the news that his estranged daughter was missing. 'Why do you say that?'

'Ask at Matilde's school. They'll tell you.'

'Simon, no,' said Stine.

Again, he ignored her, freeing himself of her imploring hand. Henrik's dislike of the man grew.

'He was caught looking through the fence at the little kiddies, wasn't he?' said Simon. 'One of the other parents complained.'

'When was this?' said Henrik, leaning forward.

'More than six months ago. He just wanted to see Matilde,' said Stine.

Simon looked at her. 'He had his phone out to take pictures.'

'Were the police called?' said Henrik.

'Yes, but of course you guys let him go with a slap on the wrist.'

'He hadn't done anything,' said Stine.

'He's a paedophile,' said Simon.

'He wouldn't harm his own daughter,' said Stine. She turned to Henrik. 'Simon and I got full custody of Matilde in the spring. The thing at the school happened just after that. There's been no repeat.'

'So, Rasmus never sees Matilde?'

Stine shook her head. 'Not anymore.'

Henrik nodded and got up, his knees creaking. 'OK,' he said. 'We'll check it out.'

Big tears rolled down Stine's cheeks as she looked up at him, seized with fear and desperation. 'Someone's taken her, haven't they?'

Henrik believed in being straight with people. He tried desperately to think of something truthful that would reassure the woman but drew a blank. 'We have to face that possibility, yes,' he said.

Stine screamed like a wounded animal, a thin, heart-rending sound.

'Have you slept?' he said. 'If you're struggling, your doctor may be able to give you something to help.'

She made a strangled sound, as her hand flew to her mouth. 'I'm going to be sick,' she said, rushing for the door.

Simon followed her out.

Henrik found Mark in Matilde's bedroom. He was shaking his head. 'No clues in here, Boss. The guys took her iPad last night but found nothing on it of any use.'

Henrik knew that already.

He looked around the room. His daughter had the same Disney poster of Elsa from *Frozen* above her bed. The same pink hues everywhere, the same array of soft toys.

'Take that, would you?' he said to Mark, pointing to a hairbrush fuzzy with blonde hair.

They might need Matilde's DNA at some stage, and this could be their best chance to get it.

There was a pile of drawing paper on the table, with an assortment of felt tips and colouring pencils in a mug. He put on his reading glasses and thumbed through the drawings. Nothing out of the ordinary: castles and princesses, Matilde and her family, mother, stepfather and baby brother.

'Who's this?' he asked, pointing to a drawing of Matilde with a woman with dark glasses, a hat and a big blue coat. There was a large red item next to her. A pull-along suitcase?

Mark shrugged, closing the evidence bag with the hairbrush and pocketing it. 'Maybe her grandmother was going on holiday?'

Henrik snapped a picture of the drawing with his phone.

Now wasn't a good time to ask the couple who the woman was. He could still hear Stine retching in the bathroom.

'Check out if Simon was at his gym yesterday afternoon between three and four p.m.'

Mark nodded, making a note.

'We need to speak to Matilde's biological father,' said Henrik. 'Get him in. And check with her school whether someone made a complaint about him loitering outside the gates six months ago.'

'Got it, Boss,' said Mark.

Henrik felt a headache coming on, the result of another poor night's sleep. He would need to pick up some pain-killers on the way to the press conference.

A press conference during which he would have nothing to say.

His phone rang. It was Pia, the search leader at Ørstedsparken.

'Please tell me it's good news,' he said, holding his breath and grimacing with his eyes closed.

'We found a green glove, same as the ones Matilde was wearing,' said Pia.

She hesitated for a split second, which told Henrik something bad was coming.

Something he wouldn't want to hear.

'It was in the lake.'

4

Every news organisation in Denmark had turned up under the pale stone colonnade circling the inner courtyard of the old police building in the centre of Copenhagen.

The journalists had formed a thick buffer in front of a row of microphone stands with colourful covers announcing the names of the country's newspapers and broadcasters.

Jensen pushed her way through to the front, her bump parting the crowd. She was freezing in her woefully inadequate raincoat. Buying maternity clothes, like signing up for antenatal classes, was something other women did.

Women who had their act together.

She had received text messages telling her off for not attending her midwife's appointments at Riget. How could she explain that she would rather do anything than think about what was about to happen to her?

She was scrolling for the latest headlines on her phone when she felt someone push in beside her. Turning to protest, she found herself staring into the red-bearded face of *Dagbladet*'s newest employee.

'Ah, the famous Jensen,' he said, towering above her. 'You left without me.'

'I wasn't aware I was supposed to chaperone you.'

'Touchy,' he said. 'I just thought, seeing as we're partners now.' He was wearing an enormous black puffer coat with a fur-lined hood suitable for the arctic. Smiling broadly with strong, straight teeth, he stretched out a gloved hand. 'Jannik.'

His handshake was crushing.

'What did you do before *Dagbladet*?' she said.

'Lots,' he said. 'Google me.'

Seriously?

'I'll take your word for it,' she said.

He pointed to her bump. 'When's the big day?'

'All too soon,' she said, turning her face away.

He sniffed as he reached into a large bag and pulled out a microphone stand, which he proceeded to unfold.

He placed the tripod at the front alongside the others, and fixed a microphone to it, running the lead back to a camera which he hoisted onto his shoulder. On the shaft of the microphone he had placed a white sticker with *Dagbladet* written in bold, black felt-tip letters.

It might as well have said *bargain basement journalism*. Was the newspaper now so hard up that it couldn't afford to advertise for itself?

'I don't do partners,' she said.

'Now, that's just not true,' said the man she would forever think of as Google Me, checking his settings. 'I'm told you've been running around with Margrethe's nephew. Now, what was his name?' He looked up, pretending to think. 'That's right, Gustav.'

Her cheeks grew hot. 'That was totally different.' She didn't elaborate. Margrethe hadn't exactly given her a

26

choice when it came to taking on Gustav as an unpaid apprentice, but none of that was Google Me's business. 'It was a temporary arrangement,' she said. 'He's back at high school now.'

'Where he belongs. I mean, I saw the work he did, and it was all right, but you can tell he was no professional.'

'As opposed to you?' She looked at him sharply. Where had Margrethe found this obnoxious man?

'Shush,' he said. 'They're starting.'

Her phone pinged, a text message from Markus, the rude receptionist at *Dagbladet*. He had sublet his flat to her when she first arrived in Copenhagen, only to throw her out with two days' notice when a failed love affair had forced him to break off his round-the-world trip and return to Denmark. She had never forgiven him.

⬜⬜⬜y n⬜⬜ ⬜⬜ ⬜o⬜⬜⬜⬜ ⬜ our ⬜⬜⬜ ⬜⬜⬜⬜⬜ ⬜or you ⬜⬜r⬜⬜ ⬜⬜ ⬜⬜⬜⬜ ⬜⬜⬜⬜r ⬜⬜⬜⬜⬜

Jensen didn't know anyone called Bodil La Cour. She responded with a thumbs-up emoji and slipped the phone into her pocket. When she looked up, Henrik was standing just a few feet away from her, squinting into the bright TV lights.

Her stomach lurched.

In his black leather jacket, black jeans, white shirt and beaten-up boots, he looked the same as the day they met, a lifetime ago.

He was staring down at a piece of paper in his hands with a grim expression. 'Yesterday at around four in the afternoon, nine-year-old Matilde Clausen disappeared from the playground close to Ahlefeldtsgade in Ørstedsparken. A search has been ongoing overnight and continues today, but I regret to say that Matilde has not yet been found.' He looked up, uncertain for a second which camera lens to look into. 'We would like to appeal to members of the public to come forward with *any* information that might help us find out what happened. If you were at the playground or in the park yesterday, no matter whether you think you saw anything or not, please get in touch with us immediately. Any questions?'

'What's your theory?' someone shouted.

'Given that Matilde is just nine years old, and it's now twenty hours since the last verified sighting of her, we have to work on the basis that a crime has been committed.'

Henrik's eyes roamed across the crowd. He still hadn't spotted her.

'Do you believe that Matilde is alive?' shouted a woman with a shrill voice.

'We've no reason to believe that she isn't.'

'If someone abducted Matilde, wouldn't it have been captured on CCTV?' came a question from the back.

'We're working through CCTV from the area as fast as we can,' said Henrik. 'I can't tell you any more at present.'

Jensen couldn't hold it any longer. 'How can a child just vanish?' she shouted, sensing Google Me pointing his lens at her. 'What do you have to say to all the parents out there who'll wonder if their kids are safe?'

She had failed to find any recent instance like it. Most missing kids of Matilde's age turned up within hours, except in cases where a disgruntled parent had smuggled their child out of the country. Not unheard of, but no one had suggested that had happened here.

Henrik found her eyes. Stunned, his gaze drifted downwards to her bump and back to her face. His mouth opened.

Then he snapped out of it, raised his head and looked

away. 'It should be remembered that child abductions are extremely rare,' he said.

'Precisely, so isn't it more likely that Matilde went with someone she knew?' she said.

Flustered now, Henrik addressed the crowd. 'We're ... keeping an open mind. I know you all want answers. We do too, and when we have them, I promise you'll be the first to know.'

Afterwards, Google Me nudged her with an elbow. 'Good questions,' he said. 'Do you know that guy?'

'Not really,' she said.

It wasn't a lie.

She had loved him like no one else. During her fifteen years in London, it had been easy to pretend that one day they could be together.

In Copenhagen, everything had become complicated.

Real.

He wasn't the man she had thought he was.

Google Me had packed up his equipment and begun to walk away.

'Where are you going?' she said, frowning at him.

'To Matilde's parents' place in Kleinsgade. Someone said they might make a statement after this. You coming?'

5

'And Stine is sure it's her daughter's glove?' said Henrik, closing his eyes and pinching the bridge of his nose.

It was the worst possible news.

'Completely sure,' said Mark. 'Apparently, there's a hole in the thumb that she'd been meaning to fix. She's adamant that Matilde was wearing both gloves at the playground.'

Henrik had held back the information from the press, hoping that the glove would turn out to have nothing to do with Matilde. After all, it had been found at the opposite end of the park from the playground, floating in the water.

How had it got there? Did it mean that Matilde had walked the length of the park to the entrance furthest away from the playground, with her abductor, and dropped her glove on the way? This would only be possible if the pair had walked along the water's edge, away from the path, and why would they have done that?

The glove could have been carried there later by an animal, perhaps a city fox, but given that the park had been crawling with people since Matilde disappeared, this didn't seem possible.

The other possibility was that Matilde had drowned after all. Maybe she had attempted to retrieve her missing glove? Wearing winter boots and a heavy coat, she would have sunk quickly.

'What shall I tell Stine?' said Mark. 'She's very upset.'

Henrik could hear her screaming uncontrollably in the background. He had been reluctant to call in the fire-service divers until now, conscious of the distress this would cause to the family. Now they had no choice but to search the lake. With their long lenses, the TV news crews would be on to them in seconds. Speculation would start that they were looking for a body.

Besides, he knew from experience that the lake was long, and more than five metres deep in places, with thick sludge on the bottom. It wouldn't be an easy job. 'Tell her it doesn't necessarily mean anything,' he said. 'That glove could have ended up there in lots of ways. We're going to be searching the lake but only to exclude it from our investigation. Tell her to try to stay positive.'

As if.

He was struggling to heed his own advice.

The ham sandwich he had bought in the canteen was sitting untouched on his desk. He had a headache despite the two paracetamol he had washed down with a Coke Zero on the way back to the office.

Seeing Jensen again had thrown him. She hadn't changed, except for the bump that stuck out from her slim frame like a football pushed under her sweatshirt.

'There's something else,' said Mark. From the way his footsteps echoed, it sounded like he had left the flat and was now in the stairwell. He lowered his voice. 'It's

31

Matilde's dad. He's a plumber, works for an industrial outfitter, but he didn't turn up for work this morning.'

'Understandable,' Henrik said.

The man's daughter was missing. Was it so strange that he hadn't felt like hanging out with his colleagues, suffering their sympathy, their well-meaning questions?

'His car is in the driveway outside his home, but he's not answering the door.'

'I see,' said Henrik.

Perhaps Nordby had got drunk to stave off his anxiety. Strange that he wasn't more interested in hearing news from the police.

Did it mean Simon Clausen was right that Nordby had something to do with his daughter's disappearance after all? Had the man harmed himself, or worse?

'And that story about him loitering outside Matilde's school?' said Mark on the phone. 'Turns out it's true. The head teacher reported him acting suspiciously, but the fact that Nordby had recently lost custody was considered a mitigating factor, and he was let go with a warning.'

Henrik got up, grabbed his leather jacket from the back of the chair. Now they had something to go on. 'I'll get a search warrant,' he said. 'Send me the address and meet me there in forty-five minutes.'

Copenhagen was choked with slow-moving traffic, the inevitable consequence of December's shopping frenzy and the heavy rain.

Henrik hated Christmas.

The schnapps-fuelled company parties that filled the roads with drunk drivers.

Spending time with his in-laws and pretending to be happy.

And when had Christmas markets become a thing? They hadn't been around when he was a boy, growing up in Brøndby.

Now they were everywhere, with their reindeer light sculptures and glorified garden sheds, stinking of mulled wine and frying fat.

The list of irritations was endless.

('You miserable git,' said his wife in his head.)

It took him almost an hour to cross town to Tåstrup, cursing at the traffic all the way.

When he got there, the team was already assembled, waiting for his signal to force entry at the yellow-brick bungalow with the silver Kia in the driveway.

A smattering of neighbours had gathered to watch, but thankfully no reporters.

Yet.

The media circus with its unsavoury atmosphere of excitement had moved to the flat in Kleinsgade, the journalists, camera people and photographers occupying a vantage point opposite Matilde's home.

Henrik had managed to talk Stine and Simon out of making a statement. Matilde's stepfather was a loose cannon with his accusations against Nordby. If he and his wife were going to talk to the press, Henrik wanted to be there.

He got out of the car and approached Mark who was waiting for him outside the bungalow.

Addressing himself to one of the uniformed officers, Henrik pointed to the onlookers. 'Get everyone's details. Ask if they saw Nordby last night or this morning and find out if they've noticed anything unusual in the past few weeks.'

'Got it.'

'And move them back, for Christ's sake.'

He and Mark walked up to the front door. Henrik nodded at the team that they could go ahead and force it.

It took three blows of the battering ram before the officers were able to stream inside. 'Police. Make yourself known!'

Henrik and Mark waited for the all-clear. It came after barely a minute.

The rooms were empty and stale, but tidy. There was a stone-cold, half-full cup of coffee on the kitchen counter, reasonably fresh food in the fridge.

'We definitely spoke to him last night?' said Henrik.

'Yes,' said Mark, wide-eyed. 'I double-checked. He was interviewed thoroughly and claimed he hadn't seen or spoken to Matilde for months. The team had a good look round. Matilde wasn't here.'

'And he seemed genuinely shocked?'

Mark nodded. 'But then you would be, if you were told that your daughter was missing, wouldn't you?'

Or if you were a good actor, Henrik thought. The officers wouldn't have searched all corners of the house last night; Nordby could have hidden Matilde under a bed.

Or something else entirely had happened, and they were wasting their time.

Since the press conference, more sightings had flowed in from all over Denmark of little girls in red coats. Almost all of them would turn out to be nothing, but they had to follow up on each one, which took resources they didn't have.

Henrik donned latex gloves and went to look around the bedroom. A small double bed was pushed up against one wall. Nothing underneath it. The wardrobe was half full, a suitcase stored on top. Impossible to tell if Nordby had taken any belongings with him.

A small, black desk was pushed up under the window. Henrik bent down, squinting at the faint dust-free rectangle on the surface.

Mark came in. 'I found this in the kitchen,' he said, holding up a beetroot-coloured passport. 'He can't have been planning to go far.'

'He took his laptop, though,' said Henrik, pointing to the empty rectangle.

Stuck to the wall next to the desk was a faded drawing of two people with big round eyes, one with long yellow hair, one with short brown hair. The two figures were marked 'Matilde' and 'Dad'.

He recognised Matilde's hand from the drawings they had found in her bedroom.

'Get someone to check out Nordby's background,' he said to Mark. 'Relatives. Former places of work. Where he likes to hang out.'

'Yes, Boss.'

Henrik opened the drawer in Nordby's desk and thumbed through the old batteries, phone chargers and letters. There was a reminder to pay an electricity bill from two months ago.

He massaged his aching temples, trying to think.

There could be a thousand reasons why Nordby hadn't turned up at work. For all they knew, the man could be out there looking for his daughter himself.

Out of habit, he moved the desk from the wall and felt along the back panel with one hand. Then he pulled out the drawer completely. The hard drive was the size of a cigarette packet and stuck to the back with gaffer tape.

Sighing, Henrik placed it into an evidence bag. He had hoped that Simon had been telling lies about Nordby, out of fear and spite.

35

The contents of the drive would make everything more complicated.

'It might not be what it looks like,' said Mark. 'There might be an innocent explanation.'

Mark.

Always wanting to see the best in people.

He wouldn't go far in the police with that attitude.

'Yeah,' Henrik said. 'And pigs might fly.' He went into the hallway and, twirling a finger in the air, signalled to the uniforms that it was time to leave. 'We're done here.'

6

WHERE IS MATILDE?

Dagbladet's headline, in giant black capitals on a yellow banner, screamed at Jensen from her laptop screen. She had finished reading the coverage in the rest of the media. Everyone was speculating. It was now almost twenty-six hours since Matilde had disappeared, and there had been no news.

Google Me had posted a video of the press conference. He had zoomed in on Henrik's face so far that you could see that his eyes were bloodshot and flickering left and right, the way they did when he was under pressure.

There had been police in Kleinsgade, and the curtains to the parents' flat had been drawn. They had waited with the other reporters for over an hour for something to happen, but in the end the wet weather and boredom had chased everyone back to their offices.

Her laptop began to ping: Markus from reception calling on Teams. As she clicked on the camera icon, she remembered his text message from hours ago.

'Your friend Bodil La Cour. You didn't call her,' he said, his angry face looming large on the screen.

'I forgot,' she said. 'In case you hadn't noticed, I've been busy covering the search for Matilde.'

'Oh, I do apologise,' said Markus.

'And she's not my friend, I've never heard of her. What does she want that's so urgent?'

'How should I know?'

'I'll call her. Soon.'

'Call her now, or I'll come up and do it for you,' said Markus. 'I swear to God, if that woman rings the switchboard one more time, I can't be held responsible for my actions.'

'OK, there's no need to—'

His face vanished from the screen.

Jensen grabbed her mobile and climbed up into her favourite spot on the dormer windowsill where she had a view of the rooftops of Copenhagen, outlined against the yellow-grey night sky.

Someone had left a stack of cardboard boxes by her desk. Most of her personal stuff would have to be thrown out in the move, including her old notebooks and the languishing spider plant she had bought when she first arrived.

Downstairs, she would be given a locker the size of a post box, barely fitting more than a pair of shoes and her cycling helmet. There would be no thinking space, little room for private calls.

She shuffled to make herself more comfortable, arching her back to breathe. Her bump was almost too big now for her to sit with her legs folded like this. A twinge in her abdomen sent a cold dart of panic through her body.

She had felt it before, a tightening deep down, like a menstrual cramp, that filled her with sudden anxiety.

Practice contractions could start weeks before birth, she had read somewhere.

I am going to have a baby.

She breathed deeply, trying to dismiss the thought. Then she dialled the number. 'Bodil La Cour? This is Jensen, from *Dagbladet*.'

'You're a woman.' The voice was elderly and posh.

'I believe so, yes.'

'I thought you were a man.'

'You're not the first. Jensen is my surname. I haven't used my first name since I was a child.'

'Whyever not?'

'Trust me, you wouldn't ask if you knew what it was. Anyway, I hear you've been trying to get hold of me?'

'Yes, I have important information.'

Jensen felt her heart start to beat faster. 'Is it about Matilde Clausen?'

'That poor missing girl?' said Bodil, sounding confused. 'I saw it on the news. Terrible. No, I want to talk to you about something I witnessed here, on Friday night – or should I say, Saturday morning.'

Jensen's heart sank. Was this a crank call? There were plenty of people with nothing better to do than tipping off the papers about things that never happened.

'Where's here?' she sighed, closing her eyes. She was going to have a long bath when she got home to Margrethe's flat, then an early night. Famished more or less constantly, she was already salivating at the thought of the lamb shawarma she was going to pick up from Nørrebro on the way.

'Peblinge Dossering where I live, by the Lakes,' said Bodil.

That figured, thought Jensen. If you had a home next to

the pretty stretches of water in the middle of the city, you were either rich or elderly and had lived there for decades.

Possibly both.

She would give her right arm for a flat on Peblinge Dossering.

It was also within walking distance of Ørstedsparken and close to Matilde Clausen's home.

'I witnessed an assault on a young woman from my window,' said Bodil.

Here we go, thought Jensen. 'An assault?' she said.

'Yes. Or murder.'

'You're not sure which?'

'The woman looked pretty dead to me.'

'Did you report it to the police?'

'Yes, but that's the thing. By the time the officers got here, the man had moved her. I called the police station yesterday, but no one would tell me what's going on. I suppose they think I made it up.'

Jensen felt a stab of guilt. Had she not devoted her career to speaking for those without a voice?

'I was hoping that if you wrote about it in your news-paper, the police would take it seriously,' Bodil continued. 'Could you come tomorrow?'

'I'm rather busy with the Matilde case at the moment. Maybe—'

'Say eleven o'clock for tea? Now, if you have a pen ready, I'll give you the address.'

Jensen smiled to herself.

Bodil wasn't backing down.

Was she an attention seeker?

Bored?

Mad?

It didn't matter. Jensen could spare an hour. If nothing

else, she would enjoy the bike ride on the path running along the Lakes; it would get her away from Google Me and the general atmosphere of doom that clung to *Dagbladet*'s office, and to the search for Matilde.

'OK,' she said. 'I'll come. But I can't promise you I'll write anything.'

7

'For Christ's sake, what is it now?' Henrik shouted at the person knocking on the door.

Only a few minutes ago, he had escaped to his office for a bit of peace and quiet to think. After a day with no material developments, and pressure from all sides, the mood among his team of investigators had become despondent.

They had continued to follow up on each lead, gather CCTV from around the park and interview the trickle of new witnesses that had come forward, but none of it had got them anywhere.

Most of the team had gone home, only Mark and a couple of the others had stayed behind to continue the search for Matilde's father. They had done the rounds of his relatives, but no one had seen him.

Or so they claimed.

Henrik's face softened when Detective Sergeant Martin Bagger stuck his head around the door. He was wearing his motorcycle leathers, with a rucksack over one shoulder. 'Only me,' he said.

'Bagger. Good to see you.'

He meant it. Bagger, a compact, athletic fifty-something cop, specialised in IT crime detection, which mostly meant finding and prosecuting those who produced and shared images of child sexual abuse.

Many of the cases dealt with by the unit of Copenhagen Police led by Henrik's boss Jens Wiese involved such material, including reports from the US National Centre for Missing and Exploited Children, or NCMEC, pronounced in police parlance as 'Neck-Meck'.

Each year, NCMEC received more than 35 million reports of suspected child sexual exploitation from electronic service providers. A not insignificant proportion originated in Denmark, and those that couldn't be traced to a specific district ended up with the Copenhagen Police.

Despite seeing some of the worst that human beings were capable of doing to one another, Bagger's eyes had somehow managed to retain their warmth and always seemed to be smiling.

Henrik liked him immensely. He was one of the few people on the force that he trusted with his life. He liked to think the feeling was mutual.

'How are you?' said Bagger.

'Oh, you know, been better.'

Henrik looked down at his hands. Sometimes he yearned to cry, but he hadn't managed it once since the murder of a detective sergeant in his team in the summer. His grief was buried deep, in a part of his brain that he couldn't access.

'Cut yourself some slack,' said Bagger.

Henrik produced a fake smile. 'What brings you here?'

'We had a look at the hard drive you found at Rasmus Nordby's house. It was as you suspected.'

'Child porn?'

'We don't call it that anymore,' said Bagger. 'It's child sexual abuse material, or CSAM for short.'

Henrik nodded. He knew why. Legal adult pornography was supposedly consensual; a child could never consent. Pornography featuring children was always the result of exploitation, assault, grooming, coercion and worse. Calling it what it was stressed the impact on the victims, rather than the product sought by unfathomable numbers of people around the globe.

He and Bagger had both investigated enough cases to know how truly devastating that impact was. 'Bad?' he asked.

'On a scale, yeah, and I'd say he was a bit of a veteran. We can see that he's deleted loads of videos and images over time, though his method of concealment is somewhat amateur.'

Henrik remembered Bagger telling him that it wasn't possible to fully delete stuff from a drive. Not without physically destroying it. 'Any pictures of his daughter?' he said.

'None so far.' Bagger gestured with his thumb in the direction of his office on the other side of the lift lobby. 'But the guys are still in there looking.'

What did it mean? Did Nordby have something to do with his daughter's disappearance? Had he been abusing Matilde? Or allowing others to do so?

The man had no previous, but that meant nothing. Child sexual abusers could go under the radar for years before they were found out. It was one of the few crimes that truly transcended society, though invariably it was those at the bottom of the pile that ended up being caught.

Nothing new there.

'Anything in his emails?'

'We're still going through those, but so far it seems mostly spam or official stuff.'

'I need to know where he's gone. Any clue, I want to know straight away. And call me the minute you find anything else of interest.'

'Of course,' said Bagger, patting him on the shoulder. 'Take it easy, Jungersen.'

When he had left, Henrik drank his fifth Coke Zero of the day. It was lukewarm and gave him palpitations.

Matilde had been missing for more than thirty hours, and they were still scratching their heads, as Wiese had reminded him before leaving in his cycling gear earlier that evening.

'Find her, Jungersen,' he had said as he disappeared down the hall.

Matilde was an ordinary child. She liked singing and dressing up. No one at her school remembered her saying anything unusual recently. She was a well-liked, easy-going, smiling nine-year-old girl who had been looking forward to Christmas.

The media had made much of the fact that her disappearance coincided with the approaching holiday season. As though that made things worse.

It didn't, Henrik thought; things were pretty much as dismal as it was possible to get.

There was another knock on the door. He looked up expectantly. Perhaps it was Bagger coming back? Perhaps they had already found something that would help them understand what had happened?

Mark entered with a spring in his step, filling him with irritation.

'Nordby didn't lose custody, Boss,' said Mark. 'He gave it up voluntarily six months ago.'

'Gave it up? Why would he have done that?'

Mark shrugged. 'It was also him who left Matilde and

her mother, not the other way around. All very amicably, apparently.'

'Did you talk to his colleagues?'

'Not yet, but I spoke to his boss. He said Nordby isn't the sociable type. I got the impression no one knows him particularly well. He's a good worker, organised, always shows up on time, except for this morning. They said it was out of character for him not to call in sick. It came as complete news to them that he's Matilde's dad. He hadn't ever mentioned that he had a daughter.'

Henrik frowned. 'Any hint as to where he might have gone?'

'No,' said Mark, 'but we're tracing his mobile.'

'Good work,' Henrik said. 'Now go home. There's nothing more we can do, and I need you fresh first thing in the morning.'

'What about you?'

'I'll be all right.'

When Mark had gone, he walked through the empty, unlit office, standing by the window and looking out at the city.

His city.

He couldn't explain it, but it felt like the ground out there had shifted and cracked, releasing something old and putrid into the air. And it was up to him, only him, to put things right.

46

Day Two

8

After tossing and turning for ages, Jensen finally conceded victory to her insatiable hunger. She got out of bed and padded barefoot into Margrethe's kitchen in search of food.

The grey-painted, glass-fronted cabinets stretched high into the darkness under the stuccoed ceiling. Uninterested in decor, Margrethe had left the Østerbro flat virtually unchanged since her mother's time. It was huge and rambling, full of stuff accumulating dust in dark corners.

Jensen's laptop was still on the dining table in the golden pool of light from the low-hanging Poul Henningsen lamp, next to the giant ceramic bowl filled with gently rotting oranges.

She had spent a couple of hours before going to bed researching a piece on the rare instances in Denmark where a young child had disappeared without trace for more than a few days.

It had made for unhappy reading.

She had her head in the fridge, debating what to eat, when she heard the front door slam followed by three clunks as a rucksack, then one trainer and another were dropped on the floor. The dragging footsteps down the corridor were familiar. 'Gustav?'

'Be quiet, you'll wake Margrethe,' he said, holding a wobbly finger to his lips.

He was smiling cheekily, headphones around his neck, looking far from the sulky teenager he had been when they had first met. There was a swagger to him in his grey sweatshirt and tight black denims torn across both knees. She had barely seen him for months.

'Is that weed?' she said, catching a pungent smell on his clothes.

'Might be,' he said. 'Is there anything to eat? I'm starving.'

He pushed in beside her, grabbed a bag of rye bread from the fridge and fished out four slices. She watched him begin to slather them in chocolate spread, before topping each with a slice of cheese with caraway seeds.

Chocolate and caraway cheese?

Her stomach rumbled as he crammed the first slice into his mouth and licked chocolate smears off his fingers.

'Where have you been?'

'Out,' he said, with his mouth full.

'Out where?'

'School party.' He avoided her eyes as he started on his second slice.

He jumped onto the kitchen counter and began to bump his heels rhythmically against the cupboard door below. 'Anyway, what's up with you?' he said.

'Couldn't sleep,' she sighed.

'Because of the missing girl?' He sounded eager to talk about it or, more likely, keen to move the conversation on from the party and what he had been smoking.

'That and other things.'

'Such as?'

'This old lady phoned me today. Says she saw a murder. Wants me to find out why the police haven't arrested anyone for it yet.'

'And why haven't they?'

She shrugged.

'Can I help you? We could shoot a cool video, then tweet about it, ask if anyone saw it or knows anything?'

'No, Gustav.'

'Why not?'

'Number one, you've got school.'

'Then after school.'

'After school, you have homework, that's number two. And, number three, your aunt has just hired a guy to create videos for *Dagbladet*.'

'What? But I could do that. I bet I'd be a lot cheaper.'

Yes, and a damn sight more pleasant to work with, thought Jensen.

'Who is he anyway?' said Gustav.

'No idea. His name is Jannik Fogh. Claims to be a genius. Suggested I Google him, which of course I didn't.'

Gustav quickly got to work on his phone. 'Looks like a right bellend,' he said, scrolling.

'I'm not disagreeing with you,' she said. 'But I don't think he'd take kindly to you butting in. Besides, your aunt would kill me.'

Gustav pretended to cry, his shoulders heaving. Then he grabbed a carton of milk from the fridge and drank from it for a few long seconds, wiping his mouth on his sleeve afterwards.

'That's disgusting,' she said. 'Margrethe puts that milk in her coffee.'

'Stays in the family then,' he said, burping loudly.

She smiled despite herself, dropping heavily onto a kitchen chair. 'How's high school?'

'It's OK.'

'The teachers?'

'They're OK.'

'Made any friends yet?'

Gustav rolled his eyes. 'Quit giving me the third degree, Jensen. You sound like my aunt.' He jumped down from the counter, grabbing another slice of bread. 'I'm going to bed,' he said.

He turned in the doorway, smiling broadly. 'What if I come along after homework?'

'I'll think about it.'

'Yes!' Gustav did a fist pump before disappearing down the hall.

She looked at the detritus he had left behind. 'Hey,' she hissed. 'You forgot to clean up after yourself.'

His bedroom door slammed.

She followed him but didn't have the energy for an argument. Returning to school, after everything Gustav had been through, had been a big step. If he was partying, that had to be a good thing under the circumstances.

She looked at his rucksack, then at his door. A quick peek couldn't hurt.

The rucksack felt curiously empty. She unzipped it slowly so as not to make a noise. Inside was a water bottle, several empty vape canisters and a squashed chocolate bar. Her hand came away sticky.

No schoolbooks, no laptop, no pencil case. Perhaps he had emptied out his stuff before going out? She would have to talk to him about it. Tomorrow, when he was sober.

She went back to the kitchen, leaned against the counter and drank the rest of the milk.

It was sweet and cold. A few drops ran down her chin. She wiped them off with the back of her hand, while eyeing up the slice of rye bread with chocolate spread and cheese that Gustav had left behind.

She took a small bite, then a bigger one. It was surprisingly delicious.

'Not bad, Gustav, not bad at all,' she mumbled as she reached into the bag of rye bread for another handful of slices.

9

'Kirsten Nordby?'

For a moment, the older woman in the pink towelling bathrobe appeared to consider shutting the door in their faces. Then she nodded slightly.

She looked exhausted.

Henrik knew the feeling, having opted to stay the night on the couch in his office. It had been a poor decision. He had a kink in his neck and yearned for a shower and a change of clothes.

No chance of that happening any time soon.

He held up his warrant card. 'Detective Inspector Henrik Jungersen, Copenhagen Police, and this is my colleague Mark Søndergreen. Is your son here?'

'Why?' she said, not budging.

'We'd like to speak to him in connection with his daughter's disappearance.'

She blinked at the mention of Matilde. Briefly, but long enough for Henrik to notice. 'Your son is staying with you at the moment, is that right?'

She shook her head. 'No. He's not here, I haven't seen him.'

'Could we come in and talk to you for a moment?'

'I'm not dressed yet,' she said. 'Come back later.' She tried to close the door, but Henrik had already pressed his builder's boot against it.

If Kirsten was like most people, she would care what her neighbours thought. He raised his voice. 'Your nine-year-old granddaughter is missing. How come you're not more concerned about her?'

Kirsten's face cracked into a grimace of pain. 'I'm in pieces. I haven't slept,' she said quietly. 'But my son has nothing to with it, I swear to God.'

'How can you be sure, if you haven't seen him? You want Matilde to be found, don't you?' he said, trying to keep a lid on his fury. 'Perhaps you know something that could help us locate her.'

It wasn't even an hour since he had been woken by a call from Mark telling him that Nordby's mobile had been triangulated to the area around Enghave Plads where his mother lived.

Kirsten had been interviewed by his team last night but managed to persuade them that, while she had spoken to her son on the phone about Matilde's disappearance, she had not laid eyes on him for months.

An obvious untruth.

They heard a door being opened in the stairwell above them, the jangling of keys.

Kirsten glanced up anxiously, before finally opening her door wide and ushering them in. The flat was tidy, well kept. On the hall table, there was a picture of Matilde blowing out candles on a birthday cake. She looked to be about three years old.

'Thanks,' Henrik said. 'Now, my colleague needs the toilet very badly. I don't suppose he could use yours?'

Mark glanced at him in surprise and opened his mouth to speak but refrained when he caught the meaningful look on Henrik's face.

'End of the hall,' said Kirsten.

'He'll be back in a moment,' said Henrik, leading her into the darkened living room, as she glanced after Mark over her shoulder. 'Now, is there somewhere we can sit down?'

She sat in the armchair facing the TV, he on the sofa. There were two mugs of coffee on the table, half full.

She saw him looking. 'They're from last night,' she said. 'My friend was here.'

He nodded as he put one hand around one of the mugs. It was still warm.

She knew that *he* knew she was lying.

'Are you and your granddaughter close?'

She shook her head. 'I haven't seen Matilde since she was five. Thanks to *her*.'

'Who? Matilde's mother?'

'Yes.'

'And why would that be?'

'She won't get off my son's back. Everything is his fault. Even this ... Matilde going missing.'

'Did she say that?'

'No, but her new husband did.'

'Beg your pardon?'

'Came around to his house last night and scared Rasmus half to death.'

Simon Clausen hadn't told them about that. Henrik wondered what else he had kept to himself.

'Is this going to take long?' said Kirsten. 'You can see for yourself that my son isn't here.' She got up. 'Where is that colleague of yours? I thought you said he was only going to be a moment.'

Henrik held up his hands to appease her, but she was having none of it. 'He's looking for Rasmus, isn't he?' she shouted, moving towards the corridor. 'He's got no right to—'

She was interrupted by a loud commotion, the sound of something heavy crashing to the floor and Mark crying out. 'He's here, stop him!'

Henrik wasn't fast enough to catch the shadow that sped past him, though he did notice that Rasmus Nordby had a black eye.

Simon Clausen had obviously done more than scare him.

Henrik leapt out of the door after him, and ran down the stairs, but Rasmus soon added distance between them.

Mark was back on his feet and giving chase from the flight above, but he was too far away to make it.

If a young man with a bicycle over his shoulder hadn't been making his way out of the building at the exact time that Nordby tried to leave, they would have lost him.

With the terrified cyclist looking on, Henrik wrestled Rasmus to the ground.

'Rasmus Nordby,' he panted, out of breath. 'The time is six forty-seven and you're under arrest.'

10

Bodil La Cour lived in a pretty, old apartment block with white casement windows and a dark-green front door. The yellow building was squashed between two larger and more modern neighbours, on the west side of the Lakes that divided Nørrebro from Copenhagen's inner city.

Jensen chained her bike to the white picket fence, lingering for a moment to watch the cyclists and runners under the big trees on the lakeside path. It was an idyllic spot.

There was an old lift, covered in mesh, with a clanging door that had to be pulled tight before the button for the fourth floor would light up and set the old mechanism in motion.

Jensen looked at herself in the mirror as she rose through the dark stairwell. Her eyes were wide and sombre with worry about Matilde.

The lift came to a stop, and she pushed open the door to find Bodil La Cour standing in the entrance to her flat.

She was tall and thin, her body stooped and skewed, her left hand clutching a walking stick. Her clothes were immaculate: a grey trouser suit and red silk blouse with a big bow at the side of her neck, the colour matching her lipstick. Her long, grey hair was wound into a bun on top of her head, her glasses strong, enlarging her large, curious eyes, outlined in heavy black kohl. 'Jensen,' she said. 'I see you're expecting.'

'Yes,' said Jensen. 'So definitely not a man.'

Bodil laughed, her wrist tinkling with gold bangles as they shook hands.

Jensen wondered what she had done for work before retiring. Had she been married once? Had children?

The flat smelled faintly of coffee and gas. It was deathly quiet, aside from a loudly ticking grandfather clock.

A grey cat with extraordinary blue eyes and a tinkling bell on its collar rubbed itself against Jensen's leg.

'That's Wolfgang,' said Bodil. 'There was a Ludwig too, but he died last year.'

Beyond the hallway, Jensen sensed spacious rooms stretching away in either direction.

'Come,' said Bodil. 'Let me show you where I saw it.'

They walked past French doors opening onto a huge living room. The walls were covered in paintings and photographs to the ceiling. On every surface, there were stacks of books, fine china, candlesticks, house plants and ornaments. Persian carpets covered the parquet floors.

The view towards the city centre, across the Lakes, was breathtaking: deep blue water dotted here and there with swans and bordered by a row of tall, white apartment buildings disappearing in the mist on the opposite shore.

It was as if the lift had not just transported her upwards, but also back in time.

'In here,' said Bodil, entering a large bedroom and heading for the window.

Jensen followed, trying to keep her eyes from straying

to the quilted, rose-silk bedspread, the vanity table and bevelled mirror hung with necklaces.

'Down there,' said Bodil with her nose to the pane as she pointed into a cobbled courtyard.

There was a red building opposite, with yellow-brown vines almost smothering two old gas lamps set into the wall. A steep set of steps led to a dark-green back door. Enclosing the courtyard on either side were the gable walls of the neighbouring buildings. The small space, sleek with moisture, held a wooden picnic table surrounded by terra-cotta pots with dead geraniums. To the side was a wooden bike shelter.

'They were just there, on the ground by the table,' said Bodil. 'The woman was bent backwards, and the man had his hands around her throat.'

'What time was it again?' said Jensen, wondering how Bodil could have seen anything at all in the dark.

'Just after three in the morning between Friday and Saturday,' said Bodil. 'But the moon was full, and the lamps were lit.'

'Did you recognise the man? Could it have been one of the other residents?'

She shook her head. 'I couldn't see his face. There was something over his head, a hat, or a hood, and he had his back turned.'

'And the woman?'

'Very pale, short blonde hair.'

'Someone you've seen around here before?'

Bodil shook her head again.

'What was she wearing?'

'This long white thing without sleeves.'

'In November?'

'Yes, now you say it, that *is* odd. She wasn't wearing a

coat. I don't think he was either. Her eyes were big. She looked frightened.'

'Was the woman screaming?'.

'No, that was the strangest thing. She didn't make a sound. After a while she went limp and slid onto the ground. The man bent over her and grabbed her arms as if he was about to drag her away.'

'What did you do?'

'Called the police, of course, but my telephone is in the hall and, as you can see, I'm not fast on my feet. By the time I got back, there was no sign of them.'

'How long before the police got here?'

'Not long. Ten minutes at most. It was a man and a woman in uniform. They spoke to me first and I told them everything. Then they searched the place, but they didn't find anything, or so they said. I must say the man was an oaf, terribly rude.'

'Did any of your neighbours see anything?'

'Not according to the officers, but they can't have spoken to everyone,' said Bodil.

'It's strange,' said Jensen.

'What is?'

'That you happened to be awake and standing by your window at that exact moment in time.'

'Yes,' said Bodil. 'I thought about that. I mean, I often stand by the window when I can't sleep, but I wonder why I was awake. Perhaps it was some sort of noise, or a scream, that woke me in the first place.' She clasped Jensen's hand in a bony grip. 'You believe me, don't you?'

'Yes,' said Jensen, surprising herself with the firmness of her answer.

Bodil's story was far-fetched, but precisely for that reason it was credible. Unlikely that she would have made something like that up.

'I don't think those police officers did. Or surely, they would have investigated properly.' Bodil sighed deeply. 'Now,' she said. 'You will have a cup of tea, yes?'

Jensen followed her into the kitchen where Bodil filled the kettle and turned on the gas.

A silver tray stood to one side, arranged with cups, milk, sugar and a plate of round golden biscuits, thin like coins. 'They're my favourites,' she said. 'Palle got them for me, from La Glace.'

Jensen knew the place. It was Copenhagen's oldest patisserie and an institution in the city, no more than a few minutes' walk from the newspaper, but a significant distance from the Lakes.

'Who's Palle?'

Bodil pointed out of the kitchen window to the red building.

'He's the caretaker, lives over there,' Bodil said, measuring loose tea into the pot. 'God only knows where I'd be without Palle.'

'What does he do?'

'Everything. My shopping. Email. He even got me a mobile phone. I can't bring myself to tell him that I still don't know how to use it, although he's explained it to me a thousand times.'

Jensen smiled. 'Have you lived here long?'

'Born in this flat, eighty-nine years ago,' said Bodil. 'My parents died within two days of each other just before I turned sixty-one. They were book publishers.'

'You never married?'

'God no,' said Bodil. 'Why on earth would I have done that? I've had a wonderful life. Worked now and again for my parents, travelled around the world with them.' She smiled. 'When is your baby due?'

'February.'

'You and your partner must be excited.'

'Actually, I'm having the baby on my own. My mother was a single parent too, and she managed all right, so I must be able to.'

'Good for you,' Bodil said.

'I don't know. I'd feel better if I had a place to live, but rental flats in Copenhagen are madly expensive, and that's if you can find one.'

Bodil lit up. 'You can live here, with me. I've got nothing but room. You could be my lodger.'

'That's kind of you.'

'I mean it. I'd enjoy having a baby around.'

'I'm staying with my editor at the moment. She has plenty of room too.'

Margrethe would like Bodil, Jensen thought. The old woman was warm, kind, interesting. 'Look,' she said. 'I'll find out as much as I can. The police may still be investigating. And if they're not, maybe I will. I'll be back within a few days. Will you be here?'

A smile slowly spread across Bodil's face as the kettle began to whistle.

'My dear girl, where else would I be?'

'Did you like the biscuits?'

Jensen came out of the lift in the dingy entrance hall to find herself faced by a tall, big-boned, fifty-something man in blue overalls. His glasses were pushed up into his unruly, grey hair.

'I'm Palle,' he said, wiping his large hands on a rag. 'Did Bodil mention me?'

'Ah yes, you're the caretaker,' she said.

He laughed, showing grey teeth. 'Not officially. I work

freelance as a structural engineer. Only, I help Bodil out now and again. She doesn't have anyone else. Anyway, she said you were coming. I suppose she told you all about what she saw?'

'She did.'

'I helped the police,' said Palle. 'They looked around with torches. I showed them the basement, unlocked the doors to the storage rooms, but there was nothing there.'

'Did you see or hear anything strange yourself that night?'

'No. I was in bed asleep. First I heard of it was when the police got here, and the commotion woke me up. That's why ...'

'What?'

'Why I'm glad I caught you,' he said. 'I don't want to speak out of turn, but I do worry about Bodil.'

'What do you mean?'

'It's not the first time she's reported something to the police.'

'It's not?'

Palle shook his head. 'About three weeks ago, she called them in the middle of the night, saying that someone had been in her flat, but when they got here, there was no sign that anyone had tried to force the front door, and nothing was missing. One of the other residents is a nurse, works at Riget. She reckons Bodil is showing signs of dementia.'

'What's her name?'

'Katja. She and Thomas live in the flat below mine with their daughter. He's a builder. She's expecting a child, like you,' he said, pointing.

Jensen wrapped her jumper tightly around her bump and folded her arms across her chest. There was something odd about Palle.

'So you're saying that Bodil imagined the incident on Friday night?' she said, taking a step backwards towards the door and the daylight.

'I don't know,' Palle said, following her. 'Perhaps I shouldn't have said anything. Only, I don't want her to be made a laughing stock.'

'Thanks,' said Jensen. 'I appreciate it. Bodil seemed certain about what she saw, though.'

'She was certain about the break-ins that never happened,' Palle said.

Was he trying to tell her to get lost?

Good luck with that.

'Sounds like you know this place pretty well,' she said, fishing out a crumpled business card from her coat pocket. 'This is my email address. If you really want to help Bodil, perhaps you could send me the names of everyone who lives here, and their approximate ages?'

'Why?' he said, looking bewildered.

'So I can speak to them, of course, and check whether anyone knows something. Maybe the man Bodil saw was one of the residents.'

Palle's eyes widened. 'If she really saw anything, and I'm not convinced she did, then it might just as easily have been someone coming in from Wesselsgade at the back.' He pointed to the red building across the courtyard, just visible through the back door. 'There's another entrance over there.'

'Isn't it locked?'

Palle shook his head. 'People are forever leaving the door ajar, although I've put up a sign telling them not to. I suggested getting spring locks fitted, but some of the other residents objected to it, the idiots.'

'Still,' Jensen said. 'It would be worth speaking to

everyone, so we know for sure. Will you send me those names?'

'If you think it's important,' he said. Then he looked at her nervously. 'Say, you won't quote me for anything, will you?'

'I'm not even sure I'll be writing anything yet,' she said. 'I'll be making a few enquiries with the police, speak to your neighbours, and then decide.'

The police.

Henrik.

It was time they had a conversation.

11

'What is it? What have you found?' Henrik stood panting in the doorway to Bagger's office, hands on his thighs.

Bagger had refused to tell him over the phone. 'It's a little delicate. I'd rather you take a look for yourself,' he had said.

Henrik had run all the way.

The large, dark room that Bagger shared with his team was dusty and smelled of electronics, sweat and coffee. Four men in jeans and trainers, wearing their warrant cards around their necks and guns on their belts, looked up from their desks.

On a shelving unit taking up one entire wall were hard drives, laptops and mobiles, each marked with a sticker. He shuddered to think what was on them.

A picture of Bagger's wife holding a grandchild stood on his desk, a reminder perhaps that, notwithstanding what he did for a living, life was still good, that there were things worth fighting for.

It was possible to forget at times.

'We found an interesting photo in amongst the stash that Nordby tried to delete from his hard drive,' Bagger said.

'Now, I'm not saying it has anything to do with Matilde, but I'd like to hear what you make of it.'

'Show me,' Henrik said.

Bagger brought up a photo. It showed a skinny, blonde girl, lying naked on blue bedsheets in a messy, dark room. Her eyes were closed, but the concentrated look on her face suggested she was awake.

It was a girl he knew.

One he had never forgotten.

'Is that . . .? But it can't be.'

'Lea Høgh, yes, I think so,' said Bagger. 'I wanted to see if you agreed.'

Lea had gone missing barely half a kilometre from her home in Dragør. He and Bagger had worked together on the case. Bagger was the only one who knew how close he had come to losing everything in the aftermath.

His marriage.

His job.

Nothing had been seen or heard of Lea in more than six years.

Henrik felt his pulse rise. 'I don't understand,' he said. 'When was it taken?'

Bagger clicked on his mouse and the screen changed to a picture more familiar to Henrik.

It was the photo that had done the rounds in the media when Lea had first gone missing. She was gurning at the camera with a pronounced overbite, standing in the family kitchen wearing an apron, with her hands in a bowl of cookie dough.

The photo had been taken by her father, Jon, the day before she disappeared and the life of her family was turned upside down.

'We'll do some further analysis, but she appears to be

around the same age in the two photos, with a similar length of hair. It was probably taken in the months before she disappeared.'

'By whom?'

Bagger shrugged. Henrik put his hands on his bald head and tried to make sense of it all.

The Høghs had been the kind of people to whom everything bad had happened. A surprisingly common phenomenon in Henrik's experience.

Months after Lea disappeared, her mother died of cancer, and her twelve-year-old brother Sebastian turned out to have been sexually abused by a local businessman in Dragør.

Jan Loft, the unmarried proprietor of a construction firm, had been a popular member of the community, a friend to all who had generously opened his home to the neighbourhood's prepubescent boys. He had lots to offer: a swimming pool, a quad bike, table tennis, pizza, an endless supply of fizzy drinks, even trips away to fancy hotels.

It had all come at a cost that Sebastian and his friends had been too young to recognise at the time, or too ashamed to talk about.

Lea had been walking home from Loft's house on the day she went missing, after failing to persuade her brother to come with her.

Loft had always denied having anything to do with Lea's disappearance, claiming that he was only into boys.

There had been no evidence that Lea, too, had been sexually abused by anyone.

Not until now.

The case had crossed Henrik's mind frequently in the past few days. The lack of any progress in finding Matilde had brought back the old feelings of inadequacy and failure.

'Why would Matilde's dad have a picture of Lea on his laptop?'

Bagger shrugged. 'It's probably a coincidence.'

'Coincidence?' said Henrik. 'We went to the ends of the earth to find Lea. I would have settled for anything, just the tiniest of clues as to what had happened to her, but there was nothing. You know that, Bagger – you were there, for Christ's sake. Now this picture turns up, on a laptop belonging to the father of another girl who has disappeared, and you tell me it's random?'

'There's no evidence that Nordby is a producer. He could have picked up that photo from anywhere. It might have been circulating for years and only surfaced now.'

Producers and consumers. Bagger had once explained to him the pecking order of the online sewer. You either supplied child sexual abuse material, which gave you access to pretty much anything you wanted, or you paid the going rate, usually from a crypto wallet.

'What about Loft then? He was a producer.'

'You know as well as I do that we turned Loft's history inside out. Never found anything.'

'Well, he knows something, the smarmy bastard, I'm convinced of it.'

Loft was due for release from prison in a matter of days.

Henrik would have to persuade Wiese to reopen the case so Loft could be interviewed.

It wouldn't be easy, given that Loft had lodged an official complaint against Henrik for assault, a heat-of-the-moment thing when he had lashed out at the man in anger and frustration.

In the end the complaint hadn't been upheld, but the damage had been done. 'Have you been through everything on Nordby's laptop?' he said to Bagger.

70

'Not yet.'

'So there might be other pictures of Lea?'

'I suppose there's an outside chance, but I wouldn't hold your breath. There are more than twelve thousand videos and images here. We need time to go through them all.'

'We don't *have* time, Bagger. Get everyone you've got on it and let me know the minute you find anything else.'

Bagger looked at him squarely. His team had returned to their work and were pretending not to listen. Henrik knew and liked all of them. They worked on cases others would rather not think about, unable to discuss any of it with their family and friends. As a result, they had bonded with each other, developing a sense of humour most people would find offensive. Henrik knew it for the survival mechanism it was.

Fighting online child sexual abuse was a hard slog, brutal and thankless, with little hope of ultimate victory against a growing tidal wave of offences. Yet, his team turned up day after day, with their packed lunches, spending hours staring at horrific content, while knowing that if they did well, they would catch but a fraction of offenders.

'A fraction is better than none,' Bagger had told him.

The camp bed in the corner of their office was testament to their dogged persistence in finding and persecuting the perpetrators.

'I was just about to have some coffee,' Bagger said. 'Would you keep me company?'

He didn't wait for an answer but led Henrik through to the kitchen with a warm hand on his shoulder, then made him sit down as he poured a cup from a thermos and added milk from the fridge.

Plenty of milk, the way he liked it. Henrik was oddly pleased that Bagger had remembered. 'How can you stand it?' he said, clutching the warm mug. 'Watching so much shit every day, and knowing there's no stopping it?'

Bagger sat down, sipping coffee. 'To tell you the truth, it's the boys who keep me here,' he said, indicating his colleagues in the other room.

'Do you ever cry?'

'No,' he said. 'Maybe when I first started in this job, but not for many years now.' He looked intensely at Henrik. 'And you, Henrik, do you cry?'

He wished to God he could.

He shook his head. 'No, but then I'm not the one spending my days looking at children being abused.'

'Henrik, you seem rattled.'

'Not you as well,' Henrik said. 'Wiese just had a go. I'm sick of everyone fussing over me.'

'I get that. But to do a good job, you must be dispassionate, leave the emotion out of it. If not, you'll be no good to Matilde, or anyone else.'

'I'm fine.'

'You sure about that? Remember last time. Loft really got to you. This case could be worse.'

Henrik got up. It wasn't a conversation he wanted to have, though he knew that Bagger was right. 'Thanks for the coffee,' he said, draining his cup. 'I've got to go now. Send me that photo of Lea, will you?'

Bagger frowned. 'You're not going to show it to Jon Høgh, are you? I mean, we haven't finished our analysis. I don't want you to set him off on one. You know what he's like.'

Having lost his wife to cancer shortly after his daughter disappeared and learning that his son had been sexually abused for months, Lea Høgh's father had devoted his life to exposing paedophiles.

It had landed him in hot water with the police several times.

'Of course not,' said Henrik, feeling his phone buzz in his pocket. 'I'm not that stupid.'

12

'Jensen, I was wondering when I might hear from you.' Henrik sounded wary.

During her time in London, their calls had felt like one continuous conversation, punctuated by weeks and months. They had been like two souls connecting effortlessly across dimensions, each time picking up where they left off.

There was none of that easy intimacy left now, and she mourned its loss.

'Calling to give me a hard time again?' he said.

So, he was sore about her questions at the press conference. 'I was doing my job. I'm a crime reporter and you're a detective.'

'Well, next time just call me. As I've told you repeatedly, I'd rather we didn't talk in front of an audience,' he said.

'I didn't feel like calling before,' she said. 'Anyway, you looked uncomfortable.'

'And you looked like you've put on weight,' he said, but his heart wasn't in the joke, and it fell flat.

Jensen waited, sipping from a bottle of water. On the way

back from Bodil's, she had stopped off at a café she liked, polishing off an open rye bread sandwich with avocado, smoked salmon and radishes, which now lay heavily on her stomach.

The café was half full of people chatting, cosy with lit candles on every table and a small Christmas tree on the counter.

'Listen Jensen,' he said, his voice suddenly serious. 'I'm sorry I haven't been in touch. Do you know what you're having yet, a boy or a girl?'

She didn't.

Hadn't wanted to find out.

Knowing the gender of the child would make it all too real. 'This isn't a social call,' she said. 'Any news about Matilde?'

'We're not having this conversation, but no.' He sighed. 'I'm also rather busy, so if that's all you wanted?'

'It's not,' she said. 'I've got this other story on the go. I wondered what you can tell me about it.'

'Well, make it quick,' he said.

'I was contacted by a woman who lives in a huge old flat by Peblinge Lake. She told me that she saw a man strangle a woman in the courtyard behind her building in the early hours of Saturday. She happened to be looking out of her window at the time.'

'Did she report it?'

'Yes. A couple of officers turned up, but they didn't *do* anything. I mean, the couple had gone by then, so they searched the place, but nothing has happened since.'

'I don't recall hearing about it, but the fact that we haven't been around to see your witness again doesn't mean there's nothing going on, of course.'

'That's what I mean. Could you find out for me? Perhaps

the woman who was assaulted has come forward, and it's all being dealt with?'

Henrik was silent for a few seconds. 'Any other witnesses?' he said.

'No.'

'OK, so you've got one person saying they saw an incident, and no corroborating evidence. Jesus, Jensen, where do you find these people?'

'Just because no one else saw it, doesn't mean it never happened.'

'Believe me, Jensen, people think they see stuff all the time. You're best to forget it.'

'No,' she said. 'What if it was me that had happened to? Or your wife, or your daughter?'

'And if the victim hasn't contacted us?'

'There could be a hundred different explanations for that. One, she's dead, and the man has disposed of her body. My witness says that the woman slid onto the ground and went limp, and that the man leaned over her as if he was about to drag her away. Two, the victim knows the man who assaulted her and is afraid of him. Three, the victim has had a brush with the law herself and is afraid that the police won't believe her. Want me to go on?'

'Please don't,' said Henrik. 'You've watched too many crime shows on TV. What do you want from me, Jensen?'

'I want you to check it out. Is there any CCTV from the area that could help verify the story? Anyone reported missing of the victim's description? Anyone else who has come forward?'

'I'm trying to find a nine-year-old child. I don't have time to run around investigating your crazy theories.'

'Then ask someone else to do it,' she said. 'How about that deputy of yours?'

'Mark? He hasn't slept for three days. None of us have.'

'Well, someone else then. Please, Henrik, I wouldn't ask if I didn't think there was something to it.'

He paused.

She knew he wanted to tell her to go to hell, but also that he still felt guilty.

As he should.

For not telling her he was married all those years ago when they had first got together.

For refusing to let her go, yet never being there when she really needed him.

She saw a message from Google Me flash across her phone screen.

I got us an exclusive with the parents. Meet me in Kleinsgade in 45.

'Henrik, just check it out. You owe me that at least,' she said.

He sighed. 'I'll think about it.'

'Does that mean yes?'

'It means I'll consider it. And now I really must go.'

13

'Why did you run?' said Henrik for the third time in twenty minutes. The harsh overhead light in the interview room was doing his headache no favours. Outside the vertical blinds, it was barely daylight in the urban hinterland of car parks, building sites and modern apartment blocks where someone in their wisdom had placed the investigators of the Copenhagen Police.

Rasmus Nordby, seated on a chair in the corner, with his defence lawyer by his side, was refusing to answer.

Henrik was trying to keep his voice even, conscious that with every tick of the second hand on the wall clock, Matilde was slipping further out of their grasp.

There had been no credible sighting of her anywhere in the country, and none of the witnesses who had been present at the playground on Sunday afternoon remembered seeing a little girl in a red coat talk to anyone or be led away.

A large team of people was still combing the streets for CCTV. So far, they hadn't found any camera covering the entrance to Ørstedsparken on the corner of Ahlefeldtsgade, but they had started to go through a list of the cars that had passed through the area on Monday afternoon, excluding them from their enquiries one by one.

Pressure was mounting on the team to show progress, but right now the only lead they had was Matilde's biological father, and he wasn't being straight with them.

Nordby was wearing jeans and a sweatshirt. He had a stubbly beard and horn-rimmed glasses, slightly enlarging his flickering eyes, one of which was sporting a serious bruise.

'We found your hidden hard drive, so we know the sort of thing you like looking at,' Henrik said. 'Was that why you tried to run?'

Nordby glanced up, his eyebrows approaching his hairline. 'I know it's wrong. I deleted the pictures straightaway.'

'Not well enough,' said Henrik.

He pulled a photocopy of the image of Lea out of his breast pocket. 'We found this among the pictures you had tried to get rid of. Do you recognise this girl?'

Nordby looked at the photo. 'No,' he said, frowning. 'Should I?'

'You sure?'

'Positive.' Nordby glared at him unblinkingly. He appeared to be telling the truth. 'Who is she?'

'Lea Høgh, disappeared aged ten, six years ago, in much the same way as your daughter. Here one minute, gone the next,' said Henrik. 'Can you explain why you were in possession of a photo of her?'

Nordby looked horrified. 'No,' he said. 'I've looked at lots of photos. I don't remember this one. I swear to you, I've nothing to do with it.'

'Where did you get the photo of Lea from?' said Henrik, his voice rising in anger.

'I don't know,' said Nordby. 'You buy this stuff in batches. I didn't even know it was there.'

'I see,' said Henrik, pretending to indulge him. 'Though, here's the thing. Your daughter disappears from a playground on Sunday afternoon. That evening, you claim to know nothing about it. Then on Monday, you fail to show up for work and hide out at your mother's, and now there's this photo of Lea Høgh on your hard drive. Now, if you were in my position, what would you make of that?'

Nordby looked at his lawyer, who nodded at him encouragingly. Then he turned his bloodshot eyes on Henrik. 'I love Matilde,' he said, his voice high-pitched. 'That's why I gave her up. I know I'm sick. But I've never hurt anyone, you've got to believe me.'

'Just because all you do is sit at home watching, doesn't mean no one's getting hurt. You're witnessing children being sexually abused.'

'Not by me.'

'They're being abused because you like to watch.' Henrik didn't press home his point. No need to stop the man's flow now that he had finally managed to unblock it.

'Simon came around Sunday night,' Nordby said, looking at his hands. 'Threatened me, said he'd tell the police that I'd taken Matilde. That he'd tell you about . . . me.'

'How did Simon know what you like to look at?'

'It was after that thing at her school, but that wasn't . . . I just wanted to see Matilde, none of that . . . other stuff.'

Had Simon's accusation been a shot in the dark, a good guess based on Nordby's behaviour, or had someone whispered in his ear?

'What did you tell Simon?'

'Same as I told you. I wish I knew where Matilde was,

but I don't, I really don't. I've been going out of my mind with worry.'

This had a ring of truth about it. Since arriving, Nordby had asked for news of his daughter a handful of times.

Henrik was puzzled. Why, just hours after his step-daughter's disappearance, would Simon Clausen have left his wife's side to go and threaten Nordby with implicating him? And why had Simon omitted that part when they had interviewed him?

'How well do you and Simon know each other?' he asked.

'We don't. I saw him a couple of times when I came to pick up Matilde. Never liked him. He wouldn't speak to me, just stood in the doorway staring at me menacingly. No wonder Matilde is scared of him.'

'She is?'

'Well, she never said as much, but I could tell when-ever I dropped her off that her mood sort of fell, and she became quiet. The man's a bully. I don't know what Stine sees in him.'

'Yet, you gave up your right to see your daughter.'

'Yes. To protect her.'

'From you?'

Nordby nodded miserably.

'What about protecting her from Simon?'

'Stine would never let him hurt Matilde. She's all right.'

'Your mum doesn't agree. Says Stine won't get off your case. Is that true?'

'Mum doesn't understand. She doesn't know about me. I've tried to tell her, but it's like she can't hear me.'

Henrik's heart had sunk to somewhere near the soles of his shoes.

Nordby's answers were plausible, but not the ones he had

been hoping for. The interview was starting to feel like a dead end, and yet there was something else the man wasn't telling them.

Something that was making him afraid.

Afraid enough to run.

Henrik rubbed his mouth with one hand, catching a whiff of stale breath. He still hadn't managed to go home. 'Your daughter has disappeared,' he said. 'As of this moment, we've no idea where she is, no leads, nothing. I'm going to ask you one last time, and I want you to think hard. Do you have any idea, any clue at all where Matilde might have gone, or who might have taken her?'

'No,' Nordby sobbed. 'She's just a sweet little girl, loved by me and her mother and everyone she comes across. I know there's something wrong with me, something really fucked up, but I swear to you, if I knew where Matilde was, I'd tell you.'

He began to cry. Loud, ugly, falsetto wails, his shoulders shaking, his hands clasping at his short brown hair.

'I think that's enough for now,' said the lawyer.

Henrik got up. He hadn't got what he wanted. The only option was to have a second go at Nordby when the man had stewed a little longer.

'Is my client free to go?'

'No,' said Henrik. 'He'll be taken for his custody hearing shortly. Under the circumstances, given that he tried to run, it's highly unlikely that he will be released.'

The lawyer opened his mouth to protest, but Henrik held up one hand to stop him. 'Not now.'

As Henrik headed back to his office to grab his jacket and go home, Mark got up from his desk and followed him at a trot. 'Well?'

'Nordby confirmed that Simon Clausen came round

to his house on Monday night and threatened him,' Henrik said.

'Perhaps he wanted to divert attention away from himself.'

He had managed that all right, thought Henrik, wasting precious police time into the bargain. 'Did you speak to Simon's gym yet?'

'Yes,' said Mark. 'It took a while to find out, but they have these passes, so they can see when people are in or out. It's the only way to—'

'Mark,' Henrik interrupted, a hand over his eyes. 'Say it.'

'Simon Clausen definitely wasn't at the gym on Sunday afternoon.'

'Let's go and talk to him,' said Henrik. 'I wonder what else the bastard's been lying about.'

The clock was ticking relentlessly, and Matilde was still out there in the cold and dark.

Going home for a shower and a change of clothes would have to wait.

14

Jensen followed Google Me's instructions and cycled past the turning to Kleinsgade. As she did so, she noticed a gaggle of hardy reporters, loitering in the hope that some-thing, anything, would happen.

The divers were still working in Ørstedsparken, but the police had refused to comment, and there were only so many long-lens shots you could take of the frogmen making their slow way through the lake.

The reporters were drinking takeaway coffees and stamp-ing their feet in the cold, chatting and laughing with each other, as though they had forgotten why they were there.

Turning into the parallel street, she found the gate to the courtyard behind the Clausens' block of flats. She locked up her bike and entered the steep and narrow back stairs, climbing to the second floor and knocking on the door.

Google Me let her in, wearing headphones around his neck. 'About time. Everything is ready,' he said, ushering her through the kitchen to the hallway.

'How did you get them to agree to this?' she whispered.

'I have my ways.'

She looked at him sternly. 'Do I want to hear this?'

'Come on, they're waiting,' he said, leading her through to the living room where Matilde's parents were seated by the dining table.

Simon Clausen, the stepfather, wore a pained, stiff expression. Stine Clausen looked up at Jensen with eyes worn out from crying.

'She's here,' said Google Me. 'The reporter who solves cases faster than the police.'

Jensen shot him an angry glance. So this was how.

'Will you help find Matilde?' said Stine. 'Please, please, find my daughter.' She broke down.

My daughter. Not *our* daughter.

Simon folded his arms across his chest and stared at Jensen. The interview obviously hadn't been his idea.

'You sit there,' Google Me said to Jensen, pointing to a chair behind which he had set up his camera on a tripod.

'You're pregnant,' said Stine, sobbing. 'Your first?'

'Yes.'

'Then you don't know yet what this feels like. I'm in agony. I can't sleep, can't eat, can't think.' The last word came out as a wail. She clawed at her cheeks, leaving a red-and-white trail.

'You're right,' said Jensen. 'I don't.'

Her baby was barely more than a concept in her mind, not actual flesh and bone, a being she might one day feel like this about. She shuffled in her seat, leaning forward to make her bump look less conspicuous.

'Right,' shouted Google Me, ending the moment abruptly. 'I want you over there, Stine, and Simon on your left, a little bit in the background with your arm around Stine. No, closer, more, more, no—'

'For fuck's sake,' said Simon. 'Will you get on with it?'

The interview was tense and awkward. Stine almost clammed up completely, blinking anxiously at the lens. Simon dominated the conversation, blaming the police for not doing enough for Matilde.

They needed a change of tack.

'Stine,' said Jensen. She put her hand on the woman's arm. 'Let's go back to before all this happened. Do you have any pictures of Matilde that you could show us?'

'They're on my phone,' said Stine, glancing nervously at Simon, who nodded slightly.

'That's fine, we can cut the photos in later. You can just talk about her, give us a flavour of what she's like.'

Stine wiped her eyes with the back of her hand and began to scroll through her photos. 'Matilde is quiet, almost timid; not at all like her little brother.'

'How old is he?'

'Nine months. She's the perfect big sister. Kind, considerate of others, careful.' Stine looked up. 'That's how I know that she wouldn't just go with someone or get into a car voluntarily. We talk about it all the time.'

'When do you last remember seeing her?'

'She was playing in the bushes. One minute she was there, and the next she was gone.'

'So it was just a minute that you looked away?'

A hard look came into Simon's eyes. 'Stine can't look at her daughter all the time. She's nine, she runs around. You'll find out yourself one day.'

'Of course,' said Jensen. 'Anyone would understand that.'

She paused for a few seconds while she thought about how to phrase her next question. 'Is it possible that Matilde could have run away, or be hiding somewhere? Maybe if something had upset her?'

Simon shifted in his seat, agitated.

'No,' Stine said. 'I mean we hadn't had an argument or anything. I've been racking my brain, but as I've told the police, there was nothing unusual about that day, there really wasn't.'

'It's her biological dad you should be looking at. Rasmus Nordby is the name,' said Simon.

Stine flicked him an anxious look, but he ignored her. 'He's a paedophile. We already told the cops. Of course, he says he's got nothing to do with it, but a man like him has connections, doesn't he? Friends who are into the same filth that he is.'

'What do you mean?'

'Why don't you ask the police?'

'Maybe I will,' said Jensen.

Henrik might have told her. Why were the police keeping it a secret?

In any case, they would have to edit out Simon's comments, or they could lead to all kinds of trouble.

'Stine,' she said. 'Is there anything you want to say to the public?'

'Look straight into the camera,' said Google Me. 'Yes, like that.'

Stine cleared her throat. 'I would like to say ... whether or not you live in the area near Ørstedsparken in Copenhagen, or were at the playground on Sunday, if you have seen someone you think might be Matilde or heard anything suspicious that could be related to her disappearance, please, please come forward. Help us find our little girl. And if you're holding Matilde somewhere, we don't care about you or what you've done, we just want her back.'

'That was good,' said Jensen. 'Really good. I'm sure it'll help.'

'Right,' said Google Me. 'I need some shots of you

holding up Matilde's photo. No, don't say anything, just look into the camera.'

'Really?' said Jensen. 'I think we've got enough now. We should go, leave these people in peace.'

The doorbell rang. Stine and Simon exchanged a glance, before he got up and walked down the hall.

Jensen recognised the voice through the open door.

Henrik.

A minute later, he stood in the living room, his eyes roaming over them, furious. 'What the hell is going on here?'

15

'Unbefuckinglievable,' said Henrik under his breath when Mark had ushered Jensen and her obnoxious colleague out of the flat, and Stine had gone to lie down. 'I told you expressly not to speak to the media without us present,' he said to Simon, not quite managing to stay calm. 'It's important or we'll lose control of this investigation.'

'Like you haven't already,' said Simon.

Henrik had demanded to see the film. The red-bearded idiot holding the camera had refused. Jensen had tried to mediate by promising that they would edit out Simon's accusations against Nordby, to which the idiot had responded that they would do no such thing.

Fucking Jensen.

Getting in the way.

The only mitigating circumstance was how uncomfortable she had looked.

Simon was on the sofa now, scrolling through messages on his phone as though he couldn't care less.

If Mark hadn't been present, ever his conscience and

minder, Henrik would have let rip. 'Matilde's father says he ran off because you threatened him with violence.'

'I hardly touched him,' said Simon, without looking up.

'Tell that to his black eye,' said Henrik.

Simon tossed his phone on the sofa and rose to his feet, jabbing his index finger at Henrik. 'What are we supposed to do, sit on our hands till you find Matilde? You haven't made any progress, have you?'

Henrik counted to five, looking at the ceiling. There was a crack in one corner, the paint bubbling where damp had taken hold.

True, there had been no sightings of Matilde, but they had received an interesting witness account. A passer-by had seen a black Audi idling near the gate to the playground on Sunday afternoon, around the time that Matilde disappeared. The CCTV team was busy looking through footage for it.

Simon had a black Audi.

And there was more, including suggestions that the man was far from the caring stepfather he was making out to be. This came from friends of the couple.

'You told us that you were at the gym when Matilde disappeared,' Henrik said. 'We checked. Turns out you lied to us. Where were you?'

Simon snorted. 'So you're suspecting *me* now? You really *are* desperate.'

'I asked you a question.'

'I was planning on going to the gym, but seeing as it wasn't raining for a change, I decided to go for a run instead.'

'Where?'

'Around here,' said Simon. He smiled.

'You seem to be finding this funny,' said Henrik, squaring up to him.

Mark stepped in between them, holding up his hands. He would have a brilliant career as a war-zone mediator if policing failed, Henrik had always thought.

It didn't look to him as if Simon had been crying. 'We've been told you don't much care for Matilde, is that right?'

'Who said that?' Simon spat.

'Never mind who said it, is it true?'

'Matilde can be a handful. Doesn't mean I don't love her.'

'That's interesting, because everyone else says she's a sweet little girl. Do you want her out of the way, is that it?'

'You're crazy,' Simon shouted, twirling an index finger at his temple. 'Proper insane. I'll speak to your boss, get them to put someone else on the case.'

'Answer my question,' Henrik shouted.

'I told you, the person you want to look at is Matilde's dad,' said Simon. 'And what have you done about it? Nothing.'

'Actually, we arrested Rasmus Nordby this morning,' said Henrik, instantly regretting that he had volunteered the information.

'Finally,' said Simon. 'And what did he say?'

'None of your business. Nordby is cooperating with our enquiries. You, on the other hand, seem to be telling lies and I wonder why.'

16

Jensen turned from her screen, cringing.

GIVE US BACK OUR DAUGHTER

EXCLUSIVE INTERVIEW WITH
SIMON AND STINE CLAUSEN

The video was ugly and crass, virtually unedited, with a bright yellow 'Breaking' banner pasted at the bottom.

She had fought Google Me, arguing that Rasmus Nordby deserved the right to comment, but Margrethe had overruled her, insisting that the video was a great piece of work.

The press release from the police, confirming that Rasmus Nordby had been arrested, and was helping the police with their enquiries, had done little to stem speculation that he, or someone he knew, had taken his daughter.

She had tried to get in touch with Henrik, leaving several messages on his phone, but these had been met with stony silence.

Asking him if he had made any progress on checking out Bodil's story would be a lost cause now.

Her office was dark except from the weak, phosphorescent light coming from the dormer window. There was no sound to be heard anywhere in the building. Everyone had gone home.

She was tired and hungry, but she couldn't stop thinking of Matilde.

Where was she?

Was she frightened, hurt, sick?

Or dead?

Finding her felt like an insurmountable task, yet the likelihood of her suddenly turning up now seemed remote. Stine Clausen had appealed to her for help, sick with worry for her child.

Jensen couldn't remember her mother ever showing concern for her welfare to the same extent. She got out her phone. It had been a few weeks now since she had last spoken to Marion. This made her feel guilty. What if something had happened?

For better or worse, it had always been just the two of them. No cousins, aunts or uncles. There had been a grandmother once, but she had died when Jensen was a girl.

'Hello? Mum?'

'Hello *you*,' said Marion.

She sounded as though she was in bed, drowsy or high. Probably both.

'Is there anyone there with you?' said Jensen.

Getting hold of weed was beyond her mother's powers of organisation, and she lived in the middle of nowhere in North Jutland without a car, which meant someone must have come for a visit.

'Bo and Lisette just left,' Marion said.

Marion had a whole army of loose acquaintances, and new people kept appearing whose names Jensen couldn't remember from one time to the next. They treated her mother like a charity case, filling her kitchen cupboards and driving her to town to pick up paint and canvases.

There had been times when Jensen had wished her mother was like the parents of her friends: capable, resourceful, interested, even irritatingly strict and laying down rules, like when to be home and how to dress.

During her early childhood, their flat in Copenhagen had been different to other people's, the door always open, virtual strangers wandering in and out. For this reason, Jensen never brought friends home, and eventually others stopped inviting her. By the time she and her mother moved to Jutland, she had lost any expectation of a social life.

'How is my baby?' said Marion.

'Fine,' Jensen said.

'And my baby's baby?'

'Kicking a lot.'

Her mother didn't own a TV and had only an old Nokia mobile phone. She didn't watch the news and had even less of an idea of what Jensen did for a living. They never spoke about her work.

Marion had to be the only person left in Denmark who didn't know about Matilde Clausen.

'Have you been eating?' said Jensen. 'Heating working OK?'

'I'm fine,' said Marion.

'I've been thinking,' Jensen said. 'When you found out you were pregnant with me, were you—'

'Is this about your father again?' said Marion, her voice instantly hitting a lower, wearier register. 'You know I can't tell you who he was. There were several guys around the time. I'm sorry, I wish I could do better.'

'I know. But I wondered . . . did you ever consider having an abortion?'

'Never. I mean, not because I was against it or anything, but I was twenty-eight, you know, and I wanted you, I really did. It was fate.'

'Even though my father could have been anybody? I mean, you didn't know how I'd turn out. I could have been, I don't know, insane.'

Marion's laughter ran down the line, like tiny hard pearls. 'But you weren't. Besides it's not all about genetics. There's nurture as well.'

God help me if nurture was all I had to rely on, thought Jensen.

The same endless stream of friends who surrounded her mother had more or less brought her up. Marion considered motherhood a communal endeavour.

'The thing is, I'm not really like you,' she said.

She had often thought about it. She and Marion had the same dark-blue eyes, but Marion, an artist, was considerably taller, and it was hard to find two people with more dissimilar personalities.

Jensen had a temper and not a single creative bone in her body, and Marion had zero curiosity about the world around her.

'No, you're your own person,' said Marion. 'Isn't that a wonderful thing?'

She sounded like she was drifting off to sleep.

Jensen thought she could hear the perpetual wind from the North Sea whistling around the cottage, a mournful, lonely sound.

'I'll come and see you at Christmas,' Jensen said. 'We can celebrate together.'

'Good,' said Marion.

Margrethe was spending the holidays in Copenhagen with her brother Claes. But Jensen didn't fancy the bad atmosphere between Gustav and his dad, or Margrethe's terrible cooking.

For once, she was glad that Marion didn't ask any questions about where she was going to live. How she was going to manage when the baby came. What the midwife had said.

Instead, they talked about nothing as, slowly, her mother's pauses lengthened, before eventually she fell asleep, her rhythmic, heavy breathing coming down the line.

She would be next to no help with the baby when the time came.

Jensen was on her own.

Completely on her own.

17

Henrik glanced at his watch, glad that only ten minutes remained of his appointment, the last of his counselling sessions after the incident in the summer.

Incident.

The clinical term used in the official reports was strangely comforting, reducing the horror and chaos to something manageable, clean.

Isabella Grå caught him looking and smiled at him benignly. 'You seem to be in a hurry, Henrik?'

She looked relaxed in her white linen shirt. Her greying hair hung loose over her shoulders and dangling by her long neck were gold earrings in the shape of leaves.

Beyond the door to her consultant's room, you could hear gentle cooking sounds and someone practising the piano.

Her husband had to be rich. The terraced houses in the area known as the Potato Rows were some of Copenhagen's most expensive. Henrik felt dirty and rough among the sparse designer furniture and modern art.

His own house was wrecked, run down by the kids, full

of the detritus of family life. 'We're in the middle of a major missing-person investigation,' he said. 'I've got to get back to the office.'

Isabella glanced at his legs. They were bobbing up and down. He ordered them to stop, ran a hand over his mouth.

'I saw it on the news. But you have a team,' she said. 'It's not all on you, is it?'

'Feels like it sometimes.' His laughter came out hollow. 'Besides, you've had four months. If you haven't fixed me by now, you're hardly going to do so in the next few minutes.'

'It's not my job to fix you,' said Isabella.

He looked at her in surprise. 'It's not? Then what am I doing here?'

'Learning how to help yourself.' Her brown eyes were still smiling, her voice even and calm. 'Do you know what I think, Henrik? I think you're right. You're wasting your time. You should go.'

The blood rushed to his cheeks. 'What do you mean?'

'You're not telling me what's really going on inside your head.'

'We've talked, haven't we? I've answered all your questions.'

'Is that what you think this is, a test?'

'Of course not.'

He looked at his legs. They had begun to bob up and down again. The truth was, he hadn't wanted the sessions with Isabella, but Wiese had insisted.

A police officer had been killed on his watch, mowed down like an animal. He could still see her blood on his hands, still woke up in the night, drenched in sweat, convinced he had just heard a shot ring out in the silent house.

What good was talking about it? She was still dead. In his mind, she had died a thousand times.

Officially, he had been cleared of any wrongdoing as her superior officer, but in his heart, he knew that all of it was his fault.

Sometimes, when he looked behind him, all he could see were failures and mistakes.

The Matilde case was shaping up to be no different.

'You seem tense,' said Isabella. 'How are you sleeping?'

Hardly at all.

'I get the sleep I need,' he lied.

'Nightmares?'

Every night, he thought, but shook his head. 'Look, I'm fine. I just want to go on with my life, focus on my work, catch the bad guys. Same as always.'

She made a note. 'Tell me about that. How does work make you feel?'

'I like to keep busy.'

It was far more than that, he thought. Work was his salvation, knowing what to do and doing it. Going through the motions.

Each case was like being given another chance.

To not fuck up.

To put things right.

'Working won't make it go away, you know,' said Isabella.

'Won't make what go away?'

'What happened to your colleague. It seems to me you're beating yourself up. You're trying to distract yourself from what's hurting by fighting it. You need to feel it, accept it.' She kept her gaze fixed on him. 'Last month, we talked about you visiting your colleague's widower. Have you made contact yet?'

He shook his head, guilt welling up in him. 'I've been up to my neck in cases.'

'You've had a long time.'

He looked at his hands. His knuckles were white, sweat pooling inside his palms.

'Are you afraid of what might happen, or what you might feel?'

He flashed her a look but saw no malice in her face, just genuine interest, the opening of a door for him to step through.

Don't be kind to me, he thought. *I don't deserve it.*

'Nah,' he said, slamming the door in her face. 'The only thing I fear is Brøndby losing to FCK in the league final.'

He got up, jangled his car keys and made for the door. He was going to head to the gym, then pick up some food on the way back to the office, go through the files on Jan Loft.

And wait for news of Matilde.

He had asked the team to start going through the entire list of registered black Audis in Denmark.

There were thousands.

'I really have to go now,' he said.

'Wait,' she said.

He cut her off, before she had time to say anymore. 'Thanks anyway. See you around, doc.'

Day Three

18

'No way,' said Wiese. 'We're not reprioritising the Lea Høgh case based on a single photo. Bagger is right, it must be a coincidence that Matilde's dad had the photo in his possession.' His gaze was obscured by the light from the Anglepoise lamp reflecting in his glasses, his face an unreadable mask.

Henrik suppressed an urge to scream.

After seeing Isabella Grå, he had spent two hours in the gym, pedalling furiously on his spinning bike until his mind was numb and there was a puddle of sweat on the floor.

He had brought a takeaway to the office, texting his wife to say that he wouldn't be coming home to sleep.

He could still taste the onions from the kebab he had wolfed down as he pored over the files on the Jan Loft case.

It had all come back to him in the empty, silent office. His fury at Loft's refusal to speak about his contacts, or tell them what he knew about Lea. The gradual destruction of the Høgh family, like a car crash in slow motion. His own endless drives around Dragør looking for Lea, carrying her photo, asking random people in the street.

He had fallen asleep at his desk, only waking when the cleaners started up their vacuums shortly after five. After washing his face in the bathroom, he had made coffee in the galley kitchen and taken it to Wiese's office.

His headache had intensified. He imagined a vice screwed into his cranium that some evil force was tightening by the hour.

He couldn't think straight. They had run up one blind alley after another.

What now?

Simon Clausen was an arsehole, but they hadn't been able to make anything stick during the interview. Could he have harmed his stepdaughter, or asked someone else to?

They would have to investigate further. The answer to cases involving young children was often to be found in the family. *Dagbladet*'s video interview with Simon and Stine, plastered across the internet, had made everything ten times worse.

And then there was Rasmus Nordby. He clearly didn't know where his daughter was, but he was still hiding something from them. What was it?

Wiese liked to be first in the office in the morning. It was how he maintained his reputation as a hard worker. Henrik had listened as Wiese approached down the hall in his cycling shoes, then watched him almost fall over in fright when he opened the door, realising that he had a visitor.

'Never do that again, Jungersen,' he had said, one hand on his chest.

Despite cycling in from Hellerup where he lived with his wealthy wife, Wiese had barely broken a sweat.

'But the photo is new evidence,' Henrik said, watching Wiese opening his laptop and entering his password. 'Knowledge we didn't have before. Lea was abused too, just like her brother. That's significant. I want to question Jan Loft.'

Wiese shook his head. 'Not going to happen.' He pretended to sniff the air, wrinkling his nose. 'Your breath stinks, Jungersen. Ever heard of brushing your teeth?'

Henrik felt himself blush. 'I'm investigating a suspected child abduction, with a potential link to another missing-persons case from six years ago, and you're concerned about my personal hygiene?'

'There *is* no link.'

'There's a photo.'

'You're proving my point.'

'What point is that?'

'You're not thinking clearly.'

Wiese had tried to persuade him to go on leave before, to consider his options, perhaps ask for a transfer into another team. Henrik had always refused.

'I'm fine,' he said now. 'You don't need to worry about me.'

Wiese took his glasses off, breathed on each lens in turn and polished them carefully with a white cloth before replacing them and obscuring his eyes once more. 'See, Jungersen, I wonder if that's entirely true.'

'What do you mean?'

'I think we all recall that the business with Jan Loft took quite a toll on you.'

Henrik was surprised. The investigation had threatened to blow his life apart, but outwardly he thought he had held it together, with the exception of the one slip of his temper with Jan Loft.

Who had Wiese been speaking to? Not Bagger. Bagger wouldn't snitch on him, nor Mark.

Plenty of others to choose from, though. People who

would go out of their way to poke at his weak spots. 'A ten-year-old girl went missing walking home from Jan Loft's house,' he said patiently. 'A few months later it turns out the same man had been sexually abusing the girl's twelve-year-old brother and four other boys over the course of two years. It was a major case, and I took my responsibility seriously. Did it take its toll? You bet it did. Unlike some, I'm not a machine.'

There was more to it than that, of course there was, but he had been softer back then, less experienced.

He and Jensen had known each other for nine years at the time. Shortly before Lea disappeared they had rekindled their contact after a long absence, and promptly fallen in love, all over again.

It had felt urgent, like an insatiable hunger, a rush of teenage hormones. Dangerous. Wonderful.

Until his wife had suspected, throwing their marriage into another major crisis, and then the Lea case had floored him.

He had virtually been living in the office during those weeks.

They had nailed Loft, but the images and videos he had created of his abuse of the Dragør boys would be circulating in the digital sewer for eternity.

'Come, Jungersen, it's not like it was an isolated case. You go too far, and I'm afraid it's about to happen again. This thing with Lea – you're staring at ghosts, a picture from a distant past.' He sat back in his chair. 'Let Bagger deal with the photo. Focus on Matilde. If you can't, if you get worked up, or allow yourself to get distracted, then—'

'Then what?'

The door was torn open, and Mark entered the room, red-faced, flustered. 'There you are,' he said to Henrik. 'I've been calling you.'

'Excuse me,' said Wiese. 'Ever heard of knocking?'

'We're in the middle of something here,' Henrik said. 'Can't it wait?'

'I'm afraid not,' said Mark, waving his mobile phone. 'It's Rasmus Nordby. Someone's covered his house in paint.'

19

Jensen watched Google Me in disgust. He was wearing his oversized parka and a black baseball cap, and was in his element filming the red paint running down the façade of the bungalow in Tåstrup.

A uniformed police officer was trying to stop him from walking all the way up to the front door, locking the two of them in an awkward sideways dance.

The morning was misty and damp, and Jensen's hair was plastered to her face. Despite the fact that she was perpetually hungry, some of her old morning sickness from months ago had returned. Coffee was still off the menu; the smell alone turned her stomach.

She missed her friend Liron, the enigmatic Israeli coffee seller, but hadn't been able to bring herself to visit his van in Sankt Peders Stræde for months.

She shivered as she stood some distance away from Rasmus Nordby's neighbours, who were mingling with a group of journalists and photographers.

Someone had phoned the media an hour ago and the news had spread in minutes.

Had Matilde's stepfather been right? Did Nordby really have something to do with his daughter's disappearance? If he did, where had he taken her and why?

'You don't expect to wake up to this sort of thing in your own neighbourhood,' said a wide-eyed, older woman with her arms wrapped around her shoulders as if trying to give herself a hug. 'It's shocking really.'

'What can you tell us about Nordby?' said one of the journalists.

His colleagues leaned in with their mobiles set to record.

'There's nothing to tell. I see him leaving for work in the morning sometimes.'

'He doesn't speak to any of us,' said a man in his seventies with a tiny brown dog. 'We had a garden party ... when was that, Ulla?' he said to the woman.

'Midsummer,' she said. 'We invited him, he didn't show. Odd character. But you don't know about other people, do you? All this time he's been living here, and we didn't know.'

'Did you ever see Matilde with him?'

They both shook their heads immediately. 'Never.'

'And did you know about the ... his er ...?' The journalist pointed to the house where the word 'Paedo' was just about legible.

'God no,' said the woman. 'But the police were here yesterday. They forced the door with a battering ram and took away some stuff in a cardboard box.'

'Did they now?'

There was a stir among the group of reporters.

'What do you think has happened to Matilde?' said the journalist.

It was a desperate question. No one knew the answer.

Jensen looked away as Google Me came trudging towards

her with his camera. 'I got loads. Bastard wouldn't let me ring the doorbell, though.'

She looked at him in surprise. 'Nordby isn't there. Why would you ring the doorbell?'

'It would have made a good shot,' he sniffed.

Jensen felt sick. 'We did this,' she said nodding at the house.

'Us?' Google Me said, wiping his nose on the back of his hand and drinking from his takeaway coffee. 'Nah, we were just holding the microphone.'

'Yes, for Simon's claims, which Nordby had no chance to defend himself against.'

Someone must have seen their interview with Simon last night and decided to take matters into their own hands.

'Come on,' said Google Me. 'It's not as if the guy is all innocent.'

'How do you know that?'

'No smoke without fire.' He pointed to the house.

'It wouldn't have happened if Margrethe hadn't put your video online. What if Nordby hasn't done anything?'

'What if he has?'

'You don't think we should wait until we know? What happened to "innocent until proven guilty"?'

Google Me looked at her, squinting as though he was trying to work something out. Then he lifted the lid from his coffee and tipped the rest of it into the gutter.

She caught a whiff of it and almost retched.

'I see what you're doing,' he said. 'You're trying to undermine me, little miss high and mighty who doesn't do partners. Well, getting this job with *Dagbladet* is the big break I've been waiting for, and I'm not going to waste my chance. At least I'm doing *something*, rather than standing there with a face like a slapped arse. Let's see what Margrethe Skov prefers, shall we?'

He hoisted the camera back up to his shoulder and headed across to the group of neighbours and journalists.

Jensen was about to swear at him, when she saw a black car roll up and park behind the two police vehicles.

Henrik.

Tired.

Pissed off.

He got out, his white shirt and black leather jacket standing out starkly in the mist. She watched as he walked up to the house and spoke for a while to the uniformed officers. One of them pointed to the crowd.

By now the journalists had spotted Henrik and were running across to him.

Jensen stayed where she was. Henrik looked up and caught her eye, staring at her for a moment. Then he held up his hands to the reporters.

'This is an act of vandalism. We'll find the people responsible and hold them to account. At this moment, there's no news about Matilde. As soon as there is, we'll update the media.'

A disappointed sigh rippled through the crowd. After a few more questions, none of which Henrik answered, the reporters headed for their cars, leaving the neighbours shuffling on the pavement and looking at each other, suddenly surplus to requirements.

Jensen folded her arms and glared meaningfully at Google Me.

'Whatever it is you want to say, I don't want to hear it,' he said, packing up his camera. 'I'm heading back to the newspaper to edit this piece,' he said. 'There's a crowd of people gathering in town to conduct a search for Matilde. They're handing out flyers. It'll make a good video.'

He didn't offer her a lift, and she didn't want one.

They had arrived together, but no way was she getting into the car with him now. They had wasted an entire morning thanks to him. She needed to think.

Alone.

'I'll make my own way back,' she said.

'Suit yourself.'

20

Jensen looked like a drowned rat as she stood on the pavement, lost in thought.

Part of him felt sorry for her. A bigger part wanted to give her a bollocking for *Dagbladet*'s idiotic coverage in the past twenty-four hours.

He was angry. Angry with Simon Clausen for repeating his accusations on camera. Angry with the vigilantes who had sprayed red paint on Rasmus Nordby's house. Most of all, angry with Wiese for refusing to let him interview Jan Loft.

He needed a lucky break.

Just one.

An idea came to him as he strolled across to Jensen; it might work.

She turned towards him, raindrops rolling down her face and catching on her lips. He would have thought they were tears, had Jensen been the type of woman who cried.

For a moment, he wanted to return to a simpler time before she had met her psycho boyfriend, when it had been just the two of them.

('And me,' said his wife in his head.)

He shook his head and stood up straight. 'Give you a lift back to town?' he said. 'I have a proposition for you.'

To his surprise she accepted, then followed his instruction to wait for him in the next street. Some years ago, she might have ridiculed this precaution to ensure that no one spotted them together; now she didn't even remark on it.

She was quiet in the car, leaning her head against the window and closing her eyes as the suburbs flashed past.

Her lack of aggression threw him. He wanted to take her hand but refrained. 'That video last night was a shitshow. What the hell were you thinking?' he said, surprised by the gentle tone in his voice.

'You don't have to tell me,' she said. 'I tried to stop it. I had a bad feeling Simon Clausen was just lashing out.'

'You and me both.'

'I should have fought harder against that video being released.'

'You should have called me first.'

'I knew you wouldn't pick up.' There was no accusation in her voice; it was a statement of fact. 'Is it true that Rasmus Nordby is a paedophile?'

Henrik didn't say anything. He didn't have to. He sensed Jensen nodding to herself as he kept his eyes on the road.

'Is there a link to Matilde's disappearance?'

'Not one we know of yet,' said Henrik, slowing down the car as it went through a wave of green lights. 'He doesn't have Matilde. Claims he doesn't know where she is.'

He wanted the conversation to last.

'Could it be Simon who vandalised his house? He seemed very angry,' said Jensen.

Henrik had already thought about that. He had asked Mark to retrieve Simon's call records, so they could find out whom he had spoken to in the past few days.

There was another possible instigator of the vandalism, but he wasn't prepared to share that with Jensen. 'It's possible,' he said.

If they carried on at the current speed, they would be at *Dagbladet* in a few minutes, and it would be too late to ask her the question that had been forming slowly in his mind.

A turning into a residential area of Christianshavn was coming up. He indicated and left the main road. 'Where are we going?' said Jensen, perplexed.

He didn't answer her but pulled up to the kerb next to a yellow apartment building by the Church of Our Saviour with its gilded helter-skelter spire.

He switched off the ignition and undid his seatbelt, turning to her. 'I need you to do something for me.'

She frowned. 'You want *me* to do *you* a favour?'

'I realise it must be an alien concept to you, but yes. Now, hear me out. Six years ago, I dealt with another case of a missing child, Lea Høgh. She vanished on a walk home, later presumed drowned. She was ten.'

'I read about it. Awful story.'

'Then you'll also remember that it turned out that her twelve-year-old brother had been the victim of sexual abuse along with a group of other lads in Dragør. The perpetrator was a local businessman by the name of Jan Loft.'

'I was in London then, so the details are a bit sketchy. I wasn't paying as much attention to Danish news as I should have done, but I do remember the effect that case had on you.'

'What do you mean?'

'You went AWOL for months. I suddenly couldn't get hold of you,' she said. 'Feels kind of familiar in hindsight,' she added under her breath.

'If you say so, but listen, Loft is due to be released from prison next week.'

'And?'

'I want you to request an interview with him, before he disappears off the face of the earth. I want you to ask him about Lea Høgh, what he knew about her, the connections he had. At the time, we found no evidence that she'd been sexually abused like her brother, but something has turned up, suggesting that maybe we were wrong about that.'

'What?'

He hesitated, but decided he had to trust her, if his plan was going to work. 'A photo. If you get the interview, I'll send it to you. I want you to look at his face when you show it to him and tell me how he reacts.'

'Why can't you do it yourself?'

'It's complicated. Let's just say that my boss has refused.'

'But I don't understand, why are you asking me about this now? Does it have something to do with Matilde?'

'No, no,' he said.

He couldn't tell her where they had found the photo, not without setting off another reckless witch hunt against Rasmus Nordby.

The man was a mess. He had cried inconsolably when they spoke to him last night. He might be a paedophile, but his daughter was missing, the daughter he had given up in order to protect her from himself.

In due course, he would receive his punishment for the pictures and videos he had bought, held and shared online. Not enough in Henrik's view. The sentences for such offences were notoriously light. And without treatment, the chances of him reoffending were high.

If Bagger was right and the old photo of Lea had been circulating online for years, there had to be more like it.

116

Henrik was anxious to hear if Bagger's team had found any. But not before he had got what he wanted from Jensen. 'So, will you do it?' he said.

'I don't see why Loft would agree.'

'I think there's a good chance. I heard he's claiming to be a reformed character. I'm sure he'd love a platform to tell everyone about it. Appeal to his ego, that should work.'

'Anyway, you called it a proposition. So what's in it for me?'

'You get to write the story for *Dagbladet*. Only you can't say that I put you up to it.'

She looked pensive. Something calculating had entered her eyes, a look he knew well. 'You know that story I told you about, the woman who said she witnessed an assault in the courtyard behind her flat by the Lakes? Made any headway on your enquiries yet?'

'Fuck's sake, Jensen, you can't expect me to drop everything for your crackpot witnesses. Not in the middle of the Matilde case.'

'I see,' she said.

She folded her arms across her bump and looked out of the window as though she had all the time in the world.

A postman walked past, pushing a trolley.

Henrik glanced at his phone.

No messages.

He needed to get back to the station as soon as possible. The vandalism of Nordby's house had been an intolerable disruption.

He didn't have time for this.

'All right,' he said. 'I'll get someone to look into it, but I wouldn't hold your breath.'

She smiled at him, her dark-blue eyes sparkling in the

winter gloom, and for just a moment there was a glimpse of her usual self.

Jensen.

The most annoying woman in Copenhagen.

She shook his hand. 'You have yourself a deal.'

On the way into town, they picked up speed. He had already lost too much valuable time.

As they passed the parliament at Christiansborg, ringed by its protective chain of granite boulders like giant pearls on a string, Jensen suddenly shouted, 'Stop the car! Stop it now.'

His heart leaped into his throat. 'What is it? What's wrong? Is it the baby?'

Jensen already had her seatbelt undone and the car door open. She stepped out.

'No,' she said, pointing to a familiar-looking lad sitting on a railing on the other side of the road with his head in a cloud of steam. 'It's Gustav. And he's nowhere near where he should be.'

21

Jensen crossed the corridor to Henning's office and pushed open the door, startled to find someone already in there. A man in workman's trousers and a zip-up fleece, headphones in his ears, was busy emptying the filing cabinets that lined one wall. He was singing badly to himself, unceremoniously dumping folders fat with clippings into cardboard boxes.

'What the hell are you doing?' she shouted.

He recoiled, horrified, stared at her face then at her bump. 'What?' he said, blushing.

'Henning's off sick. You can't just come in here and pack up his office.'

'I was told to.'

'By whom?' she demanded.

'Margrethe Skov. She's asked us to clear out the whole floor.'

She knew this, of course.

She would need to pack her own office too, but seeing the stranger trampling all over Henning's things was infuriating. 'Where are you taking everything anyway?' she said, her voice softening.

The man looked flustered as he tried to recover his composure after the shock of her intrusion. 'To the tip, I guess. It's just loads of old paper, isn't it? It's all online now.'

She looked at him, hands by her sides. 'Do you know how long it took to cut out all these articles and mark them up and file them away?' she said.

He shrugged and resumed his work. 'Nothing to do with me,' he said.

'I want you to leave,' she said. 'Right now.'

The workman finally left, shaking his head. 'Crazy woman,' he mumbled under his breath.

When she had calmed down, she felt embarrassed. No one, not even she, could hold back the wave of change that was crushing the newspaper industry to death.

Seeing Gustav in the street earlier had set her in a bad mood. He had been sitting on railings by the canal, vaping without a care in the world.

'Why aren't you at school?' she had asked him.

'First couple of lessons got cancelled,' he said, refusing to look at her as he jumped to his feet.

'Gustav, do I look stupid? Your high school is two kilometres from here,' she shouted, ignoring the passers-by who were staring at them.

'So what?' Gustav said. 'There's no law says I can't go where I want in my free period. Get off my case, Jensen.'

He picked up his rucksack and started to walk away, then changed his mind. 'What about the story of the assault down by the Lakes? Find any clues yet?'

'Nice try, Gustav, but this isn't about me. This is about you not being at school.'

'Sure, Mum, whatever you say.'

'I looked in your rucksack last night . . .' she began. 'I didn't see any schoolbooks in there.'

But he had already put on his over-ear headphones and was walking away without looking back.

She needed to speak to Margrethe about him, and soon.

The workman had only got as far as 'C'. The rest of Henning's alphabetically organised files were still in their drawers. Carefully, she opened the one marked L–M, and picked out Jan Loft's file.

She took it to her office and sat down by her desk to read the newspaper cuttings.

Lea Høgh and Matilde Clausen were both skinny and blonde and close in age when they disappeared. Aside from that, there seemed to be very few similarities between the two cases.

The last person to see Lea before she disappeared had been her older brother Sebastian. She had walked off when he refused to come home, though he had been supposed to babysit her.

Later, after the sexual abuse of her brother had come to light, the newspapers had speculated that Loft had got some of his paedophile acquaintances to abduct Lea. She had left Loft's house around three o'clock in the afternoon. When Sebastian had returned home at a few minutes to five, there was no sign of his sister. It was assumed she had taken a shortcut that ran behind Loft's house. Sebastian had gone out to look for Lea himself; the alarm had only been raised when the children's father Jon had returned from work to find Sebastian in floods of tears.

Several witnesses claimed to have seen Lea after she vanished, including a group of teenage boys who said they saw a girl matching Lea's description walk into the sea from a nearby beach.

After the clothes and sandals she had been wearing that day were found folded yards away from the water's edge, it was assumed that Lea had drowned.

The search continued along the coast for several days, joined by hundreds of members of the public, now focused on finding Lea's body.

A mission never accomplished.

Later, when Jan Loft had been arrested for sexually abusing Sebastian and his friends, suspicion had fallen on him, but he had denied involvement, and the police hadn't been able to produce any evidence.

All the *Dagbladet* articles in Henning's folder had been written by Jensen's predecessor, Frank Buhl. She wished she could talk to him about it but knew the feeling wouldn't be mutual. Last time she had seen Frank, as he walked away from the office with his possessions in a cardboard box, he had practically accused her of stealing his job.

Still, if she was going to interview Loft, she would need more information than the articles in front of her.

Who was he? What had really happened on that summer's day six years ago? What else was there to know about the case?

She added Frank Buhl to the list of people she had to speak to.

She had already emailed the request to see Loft. The weekly visiting day was Saturday. If he responded quickly, she could be seeing him as soon as the weekend.

One thing was certain: Google Me wouldn't be anywhere near when she did.

Her story about the vandalism at Rasmus Nordby's house had been given top billing in *Dagbladet*'s digital edition, along with Google Me's video. The whole thing filled her with embarrassment.

She climbed into the dormer windowsill and looked out at Copenhagen.

Somewhere out there was Matilde.

Alive or dead.

Hiding or being hidden.

Jensen put her hand on her bump and felt a bone digging into her palm.

22

Henrik was relieved to see Jon Høgh's locksmith's van parked in front of the house in Dragør. He hadn't called ahead, not wanting to alarm the man or give him a reason to refuse the visit.

He still hadn't decided whether to show Høgh the picture of Lea that they had found on Nordby's laptop.

A rhythmic thumping was coming from the back of the carport. Henrik followed the sound and found Høgh drenched in sweat, beating the crap out of a punchbag suspended from a small overhang. Eventually, he stopped and wiped his face with the back of his boxing glove. Høgh was about the same age as Henrik, but significantly taller and more muscular.

'What are *you* doing here?' he said.

A thin, blonde woman passed behind the kitchen window, staring at them both with frightened eyes. Høgh's latest girlfriend, presumably.

He had been arrested a couple of times for harassing convicted paedophiles, and already had a suspended sentence. Next time he might not be so lucky.

'How are you doing, Jon?' Henrik said, then held up his hands. 'Nothing's happened. I was just passing.'

'Shouldn't you be out searching for that missing girl?'

Henrik didn't reply. To his immense disappointment, there had been no major development when he had checked in with the team back at the station.

Hundreds of people had gathered outside Ørstedsparken to hand out flyers and search through the city. Though well-meaning, they were a nuisance, getting in the way and adding to the already substantial fear among the public.

Wiese had caught him in the corridor, pushing him for progress, and Henrik had assured him that they were doing everything they could.

This had left him uneasy.

Were they really? Doing everything they could?

'Oh, I get it,' said Høgh, a cynical smile slowly spreading across his face. 'I saw the news. If you're here to ask me if I had anything to do with that paint job in Tåstrup this morning, save your breath. I haven't done anything for ages.' He resumed his punching with what felt like excess aggression.

Henrik stood silently by, keeping his eyes friendly and fixed on Høgh. 'I'm not here about you,' he said.

'OK, if you say so,' said Høgh. 'But I haven't seen you in a couple of years, so spare me the bullshit about just dropping by.'

Henrik felt terrible, not being able to give the man what he wanted: his daughter back, or at the very least some sort of answer as to what had happened to her. The coverage about Matilde must have been triggering. 'Is there somewhere we can talk?' he said gently.

Høgh picked up a towel, wiped his brow and pointed to a bench.

Henrik sat down, but Høgh remained standing, slowly and menacingly removing his boxing gloves. Steam rose from his shoulders in the cool air.

'It's about Jan Loft. He's being released soon,' said Henrik.

Høgh spat, missing Henrik's boots by a couple of inches. 'Yeah, next week, the bastard.'

'You're not planning on doing anything stupid, are you?' Henrik said.

'What if I was? I lost my kids because of that monster. My wife wouldn't have become ill and died, had it not been for him.'

'You still have your son.'

Henrik knew that Sebastian was in his second year of high school, lived in student accommodation in Copenhagen and had a girlfriend. He checked up on all of Loft's victims from time to time. They were a shrinking bunch. One had killed himself. One had died of leukaemia. One was on drugs. With the exception of another lad who had joined the air force, only Sebastian had managed to break away from what happened to him.

At least outwardly.

Høgh shook his head. 'He stopped talking to me six months ago now. Told me he needs to move on.'

'Seems fair,' Henrik said. 'You don't agree?'

'It's not a matter of agreeing. I can't do it. Not while that pig is still alive. Not while he won't say what happened to Lea.'

'You still think he had something to do with it?'

'Are you fucking kidding me?' said Høgh. 'My daughter vanishes on the way home from a house belonging to the man who abused my son, and he's got nothing to do with it?'

'We found no evidence that Loft was involved.'

'You know as well as I do that Loft is a liar.'

Høgh sat down, so close that Henrik could smell the sour sweat coming off him. He was agitated. Telling him about the photo of Lea now would be too risky.

'The fact that Loft was busy molesting Sebastian and his friends at the time is exactly the reason why I think he was involved,' said Høgh. 'Lea saw something she shouldn't have, so he had her killed and made it look like she drowned.'

'You still don't believe that she did?'

'She couldn't swim, she was scared of the water. Why would she just walk into the sea?'

It was a good question.

It was the same question he had asked himself about Matilde and the lake in Ørstedsparken.

'There was another witness at the time,' said Høgh. 'One no one listened to.'

'You're talking about Bitten Vognmand.'

Høgh nodded.

Vognmand, a woman in her seventies, had reported seeing Lea getting into a white car, but there were problems with her statement. She had argued that Lea had been fully dressed, despite the discovery of her clothes on the beach. And the previous report Vognmand had made to the police was of a UFO sighting in her garden. 'She wasn't exactly what you'd call a reliable witness,' said Henrik.

'She's dead now, but I spoke to her several times. I have all the tapes – you're welcome to them. She never changed her story,' said Høgh. 'Do you know what I think? I think whoever picked Lea up in that white car killed her, and Loft was behind it.'

Henrik said nothing. He had heard it all before, followed up, spoken to hundreds of people and none of it had ever led anywhere except to exhaustion and bitterness.

Høgh sniffed, stood up. 'What was it that you wanted to know about Loft?'

Henrik held his hands up. 'I'm not here in any official capacity. It's just . . . what I said, regarding Loft not harming girls.'

'What about it?'

'You know we looked at his acquaintances, all of them going back several years, his staff, everyone we could think of. Well, we never found anyone else connected with child sexual abuse in any way.'

'Yes, I know that. What's the "but"?'

'There was the online side of things as well.'

'Where the bastard shared the pictures and videos. Yes, I know.'

'Before Lea disappeared, was there anything that worried you? Had there been any change in her behaviour?'

'Like what?'

'Was she more quiet than usual, for example? Did it seem like there was something on her mind?'

'What are you getting at?'

'Is there any chance that, without you knowing, Lea had been subjected to sexual abuse, in any context, before she disappeared?'

Høgh's mask was cracking and dissolving, revealing unbearable pain and grief. He jumped up. 'Has something happened? It has, hasn't it? I can tell from your face.'

Henrik knew he had gone too far.

Too far to stop now.

'We'd better go inside.'

23

'Jensen. What are *you* doing here?' said Frank Buhl, standing in the back garden of his bungalow in Albertslund. His expression betrayed an inner struggle between rage and curiosity.

Jensen had walked around the house through a garden gate after ringing the doorbell in vain a few times.

The red Toyota Yaris in the car port suggested someone was in, as did the lights in the kitchen.

Seeing Frank again, in his clogs, old jeans, red braces and lumberjack shirt, pricked at her guilty conscience.

Contrary to his accusation, she hadn't deliberately gone after his job as chief crime reporter of *Dagbladet.*

In some ways, it was worse than that. She had failed to see him altogether, neglected to consult him or show even a modicum of respect for his experience.

Not that he had offered her the hand of friendship exactly. Always her loudest critic, he had led the campaign against her when Margrethe had brought her back from London.

He hadn't changed, at least not visibly. His grey beard

was still long and unruly, growing into his nose and ears, his gaze still had the same cynical glint in it.

'Frank is old-school,' she recalled Margrethe once telling her. 'Awkward, difficult, won't relent on anything.'

You could say the same about Margrethe. And Jensen herself, for that matter.

'I know what you think of me,' she said. 'I've been tone deaf. Would you at least let me try to make up for it?' She held up the paper bag of cardamon swirls that she had bought on the way. 'I thought that maybe I could blag a cup of tea to go with these?'

Frank looked at her for a moment as if trying to decide if she was mocking him in some way. Then he threw the bunch of dead branches he had been holding into a wheelbarrow and slowly removed his gardening gloves. 'I suppose that would be OK,' he said.

He disappeared inside the house, and she caught a glimpse of a living room full of packing boxes and disassembled furniture.

The shrubs and potted plants in the garden were in various stages of dying, the parasol and dining table hidden under mildewy covers. There was a greenhouse filled with polystyrene boxes and trays of brown plants, a punctured grey football under a tree.

Jensen tried and failed to imagine the place in happier times.

'I'm smartening things up a bit for the new owners,' said Frank, appearing with two mugs and a red thermos. 'I know I don't have to.' He pointed to a couple of wrought-iron garden chairs that had once been white. 'Have a seat.'

She did as she was told. He poured their teas.

'I heard you were pregnant,' he said, taking a seat next to her.

'Yeah,' said Jensen. 'It was . . . a surprise.'

They both looked at their mugs.

'So, you're moving house?' she said, after a pause.

He nodded. 'To my summerhouse on Langeland. My other half died in October, and my daughter lives in the Far East.'

'Oh Frank, I'm so sorry.'

'Motor neurone disease. We knew it was coming, but still, too many memories in this house.'

He swallowed a couple of times, looked up into the leaden sky. 'In a way, it was just as well I lost my job, so I could look after her at the end.'

'I had no idea.'

'Guess no one told you.'

'I could have asked,' she said.

'Yeah, well.'

They sat for a long while in silence, sipping their tea. The grease-stained paper bag with the cardamon swirls lay unopened between them.

'I've been reading your old articles,' Jensen said, trying to break the awkwardness.

Frank looked pleased. 'Really?'

'On Lea Høgh. You know, the missing ten-year-old from Dragør? And the subsequent child sexual abuse case that involved her brother?'

'I remember it well,' he said. 'Jan Loft. Nasty piece of work. He must be due for release soon.'

'Next week. Apparently, he's a reformed man.'

'Oh sure,' Frank snorted.

Suddenly, he frowned at her, sitting up in his chair, the old newshound picking up a scent. 'Why are you reading up on that old story? Does it have anything to do with Matilde Clausen?'

'What? No, no, it's just . . .' She thought of a suitable reason for her interest.

She couldn't tell him about the photo of Lea, nor the interview with Jan Loft, and Henrik hadn't said there was a link, though she couldn't help wondering. 'I was thinking of writing an article about Loft on his release from prison.'

Frank chuckled. 'The whole country is searching for a missing nine-year-old, it's the biggest story around, and you're digging into a cold case? Come on, Jensen, give me some credit.'

'There's not a lot we can do on the Matilde Clausen story except run around holding up the microphone to people who at best don't know anything and, at worst, send us down paths that lead to nowhere.'

'Yeah, I saw your video interview with Simon and Stine Clausen.'

'We shouldn't have posted that,' said Jensen. 'But my point is, it's a waiting game.'

Frank shook his head. 'Nah, there's always something you can do. Someone somewhere knows something. You just have to find them. You of all people should know that.'

'You're right,' she said. 'You're a good journalist, Frank. Your articles on the Jan Loft case were great, detailed, thorough, better than anything else out there. Though, I was wondering . . .'

'Yes?'

'Was there any of your research at the time that you *didn't* publish? I mean, did you hear or see something while you were working on the story that made you develop a theory that you just couldn't substantiate? For example, it was never proved that Loft had anything to do with Lea's disappearance, but do you think that in actual fact he did?'

Frank narrowed his eyes and set down his mug. 'I see

what's going on here,' he said. 'You come to my house without notice, all nice and friendly, allegedly to make amends.'

'No Frank, I meant it, I—'

'And all along, you're just here for your own ends, to
pump me for information, so you don't have to find it
yourself.'

He stood up, jabbing his finger at her, red-faced. 'Give
me one good reason why I should help you?'

Frank was angry, but he was more than that. She saw
that he was trembling.

Was he afraid?

She rose slowly, holding up her hands. 'You've got it all
wrong, Frank. Please, listen to me.'

But Frank grabbed the paper bag on the table and thrust
it into her hands. 'Take your pastries and get out of my
house. Right now.'

24

One wheel of the patrol car was mounted on the kerb, as though its occupants had pulled over at speed to attend an emergency. A glance through the windows of the cosy Nørrebro café decorated with fairy lights made it immediately obvious to Henrik that nothing could be further from the truth.

Police constables Hannemann and Olsen were seated opposite each other, tucking into sandwiches – or at least Hannemann was. Olsen was nursing a black coffee and looking at her colleague with thinly veiled disgust.

Henrik had known Hannemann for years; he was a thin and wiry cop with an admirable metabolism, fuelled by restless energy. His eyes were deep-set and in constant movement.

Olsen, an unusually tall and broad young woman with brown, bobbed hair and a friendly, almost apologetic, demeanour, was a more recent acquaintance.

Henrik hesitated at the door, steeling himself for the conversation. He could barely think straight. Needed badly to get home to Frederiksberg, have a shower and put on a fresh shirt. Sleep for an hour or two, if he could get away with it.

Simon Clausen's car had been miles away in Hvidovre during the window when Matilde disappeared; he was still refusing to explain himself.

The black Audi seen idling outside Ørstedsparken had not been picked up on CCTV, but the footage they had found so far didn't cover the entirety of the surrounding area. By now, they had narrowed tens of thousands of registered black Audis down to just under twelve hundred of interest.

Could Simon have asked someone to remove Matilde? Staged her disappearance to cast blame on Nordby, only to find her later himself, promoting himself as a hero?

At this point they had to investigate every possibility.

Olsen looked up nervously when Henrik entered the café, as did the tired-looking woman who was drying glasses with a cloth at the back of the room.

'Jungersen,' said Hannemann, mouth full of sandwich, but nevertheless managing a sarcastic grin. 'I thought you had your hands full.'

'Nothing gets past you,' said Henrik, sitting down next to Olsen, who put down her coffee cup and stiffened. He smiled at her reassuringly.

'What are you doing here?' said Hannemann, with only a modicum of the deference normally reserved for a senior officer.

He wasn't stupid and would already be wondering why a detective inspector would have left the investigation into the disappearance of Matilde Clausen to seek out a couple of uniformed officers. If he found out about Jensen, it would be a matter of time before the whole of Copenhagen knew about it.

'I want to ask you something,' said Henrik, trying to keep his voice casual. 'A few weeks ago, you took a call-out to a property by the Lakes. An elderly woman by the

135

name of Bodil La Cour who reported witnessing a murder or serious assault?'

Henrik could tell that Hannemann remembered. 'What about it?' he said, already on his guard.

'She's a friend of my stepmother's,' said Henrik, apologetically. 'You know what it's like. I promised to find out if there was any news.'

'News? Are you kidding me? That woman is bonkers, no disrespect to your stepmother.'

None taken, thought Henrik.

Birthe was suffering from Alzheimer's and no longer remembered who his father was. She also had no friends. 'You think she was mistaken then?' he said.

Hannemann leaned back in his chair, smiling. On his chest, his radio was crackling with the voice of the dispatcher directing officers to crime scenes across the city. 'Put it this way,' he said. 'There was no body, no sign that anything had happened, and no other witnesses. I mean, what are we supposed to do with that?'

'Yeah, I get it,' said Henrik. 'Only I promised to ask.'

'Besides, it wasn't the first time your stepmother's friend reported something that didn't happen.'

'It wasn't?'

'Last time it was a burglary.'

'I see,' said Henrik.

Olsen fidgeted nervously beside him but kept quiet. Henrik wondered if she shared her buddy's version of the story. She would know that Hannemann wasn't the sort of bloke you undermined without suffering the consequences. 'No CCTV I assume?' he said.

Hannemann looked at him, his eyes narrowed to two dark slits. 'We followed due process. Conducted a search of the buildings, spoke to some of the residents. The woman probably had a nightmare and got confused, thinking it was the real thing, end of story. We filed a report. If you guys had thought it worth investigating, I assume you would have done so?' said Hannemann.

Touché.

Henrik silently cursed Jensen and the things she made him do. 'Yeah, I know, I know.' He smiled, opened his hands. 'Families, eh?'

Hannemann raised his coffee cup and drank, clearly suspicious.

'How are things otherwise?' said Henrik, hating himself for having to bow to an officer whose integrity famously fitted on a pinhead.

They chatted for a few minutes, during which he managed to make Hannemann laugh a couple of times.

'I'll get these,' he said, pointing to the coffees and sandwiches. 'It's the least I can do.'

He felt Hannemann's eyes drill into his back as he approached the waitress behind the counter and got out his phone.

By the confusion mixed with relief on her face as she took the payment, he could tell that his instinct about Hannemann had been correct. The bastard had forced her to give him a freebie.

As he left the café, Henrik braced himself for a difficult conversation with Jensen. She would be disappointed that he had nothing to tell her.

Whatever, he had kept his side of the bargain. It was now up to Jensen to keep hers.

His phone pinged, a message from Mark.

We found something, Boss. Call me.

25

Jensen looked at the building by the Lakes, the windows glowing bright yellow in the murk, and felt like going home and burying herself under her duvet.

Henrik had told her that the investigation into what Bodil saw in the early hours of Saturday had been dropped on lack of evidence.

'I know you want to do the right thing,' he had said, his tone gentler than usual. 'But take it from me, you're wasting your time.'

It had been a terrible day, even by recent standards. The fiasco over the Simon Clausen interview, the vandalism of Nordby's house, Frank's explosive reaction.

And Matilde Clausen was still missing.

The only good thing that had happened was that, to her surprise, Jan Loft had accepted her request for a visit.

She would be travelling to the prison in Jutland early on Saturday morning. Henrik had been delighted when she told him.

He had promised to brief her, and there was a lot more research she could do herself. She was going to make a start on it tomorrow morning.

But first, she had to deal with Bodil. Perhaps Palle, the caretaker, was right that her mind was going, that what she said couldn't be trusted.

But what if he was wrong?

Until she had proof that nothing had happened, she had to keep trying to uncover the truth.

Palle had sent her the promised email with the names and addresses of the residents in the block. She would have to speak to them one by one.

Of the nine flats, only two were occupied by single men, and one of them was Palle.

As she locked up her bike and walked up the garden path, she hoped she wouldn't meet him this time.

She almost ran into the lift, staring at herself in the mirror as it ascended, clanging loudly as it passed each floor.

'Jensen, I'm so glad to see you,' said Bodil on opening her door.

She led them through to the living room, the Lakes sparkling with a thousand reflected lights beyond the windows.

The radio was on, a soft, classical piano. Wolfgang the cat looked up from the sofa with his ice-blue eyes.

'So, what did you find out?' said Bodil when they were both seated, Jensen having declined the offer of tea.

'I'm afraid you'll be disappointed. The police have dropped the case.'

Bodil smile faded. 'So, it's as I suspected. They think I made it up.'

'Well, maybe not quite that. Only, they haven't been able to find anything to prove it.'

'Same thing. They think I'm lying.'

'They think that maybe you drew the wrong conclusion about what you saw. The man and woman might just have been playing around.'

'They were not.'

'Right,' said Jensen. 'Nevertheless, here we are. The police won't do any more about it.'

'Then we must do it ourselves,' said Bodil. She smiled defiantly.

Jensen smiled back. 'There *is* something we could try,' she said.

'Yes?'

'I could write an article if I can persuade my editor to publish it. It might jog someone's memory.'

Or goad the police into action, she thought.

They were interrupted by a loud banging on the front door, along with agitated voices in the stairwell.

'What on earth?' Jensen said.

Bodil went to investigate, followed closely by Jensen.

What?

Standing on the doormat was Gustav, trousers below his hips, headphones around his neck, his face a deep pink.

Holding Gustav up by his hoodie was Palle. He was looking at Bodil. 'Found this one loitering in the stairwell. Insists he knows you.'

'Let me go, you moron,' said Gustav, in falsetto. 'I told you I'm Jensen's assistant. Jensen, tell him.'

Only then did Palle notice her. 'Oh, I'm sorry,' he said to Bodil, immediately letting go of Gustav, who shook himself meaningfully. 'I didn't know you had company.'

Bodil turned to her. 'Well,' she said. 'Is it true? Is this young man your assistant?'

Gustav looked at her pleadingly, smoothing down his hoodie where Palle had pulled it.

'Yes,' Jensen lied. 'Only, I didn't know he was planning on turning up today.'

'Well, then, you'd better come in,' said Bodil.

Palle looked disappointed, as though he had been denied access to a party. He stretched his neck to see further into the flat.

Jensen could tell that he was angling to come in, but Bodil was oblivious. 'Thank you, Palle, it seems it was all a misunderstanding,' she said, closing the door on him.

Jensen and Gustav followed Bodil into the flat. 'What are you doing here?' she whispered at him angrily behind Bodil's back.

'You said I could come along, after homework.'

'I said I'd think about it. How did you even find it?'

'You left a note with the address on your desk.'

Jensen stopped in the corridor. 'You went to my office at *Dagbladet*?'

'Yeah,' he laughed. 'They still haven't changed the key-code on the back door, the idiots.'

'It's not funny, Gustav. You can't just go in and look through my things.'

'I wasn't. I just dropped by to apologise for earlier today. You know, when you saw me in my free period? I was in a bad mood, sorry.' He clapped his hands, then rubbed them together. 'Anyway, I'm here now. You said Margrethe wants more video. How about I film Bodil? You can say you did it yourself, no one will know.'

He reached into his rucksack and pulled out a tiny tripod with telescopic legs. 'I got a microphone too. Just a cheap Bluetooth one, but it should work OK. If you post it, it might help someone remember.'

She looked at him, exasperated. She had always been told she was stubborn, but Gustav was redefining the meaning of the word.

'I'm good with old ladies,' he said, smiling.

It was an understatement. Gustav knew how to be charming.

When he wanted something.

'Are you coming, you two?' shouted Bodil from the living room.

26

Henrik stood back from the uniformed officers and tried to rein in his excitement. Could they be close to a break-through? Would this be the end of the search for Matilde?

It felt too good to be true.

The row of lockups on the industrial estate in Hvidovre looked unremarkable, but a witness claimed to have seen Simon Clausen there on Sunday morning, acting strangely, and then again late in afternoon, after Matilde had disappeared.

His lockup was the third from the right. A metal grille was pulled down and fastened with a heavy padlock. A door was set into the grille, with no fewer than three further heavy-duty locks.

Simon had been cagey when they had asked him about it. He was an IT engineer for a large building society, with a flat in central Copenhagen. What was he doing with a lockup in the suburbs?

He had given them a long-winded explanation about having been offered a cheap deal and deciding to accept, in case the family grew out of space in the Kleinsgade flat.

He had refused to take them to the lockup, insisting that he had never used it, and that it had nothing to do with Matilde. However, this had been contradicted by the witness whose statement was corroborated by CCTV, clearly showing Simon coming and going, not just on Sunday but on each of the past three days.

Each time he had looked around him carefully before opening the door, and appeared again around five minutes after, before locking up.

It had not been difficult to obtain the search warrant. Henrik had driven straight from Nørrebro, meeting Mark and the team there.

'Now,' shouted an officer in protective gear, as another broke down the door. The officers piled in, shouting as they did so.

Henrik's anxiety mounted. His mouth was dry.

After a few minutes, the commander came out with a strange look on his face.

'Is she there?' Henrik said anxiously, praying that their instincts had been correct and that they would soon be looking into Matilde's face.

Frightened and hungry, but safe.

The officer shook his head. 'But there's something else. You'd better come and see.'

Someone had switched on the overhead strip lights. They cut into Henrik's eyes, momentarily blinding him. When he found his vision again, he was looking at stacks and stacks of cardboard boxes.

There was no sign of any human activity, no mattress on the floor, no red coat.

No Matilde.

'What is this?' he said, wearily.

The uniformed officer beckoned him across to a stack

of boxes, all opened. They were full of illegal cigarettes. 'Smuggled in from Eastern Europe, no doubt,' said the officer. 'Looks like Simon Clausen has been running a profitable side gig.'

Henrik stumbled out of the lockup. For the second time they had chased up a dead end. To protect himself, Simon Clausen had wasted precious time, moving his stepdaughter still further out of their reach.

'Bad luck,' said Mark by his side.

Bad luck my arse, Henrik thought.

They had no leads, no clue as to what had happened to Matilde.

'What shall we do now?' said Mark.

'Call the financial crime guys. Let them deal with the bastard.'

Wiese would flay him.

If the press didn't get there first.

27

'If these people don't know anything either, then we're stumped,' said Jensen, pressing the doorbell to the second-floor flat in the red building across the courtyard.

It had been Gustav's idea to speak to Bodil's neighbours straight away.

'We might as well, now that we're here,' he had said, after they had finished creating the video at Bodil's.

Jensen had interviewed her first, then Gustav had made Bodil change into her nightgown and housecoat to re-enact how she had woken up in the night and got out of bed.

He had filmed her standing by her bedroom window, looking down into the courtyard through a gap in the curtains.

Later Gustav would cut out Jensen's questions and turn Bodil's answers into a voice-over accompanying the dramatisation.

Bodil had been up for the whole thing, putting on a concerned face as she picked up her phone in the hallway to call the police.

There was a total of fourteen adult residents in the flats.

None of the residents matched the description of the young woman Bodil had seen attacked.

Gustav and Jensen had agreed on three questions to ask everyone:

Were you at home on the night between last Friday and Saturday between three and four a.m.?

Your neighbour Bodil La Cour witnessed an assault that night. Did you hear or see anything unusual at the time?

Have you ever seen any of your neighbours behaving strangely, or as if they had something to hide?

They had been fortunate so far, finding at least one person at home in every flat, except the one immediately below Bodil's, which belonged to a couple who were away in Australia.

No one knew much about Bodil, aside from having the odd friendly chat with her when they met on the stairs.

Nor did they know anything about the report Bodil had made to the police.

'It's generally very peaceful around here,' said a bald man with a long grey beard and tiny round glasses who lived alone two floors down from Bodil.

'So the police didn't speak to you after it happened?' asked Jensen.

'No, but then I was visiting my brother in Jutland last weekend,' the man said.

So Palle was the only single man who had been around on the night. As Bodil hadn't seen the attacker's face, it could well have been him.

They waited outside the next flat.

'Just this one and Palle to go,' said Gustav.

Jensen rang the doorbell again. She thought she could hear a child crying inside.

From Palle's email, she could see that the flat belonged to Katja and Thomas Jespersen. She remembered Palle telling her that Katja was a nurse and thought that Bodil might be suffering from dementia.

They heard the key turning in the door, and a safety chain being removed. The door opened about ten centimetres and a man looked through the gap.

'Thomas?' said Jensen.

'Yes?' His eyes were flicking between the two of them.

'Don't worry,' said Jensen. 'We're not Jehovah's witnesses or anything.' She held up her press pass, putting on her best smile. 'My name is Jensen. I'm a journalist from *Dagbladet*, and this is Gustav Skov, my colleague.' The child kept crying, a low plaintive wail that tugged at something inside of her. 'We're doing a story about an assault witnessed by your neighbour Bodil on the night between Friday and Saturday.'

'I don't know anything about that,' said the man. 'I'm sorry, but I'm trying to get my daughter off to sleep.'

'Maybe we could speak to your wife?'

'She's resting.'

'Can we come back later?' said Gustav.

'I don't know, maybe. I've got to go now,' said Thomas.

He closed the door, and they heard the lock turning and the chain being refastened.

Jensen looked at Gustav. He shrugged at her. 'Let's talk to Palle, and then we can go home, and you can get the video done,' she said.

*

Thankfully, Palle was faster at responding. 'I heard you've been going around asking people questions. Well?'

'No one else heard anything. We haven't spoken to Thomas and Katja yet. Thomas was just putting their daughter to bed.'

'They didn't hear anything either,' said Palle. 'I told you, Katja didn't believe it really happened and I'm inclined to think she's correct.'

'We also need to speak to you,' said Gustav. 'Can we come in?'

'Me?' said Palle.

'Yes,' said Gustav. 'We're asking everyone the same questions.'

Palle glared at him.

'Your neighbours were happy enough to let us in,' said Gustav.

Reluctantly, Palle opened the door. Gustav zipped past him. 'Nice gaff,' he said.

Jensen noticed a large keyring just inside the door. Each of the keys had a name tag: Bodil, workshop, lockup, basement. On the coat rack lay Palle's blue overalls.

The rooms looked sparse, with tired-looking furniture. No plants, no pictures on the walls, no books or photos.

They sat by the dining table in the corner of the living room. It faced the courtyard. You could see Bodil's windows from there. There was a light on in her kitchen and bedroom.

'What did Bodil tell you earlier when you visited her?' said Palle.

'Keep an eye on *Dagbladet*'s website tomorrow and you'll see,' said Gustav.

He was in his teenage delinquent mode, the charm he had used on Bodil to great effect all but gone. No one

149

carried a grudge like Gustav; his first, failed encounter with Palle had clearly stuck.

Jensen sent him an angry look. She had already had words with him about turning up uninvited. About letting her do the talking.

'Gustav is teasing you,' she said to Palle. 'He means that we filmed Bodil explaining what she saw in the early hours of Saturday. We're hoping that other people may come forward when they see it.'

Palle looked worried. 'That's exactly what I was afraid of,' he said. 'You've taken advantage of her. People will think she's mad.'

'And I told you that I believe her.'

'OK,' said Palle. 'Let's say she *did* see something. The police came. They searched the place but didn't find anything.'

'We found out that they didn't speak to any of your neighbours that night,' said Gustav. 'Only to you.'

Palle frowned at Jensen. 'But you just said that no one else saw or heard anything.'

Jensen sighed. 'It's more complicated than that,' said Jensen. 'They wouldn't have noticed anything unless they happened to be standing by their windows at the time. Bodil said that the woman didn't make a sound.'

'Doesn't that strike you as odd if she was being attacked?' said Palle. 'I mean wouldn't she at least have screamed?'

'It's odd, I grant you. We don't have all the answers yet. Let's go through the questions we want to put to you, and we'll leave you alone,' said Jensen.

Palle co-operated, but only just. Yes, he had been at home. No, he hadn't seen anything. No, he hadn't witnessed any neighbour behaving strangely.

'Tell me about your relationship with Bodil,' said Jensen.

'My relationship?'

'Yes, you seem very close. Bodil told us that you help her with shopping, fixing things in her flat, online banking, tax and that sort of thing.'

Palle blushed. 'Bodil doesn't have anyone else, and I'm often around. It's the least I can do.'

'She says you helped her buy a laptop?'

'Yes. It was my suggestion. You can't do anything in Denmark these days unless you're online,' said Palle. 'But what has this got to do with anything?'

'Nothing,' said Jensen. 'It just occurred to me that Bodil has placed an awful lot of trust in you.'

'Can we have a look in the basement?' Gustav said.

'What for?' said Palle.

Gustav continued, unperturbed. 'Do you have a girl-friend, Palle?'

Jensen looked at him angrily.

Palle scrambled to his feet. 'What kind of question is that?'

'Wait,' Jensen said. 'Gustav didn't mean—'

'I'd like you both to leave. Out,' he said. 'Now!'

He virtually shoved them out of his flat.

'That was clumsy, Gustav,' said Jensen as they walked across the courtyard and through Bodil's building to the front entrance. 'You went too far.'

'He's such a creep,' said Gustav.

'He's odd, but not necessarily a criminal. He might just be trying to protect Bodil, out of some sort of loyalty to her,' she said.

Still, Palle had seemed anxious about something. How come?

She put on her helmet and unlocked her bike, her stomach rumbling. 'Come,' she said. 'We'll go through everything over a burger. Then you can edit the video while I write my piece.'

Gustav smiled broadly and jumped on his e-scooter.

Day Four

28

'So it's true what the others say: you just won't collaborate.'

Jensen looked up to find Google Me standing in the doorway to her office. He was still wearing his coat, and carrying his camera bag. His hair and beard were dripping wet from the rain that was hammering against her office window.

She had been looking forward to a quiet hour of reading Henning's articles on Jan Loft before the daily editorial meeting. Her mind had been buzzing all night with thoughts of Matilde and Lea. She had slept badly, unable to get comfortable in the single bed in the spare bedroom at Margrethe's.

She frowned at Google Me. 'What do you mean?'

'Saw your video about that crazy old bat down by the Lakes.'

'Oh that,' said Jensen. She pretended to resume her reading, her heart pounding.

'Yes, that,' said Google Me, dropping his bag on her desk and spraying rainwater across Henning's articles. She looked up at him angrily. 'Hey, watch yourself.'

'We're supposed to be working for the same newspaper,' he said to her. The skin on his neck and lower face had flushed bright red.

'Look,' she said. 'It's no big deal. The woman rang me on Monday and told me her story. I looked into it, but the police won't take it any further. Seeing as I was there, I thought I'd film her, see if it helped bring any other witnesses forward. Not that it worked.'

The story hadn't had many views, and the few comments were dismissive and unkind.

It seemed *Dagbladet*'s readers were no more prepared to believe Bodil's testimony than the police had been.

'It was just a spontaneous thing,' she said.

Google Me attempted a laugh, baring his teeth. 'Oh sure. You've never created a video before, and you just thought you'd give it a go?'

'Yes,' she said, looking at the wet articles. Thankfully, they weren't completely ruined. 'I mean, it's hardly rocket science.'

'You know what I think, Jensen? I think you're lying. It was that little helper of yours again, wasn't it?'

'Gustav?' she said, looking straight at him. 'No, he wasn't there. I told you, he's gone back to school.'

'You sure about that?'

'What's that supposed to mean?'

'Why don't you ask him yourself?' said Google Me.

'Maybe I will,' she said.

He picked up his camera bag and began to back away. 'OK,' he said. 'If this is what you want.'

'If what is what I want?'

'From now on, you and I no longer work together.'

'Don't be ridiculous,' she said.

'And good luck with that dead story of yours. You and the lad are welcome to it.'

As he walked away, he laughed again, this time almost convincingly.

Jensen's phone announced a text message. She sat up. It was from Margrethe.

Margrethe only communicated in emergencies.

Her message was characteristically brief, consisting of a ward number at Riget and a single sentence.

If you want to see Henning again, come now.

29

The meeting room at Teglholmen was full to bursting, all four walls lined with investigators. Exhaustion and despair were written on their faces.

Wiese had plucked fifteen extra people from other teams, in a vain attempt to accelerate progress.

The media was going mental, coming up with all sorts of unhelpful theories.

Even the politicians were pitching in, filming themselves on social media with pictures of Matilde and appealing for information. Posters had sprung up on lamp posts and fences all over the city.

Henrik cleared his throat.

'Matilde Clausen has now been missing for almost four days,' he said. 'Last night, a member of the public tipped us off that Simon Clausen owns a storage facility in Hvidovre. Our source told us that Clausen has been seen at the site several times this week, acting suspiciously. We gained access to the unit and uncovered a large quantity of counterfeit cigarettes.'

Someone whistled.

'We're still looking for a black Audi seen idling outside the Ahlefeldtsgade entrance to Ørstedsparken. We now know it's not Simon Clausen's vehicle, but we've another few hundred left to eliminate. The car may or may not have anything to do with Matilde. She herself has not been spotted leaving the park on any of the CCTV that we've gained access to so far, but the dive team have more or less concluded that she's not in the lake.'

'Excuse me,' said Wiese, sitting just a couple of metres away, arms folded across his skinny chest. 'You're saying that Matilde never left the park, but also that she's not *in* the park. Which is it?'

'I didn't say she never left. Clearly, she did. I said, her leaving wasn't captured on CCTV. It's most likely that whoever abducted her took her to a waiting car.'

'The black Audi?' said Wiese.

'Possibly. We must remain open to all possibilities, though it does seem that the whole thing was carefully planned. The mother told us she and Matilde always go to the park on Sunday. Someone could have been watching the pair of them for weeks. If so, they would have known where Matilde likes to play, and where her mother always sits. The area where the witness saw the Audi is not covered by CCTV. Perhaps they also knew this. So, we need a list of people who have been coming to the park regularly on Sunday afternoons, and we need to find and speak to all of them.'

His colleagues nodded.

'We've already made some progress,' said Lotte Nielsen, a slim, athletic blonde who headed up one of the other violent crime teams in Wiese's department and had been drafted in to help.

Henrik cringed when he remembered how he had

come on to her in a moment of madness a few months ago. Thankfully, she appeared to have forgiven him.

'Several witnesses have said that they regularly see an elderly woman by the lake in Ørstedsparken,' said Lotte. 'She always sits on one of the benches that back onto the playground, so pretty close to where Matilde was playing. She could be a key witness. The press office has put a description of her on X, to see if anyone knows who she is.'

'Description?'

'Tall, with a blue coat, a walking stick, a dark brown hat and sunglasses,' said Lotte. 'Oh and she had this red shopping trolley with her. We've asked in the local supermarkets, but so far no luck.'

Something stirred deep down in Henrik's sleep-deprived brain.

What was it?

It slipped out of his grasp as another thought entered his mind.

Jensen's witness, Bodil La Cour, lived barely three-quarters of a mile from Ørstedsparken. Could it be her?

He shook his head. Plenty of elderly women in Copenhagen.

Simon Clausen had been released after being charged with handling counterfeit goods. Had the circumstances been different, Henrik would have liked to have added a separate charge for wasting police time.

Thankfully, there had been no more interviews to the press. Henrik reckoned they could rely on him to be quiet from now on.

If there was still no sign of Matilde in the next few days, it would be worth staging a reconstruction. Ørstedsparken was due to reopen to the public as soon as the divers had finished their search.

'Bagger,' he said. 'Have your guys found anything else on Nordby's hard drive?'

Bagger nodded. 'Seems he's been accessing the dark web using the Tor browser on numerous occasions.'

'To do what?'

'Probably to join some forum, or a chat room. Could have been buying photos or accessing a live stream.'

'Keep looking,' Henrik said.

'Why?' said Wiese. 'Do we still think Nordby had something to do with his daughter's disappearance?'

'We can't be one hundred percent sure,' said Henrik. 'The environment he moves in, someone might have exerted pressure on him to share his own child sexual-abuse material.'

'Drop it,' said Wiese. 'Nordby is a distraction.'

Henrik and Bagger exchanged a glance. The other investigators didn't know about the picture of Lea. Wiese had told them to keep it to themselves.

'Hold on,' shouted Mark, looking at his phone screen. 'It's the dive team.'

Henrik sent a private prayer heavenwards as Mark read the message.

Please, please, let her not have drowned.

'They haven't found Matilde,' said Mark. 'But they've recovered a mobile from the lake, same model and make as hers.'

The room erupted in excited voices. Henrik's palms tingled as he shushed his colleagues. He looked at Bagger. 'It's been submerged for days; won't the data be lost?'

'Not necessarily. Tell them to fill a small container with lake water and put the phone in it, then get the whole thing to NC3 as soon as possible.'

Henrik knew that Bagger had a close working

relationship with NC3, short for National Centre for Cyber Crime, located in Ejby on the outskirts of Copenhagen.

Finally, a breakthrough. The mood in the room had lifted by several degrees.

Henrik tried to keep a lid on his enthusiasm. They had been here before. Knowing his luck, it would be another false dawn.

But it was hard, even for him, not to feel a glimmer of hope.

30

Jensen darted out of the lift and ran across the polished floor, dodging trolleys pushed by porters, patients in bathrobes clinging to wheeled drip-stands, and cleaners and nurses rushing in and out of rooms.

No one looked at her.

Riget was a microcosm of human life, of births and deaths, and the whole gamut of suffering, anger, grief and joy in between.

Someone rushing to the side of a dying patient hardly warranted a second glance.

She had never found out if Henning was married. Perhaps when she entered the room, there would be a circle of children and grandchildren around his bed. Her presence might be an embarrassing intrusion. After all, she had only known him for a little over a year.

In his own way, he had become a friend to her when she had first returned to Copenhagen, feeling like a stranger in her own city.

They had talked often. In his office, as he sat cutting articles out of the Danish newspapers of the day, marking them in snarly blue ink and filing them by topic. Or in hers, when he came to scavenge the dregs from her coffee machine.

She liked to think that she had been a friend to him too, keeping him company, tapping into his large brain for information and bringing him the odd cup of fresh coffee from Liron's van by way of a bribe.

She had never seen him talk to anyone but herself and Margrethe. It was as though he was invisible to the other *Dagbladet* reporters, a ghost of newspapers past floating among them in his beige suit, an unlit cigar in his mouth.

She found the right door and pushed it open. The touching bedside scene she had imagined in her head clashed with reality and broke in a thousand pieces.

Henning was in the bed, his jaw slack, his hands still above the blue duvet. There were no machines pinging. The curtains were closed, the lights turned down low.

'You're too late,' said Margrethe, looking up from the visitor's chair.

Jensen had never seen her editor cry. She wasn't even sure she was seeing it now. Margrethe's voice was oddly strangled, but her eyes were obscured by the thick lenses in her glasses.

'When did it happen?' said Jensen, approaching the bed. Carefully, she put her hand on Henning's. It was still warm, just skin and bone.

'Ten minutes ago,' said Margrethe.

'Lucky you were here,' said Jensen, feeling the tears burn the inside of her eyelids.

Margrethe frowned at her. 'Lucky? I've been here all night,' she said. 'And the night before that and so on.'

Jensen hadn't heard her leave that morning, but there was nothing unusual in that. Margrethe never slept more than a few hours, and usually left for work before she and Gustav were even awake.

'Why didn't you tell me sooner?' said Jensen, swiping away the tears that had started to roll down her face.

Another frown. 'I'm not your keeper, Jensen. You had months to visit Henning.'

Jensen bit her lip, nodded.

She had wanted to, but somehow it had never happened. There was always work, and she had felt awkward about visiting someone who was just a colleague when he was unwell and vulnerable. Excuses that felt flimsy now.

'Are his family on their way?' she said.

Margrethe looked at her, slowly shaking her head. 'You really are oblivious, aren't you?' she said. 'There's a nephew, lives in the States. Henning never married. You could say he was in a monogamous relationship with *Dagbladet* all his life. There was no journalism school when he started his career. He was a trainee, worked his way up through the ranks until he was appointed editor.'

Jensen thought about the picture of Henning in his heyday. It was hanging on the wall of Margrethe's wood-panelled office, along with all those that had come before him.

And after.

He had retired long before Jensen had been sent to London as *Dagbladet*'s correspondent by Margrethe as a green twenty-year-old. But soon he had returned, taking up the position as the newspaper's obituary writer.

'I'll never forget the miserable look on his face at his reception when he retired. He was sixty-eight. He couldn't stand being at home. After a few months, he was literally begging to come back, said he'd take on any job, wash the floors if it came to it. Poor old sod.'

You're one to talk, Jensen thought, unable to imagine Margrethe tending to a rose bed or taking up a hobby. She, too, was married to her job at *Dagbladet*, a job that looked ever more precarious. What would she do with herself if the newspaper closed?

Jensen felt certain it wouldn't last out her own career. Here they were, three generations of newspaper reporters, and she might well be the last.

'How did it happen?' she said, nodding at Henning. 'I mean, it seemed so sudden. I thought he was recovering?'

'He had another stroke last night. His body was too weak to cope.'

Margrethe briefly rested her hand on Henning's head. The move was tender, almost loving.

'What now?' said Jensen.

Margrethe looked at her with a determined expression, any sign of grief wiped from her face. 'Now we go back to work. A nine-year-old girl has been missing for four days. It's time we cranked up the pressure on the police to find her.'

'I meant with Henning?'

'Oh, they'll take him to the morgue. Yasmine will sort the practical stuff, the funeral and so on.'

Yasmine. Personal assistant come fixer. Margrethe's life would fall apart, were it not for Yasmine.

'Can I have his filing cabinets?' said Jensen.

'Where are you going to put them?'

'In storage, until I find my own place.'

'Suit yourself,' said Margrethe. She got up with a grunt of effort and looked around for her coat and worn, brown-leather shoulder-bag. Then she moved towards the door.

'Are you going already?' said Jensen.

'What else would you have me do?' said Margrethe. 'Henning is gone, and we've a newspaper to run. It's what he would have wanted.'

31

Henrik hadn't made it more than a few yards down the corridor after the morning briefing when he heard a quiet voice behind him. 'Jungersen?'

He turned, surprised to see Maja Olsen in her dark-blue police uniform with the gold and green crest. She removed her cap and straightened her rain-soaked fringe.

He hadn't realised before how big and tall she was. He barely reached to her shoulder. It seemed nature had added one-half to her size compared to the average woman. 'Olsen, what are you doing here?'

'I hope you don't mind,' she said. 'I know the receptionist downstairs. He said you'd be here. I know you're busy on the Matilde Clausen case, and I would have called, only . . .'

She trailed off, glancing up nervously as a couple of Henrik's colleagues passed, staring at her with open curiosity. No one at his office wore uniforms.

'Of course,' he said, looking left and right down the corridor, before pulling Olsen into an empty meeting room.

'What is it?' he said, hands on hips.

'You know that friend of your stepmother's?'

'Who?' he said, confused for a moment. Then he remembered his lie. 'Ah, Bodil,' he said. 'What about her?'

'It wasn't exactly like Hannemann said. I wanted you to know, in case it's important. I suggested we search the area, call in the dog patrol, but he told me it wasn't necessary. And we didn't really speak to all the neighbours either.'

She pulled a notebook out of her pocket and looked through it, settling on a page in the middle. Her handwriting was tiny and pristine. 'We only spoke to this one weird guy called Palle Dybdal. I think he's some sort of caretaker. He showed us around the property and into the basement. Then Hannemann decided we were wasting our time and called it quits. About ten minutes, perhaps?'

'You said the guy was weird. How?' said Henrik.

'He seemed nervous, like he wanted us to leave.'

He smiled. 'We have that effect on some people.'

'No, I mean shifty.'

'OK?'

'He insisted Bodil had probably imagined it. It was him who told us about the burglaries that she had reported previously. That's when Hannemann decided we should leave. He reckoned she was probably senile.'

'Thank you, Olsen, I'm glad you told me.'

'I don't think it's fair,' she said.

'What isn't?'

'That just because a woman is old, no one believes her. Like she's got no value to contribute to society, like she's invisible.'

He looked at her more closely. 'That's an admirable stance,' he said. 'Still, it doesn't change the fact that no victim was found, no person reported missing matches the victim's description, and no one else witnessed the incident.'

'I know,' she said. 'But I thought I might check it out,

you know, see if I can find any CCTV from around the area. On my own time, of course. If I'm not successful, then at least I'll know that I've done what I could.'

'I won't stop you,' said Henrik, not wanting to quash her enthusiasm completely. Olsen was obviously a conscientious officer, and he appreciated the initiative she had shown.

He looked at his watch. 'If there was nothing else? Only I need to get on.'

'Of course. There's just one other quick thing,' Olsen said, blushing as she looked down at her black waterproof boots. 'I want to be a detective.'

'I see,' he said. 'When did you join the force?'

'Finished my training five years ago. Patrol and case work since then. All in Copenhagen. I've taken the courses. I'd like to join your team.'

He smiled. 'It's not often I hear anyone say that. Not recently anyway.'

She blushed. 'I read the report about what happened in the summer. It wasn't your fault. You couldn't have prevented it.'

'I'm not so sure.' He led her to the door. 'But I'll keep you in mind if anything should come up. Thank you, Olsen, you did the right thing by talking to me.'

He said his goodbyes quickly. His instinct on Hannemann had been spot on; the man had cut corners.

Still, what Olsen had said had led him nowhere nearer to believing anything had happened.

Jensen would disagree, but that was just too bad.

He only had to humour her until she had completed her interview with Jan Loft on Saturday. Then they would be quits.

32

'It'll be perfect for you. Ready to move in to,' said the estate agent, unlocking the door to the third-floor flat in Frederiksberg.

It would have to be, Jensen thought.

Above her budget, and with just a single bedroom, it was hardly ideal, but there hadn't been anything decent on the market for ages.

If she could haggle the price down, she might just be able to make it work.

'Is there a basement lockup, for my bicycle?' she said, noticing the narrow dimensions of the hallway. It smelled of cat.

'No,' said the estate agent, a man about her own age, with a spiky hairdo stiff with gel. He was chewing gum, his white shirt unbuttoned so far you could see the hair on his chest.

He looked at her more closely. 'I thought you said you were on your own?'

'That's right.'

'And you're having a baby soon?'

She nodded. 'In February.'

'Then you won't be doing much cycling for a while, will you? I mean, you can't strap a newborn into a child seat. Or maybe you have a cargo bike?'

She hadn't thought about that. She couldn't afford a cargo bike.

'You'll need a pram, but you can leave that downstairs in the lobby by the mailboxes. Everyone else does that.'

Pram, changing mat, clothes, toys. So many things to buy. The twinge deep in her abdomen was back, filling her with panic at the thought of what was to come.

He opened the door to a small kitchen. 'Nice and new. Plenty of storage,' he said.

She followed him in. There was barely room for the two of them.

The bathroom wasn't much better. The shower was an attachment to the two taps on the sink, and as far as Jensen could tell, would necessitate sitting on the toilet seat when bathing.

Her heart sank, as she glanced into the two main rooms, dark and stuffy.

She was still reeling from her conversation with Margrethe at Riget. A conversation which had made it seem even more urgent to find a place to live.

It had started with an innocent question in the lift as they had made their way down to the lobby. 'How do you think Gustav is doing at high school?' she had asked.

Margrethe had demanded to know why she was asking. 'I know him going back to school wasn't what you wanted, Jensen, but you've got another three years of it, so you'd better get used to it.'

'I never said I didn't want it for Gustav. I said not every-one has to go to high school. And you know that he didn't really want to go.'

'I didn't force him, if that's what you mean.'

'He wanted to please you.'

Margrethe had sent her an angry glance. 'Don't be melodramatic,' she said. 'In any case, it's my impression that he's getting on very well at school.'

'I don't know,' said Jensen. 'He never wants to talk about it. Don't you find that a little odd?'

She wanted to say: he's smoking weed. He's playing truant. There's nothing in his schoolbag.

But she didn't. It would be better for her relationship with Gustav if Margrethe discovered those things for herself.

'If I were you, I'd focus on my job,' said Margrethe. 'Jannik told me what happened between the two of you. He says you've been obstructive and rude to him ever since he started working at the paper.'

'What?' said Jensen. 'But that's not true.'

'What you don't seem to understand, Jensen, is that if we don't try something new, it'll be over for *Dagbladet*. Maybe a few years from now, but over for sure. Which means you and I will both need to find ourselves a new job.'

'I didn't mean—'

'If you weren't pregnant,' Margrethe said. 'If you were anyone else, I would have told you to leave by now.'

Jensen knew that she didn't really mean it. She had said similar things in the past and ended up regretting it. 'But Jannik is a total idiot,' she said.

'You've underestimated him. Just wait and see,' said Margrethe.

'He doesn't care about anyone but himself.'

'That's funny,' said Margrethe, smiling as she stepped out of the lift into the busy hospital lobby. 'Because that's exactly what he says about you.'

She had walked away, leaving Jensen behind in the twirling crowd of patients and visitors.

Choked with indignation, Jensen had got out her phone immediately, searched for flats to rent in Copenhagen and called an estate agent who had agreed to meet her within the hour.

'So, what do you think?' he said, jangling his keys.

'It's small,' said Jensen. She opened the door to the wardrobe. Inside, the shelves had collapsed.

'Oopsy-daisy,' said the agent. 'Easy enough to fix though.'

'I'm not sure where I'd put the baby.'

'Get a single bed. Then you can fit a cot next to it,' he said, chewing.

'Is the rent negotiable? It's a bit high for me.'

'This is Copenhagen, what do *you* think?'

'So that's a no then?'

'Look, lady,' he said, breathing spearmint on her. 'You said you were in a hurry. This flat will go today. If you want something bigger and cheaper, I'd suggest you look further out. This close to town, this is the best you're going to get. So, do you want it or not?'

33

Stine Clausen had used up the last tissue in the box on the table in the family room, and Mark had gone in search of a fresh supply. 'I don't think I can take any more,' she said, her voice hoarse and weak. 'Simon said he was doing well at work. I thought that was where the money was coming from.'

She was clutching the tea with three sugars that Henrik had made her in the galley kitchen. Her hands were shaking.

'Don't worry about that now,' Henrik said. 'It's being dealt with.'

'I just want my daughter back,' she said.

'I know,' said Henrik. 'It was good of your friend to drive you here.'

He had a whole team looking at Simon's background now. Could Matilde have been kidnapped by one of his business associates? Was there a ransom demand that he had kept quiet about? So far, he was denying this, but he had lied to them before.

Given his relationship with Stine, it was a tricky situation to negotiate.

Most of the rooms in the police building were pared down and neutral, with little suggestion of homeliness. But the family room had sofas, cushions and pot plants, a vain attempt to soften the blow for those caught up in crime either as victims or as relatives. It looked like one of the fake living rooms you saw at IKEA, a stage set for human distress.

Henrik suspected Stine couldn't care any less about her surroundings than she did in that moment.

'You wanted to talk to me?' she said.

'Remember I told you earlier that we found your daughter's phone in the lake?'

She began to cry again, her shoulders shaking. He waited for her to finish. She wiped her nose with the back of her hand.

'We've managed to recover the data.'

He couldn't believe it when Bagger had told him, had almost kissed him on the lips in gratitude.

Stine looked up at him, confusion pasted on her face. 'And?'

'We've identified almost all the numbers in Matilde's contacts – you, Simon, a handful of her friends, your ex. But there's one number that we can't account for.' He pushed a piece of paper across to her. 'Recognise it?'

'No. Whose is it?'

He sighed deeply. 'We don't know. They've used an anonymous pay-as-you-go SIM card. Can you think of anywhere Matilde might have got into contact with a stranger?'

She shook her head. 'I've already told you no. It's completely impossible. Unless ... could it be someone from school? One of the older kids?'

'We're checking that, but we don't think so, given how

they've managed to keep things anonymous. The thing is, Stine, and this is going to be difficult news for you, Matilde was exchanging messages with this person for a while.'

She jumped up. 'But I check her messages regularly. I gave you her passcode.'

'Matilde deleted the messages, so you wouldn't have known. But we were able to retrieve them.'

'What were the messages about?' she shouted, looking like she was going to collapse.

He needed to calm her down. 'It was mostly nothing. Emojis and GIFs. How are you today, and inane little messages of that nature.'

'Mostly?'

'Yes, except for a couple of messages last Saturday. The unidentified person writes, "See you tomorrow?" and Matilde responds with a smiley. They must have arranged to meet in the park.'

Stine stared at him, hands on her cheeks, pulling her mouth down in a silent scream. 'That's why she was so intent on going,' she said.

'Yes, probably. We don't know any more. It's likely they promised Matilde something. Or claimed to be a friend of yours.'

'So this person's got her?' Stine cried.

'Yes, we think so. We can't be sure, but it's an important lead. It gives us something to go on. In the meantime,' he said, hesitating for a second, 'I know we've been over this before, but can you think of anyone who might have come near Matilde when you went to the park?'

'No,' Stine snapped, pulling at her hair. 'I've told you a million times.'

'OK,' he said. 'We're trying to find people who might have seen Matilde talking to someone. A few people have mentioned seeing an elderly woman with a red shopping trolley in Ørstedsparken on Sunday afternoons. Do you recall someone like that?'

'I don't know. Maybe. Not that I've noticed.'

Henrik suddenly remembered what his brain had been trying to tell him. Could the suitcase in Matilde's drawing of the old woman in fact be a shopping trolley? Had Matilde made friends with the woman? He got out his phone. He scrolled through his photos until he found the picture and showed it to Stine. 'I found this drawing in your daughter's room. Do you recognise the person in the picture? Could it be Matilde's grandmother, perhaps your mother, or Simon's?'

She shook her head. 'My mum's dead, and Simon isn't in touch with his. Matilde has never even met her.'

Henrik frowned.

'Who is it?' said Stine.

'No idea,' he said. 'But we need to find her. Urgently.'

Day Five

34

'Did you see what that bearded clown did?' said Gustav over the phone.

Jensen sighed. She could hardly have missed it. Google Me's scoop had completely blindsided her.

'A taste of your own medicine. Now you know what it feels like,' he had told her earlier when they had met on the stairs.

She suspected this was no accident. Google Me must have been waiting for her to come in, not wanting to waste his chance to crow.

TEN-YEAR-OLD BURGLAR: THEY PAY ME IN COCAINE

His video had kicked up a media storm, pushing the Matilde case down the front page; the story was running on all channels, and across social media.

The little boy's face was obscured, his voice distorted. He fidgeted and swung his legs on the chair, as he recounted how he burgled houses in exchange for weed and occasionally cocaine.

The film then cut to a playing field and Google Me explaining on a voiceover how the boy had been recruited by a gang on his way home from a game of football.

'*Dagbladet* is in possession of the name and address of the child and has verified the story with his mother, a single parent who's too frightened to come forward or report the gang to the police,' said Google Me.

'What do you take when you burgle?' he said, out of shot, as the film cut back to the interview.

'Cash, jewellery, tablets, phones,' said the boy.

'Have you ever got caught?'

'Once, but the police just called my mum and let me go.'

In the voiceover, Google Me said that the child was now addicted to drugs and refusing to stop burgling, turning his mother frantic with despair.

There was an article along with the video, accompanied by a flattering photo of Google Me.

A psychologist was quoted as saying that children were easy prey for gangs, and that this was unlikely to be an isolated case.

Meanwhile, a spokesperson for one of Denmark's far-right parties repeated an old call for the age of criminal responsibility to be lowered from fifteen to twelve, and even questioned whether this ought now to be ten years of age.

This must have been what Margrethe had been alluding to in the lift at Riget when she claimed that Jensen was misjudging Google Me.

She had even written a leader column titled *What is happening to our children?*

'We've a duty of care to the most vulnerable in our society, and that includes the next generation,' the article said.

Jensen wasn't looking forward to watching Google Me bask in Margrethe's praise at the editorial meeting. 'Yeah, well,' she said to Gustav. 'Your aunt is loving it. She clearly thinks very highly of him.'

'He's a total dick,' said Gustav with surprising aggression. 'You can tell from the stuff he writes about himself.'

Google Me's website, however self-aggrandising, hardly warranted that degree of anger, thought Jensen. 'He does work here now, Gustav. He's only done what he was hired to do. From the looks of it, the story is something he'd been working on for a while before he joined.' She paused. 'Anyway, shouldn't you be at school?'

'I *am*,' he snapped. 'I've just popped out to go to the toilet if that's OK with you?'

'Gustav, what's the matter? You sound . . . has something happened?'

'No, it's just . . . it seems so unfair that he's doing a job that I could easily be doing, if only—'

'You weren't at school?' said Jensen. 'Gustav, it was your own choice.'

'Yeah, with Margrethe holding a gun to my head,' he said. 'It was like, "Go to school or go back to your dad, the Nazi. Your choice."'

'She only wants what's best for you. We both do.'

He sucked deeply on his vape. At least, Jensen hoped it was only a vape. 'He came round to the flat, you know,' he said, exhaling loudly.

'Who?'

'The bearded clown. Last night when you and Margrethe were both out.'

'He did?'

'Yeah, that nice *Dagbladet* photojournalist whom everyone thinks is so great came to the flat saying he needed a word. He said that unless I stayed away from *Dagbladet* . . .'

'What did he say he would do?'

Silence at the other end.

'It doesn't matter,' said Gustav.

'Did he threaten you?'

'No, it wasn't like that. He just said he'd tell Margrethe.'

'That it was you who filmed the video at Bodil's? He can't know that. He's just bluffing. It would be his word against mine.'

Not that she would necessarily win that contest, Jensen thought. Margrethe was just as likely to believe Google Me.

'No,' he said. 'Something else.'

'Tell me, Gustav.'

'I don't want to talk about it.'

She didn't want him to hang up, as he might be liable to do, if she pushed him any harder. She would have to get it out of him some other time.

'Anyway,' he said. 'Shall we meet at Bodil's tonight? Discuss what to do next?'

That's my boy.

'Sure,' she said. 'I'll call Bodil and pick up some food for us all on the way. Speak later. Now go back to class.'

He ended the call.

She grimaced at her reflection in the desk monitor.

If Google Me wanted war, then war he was going to get. Their collaboration, such as it had been, was over.

For good.

35

'I don't have to remind you that the optics here are horrendous,' said Wiese. 'Dozens of officers on the case, and so far, we've got a handful of tenuous leads, one vandalised house, and not a single clue as to the whereabouts of Matilde,' he continued.

Seated in front of his desk, Henrik and Mark exchanged a glance. They were both feeling glum and exhausted, running on fumes.

'Optics' was a favourite word in Wiese's nauseating vocabulary, but Henrik knew he was quoting the rest more or less verbatim from Chief Superintendent Mogens Hansen, AKA 'Monsen'.

He, too, had received a call from Rome where Monsen had been attending a policing conference, tacking on a holiday with his long-suffering wife Rigmor.

It was a running joke in the office that his international engagements were only ever in attractive locations.

'I leave the country for five minutes and everything immediately goes down the toilet!' he had roared into Henrik's ear.

Monsen hadn't just meant the search for Matilde, but also *Dagbladet*'s latest top story.

Ten-year-old burglars with drug habits? Henrik had encountered plenty of thirteen-year-olds busy forging a criminal path for themselves, perhaps even early maturing twelve-year-olds. Below the age of legal responsibility, kids could be valuable to criminals. But a boy of ten? It was hardly the widespread phenomenon that the media was making it out to be.

If there was a silver lining – in the most generous sense – it was that the new story had taken the heat off him and his team for a bit.

The intense media attention had made it impossible to think and triggered endless calls from the public that each had to be logged and investigated.

Matilde had now been spotted in a restaurant in Mallorca, on a plane to New York and by a Danish expat couple in New Zealand who had read the news online and were certain they had seen her on a bus in their local town.

He rubbed his face, trying to shake a bit of life into himself. He had barely slept for more than a couple of hours in the past few days, creeping into bed after his wife was dead to the world, and leaving before she got up.

Lying in the dark, listening to his wife breathing steadily next to him, he had wanted to wake her up, shake her into life and talk to her, but he hadn't known where to begin.

'What's the plan?' said Wiese.

It was a good question, the right question.

After hundreds of interviews with car owners, some of whom had wasted time with tall tales of their movements on Sunday afternoon, a black Audi on false plates had finally been tracked on CCTV, driving at speed down

Nørre Farimagsgade at the opposite end of the park from the playground on the day Matilde had disappeared.

Already, bleary-eyed detectives had looked through hundreds of hours of recordings from multiple CCTV cameras positioned at and around the seven entrances to the park.

If Matilde had been dragged off by a stranger, she would have been upset, likely crying, perhaps digging in her heels. It would have attracted attention.

Instead, their working theory was that Matilde had left voluntarily with the unknown person, whom she had been in touch with via text messages. The two had somehow made it out of the park together and left in the black car.

They had spoken to pretty much everyone else Matilde had been in contact with during the weeks leading up to her disappearance.

To make progress, they needed to track the black car and put together its journey across the city, which would take time.

Henrik didn't like waiting.

Not one little bit.

'We think we've identified a crucial witness,' he said. 'An old woman with a red shopping trolley was seen by several people on consecutive Sundays. We think Matilde might have spoken to her, or at least noticed her. We found a drawing in her room of someone matching the woman's description. The other possibility is that the old woman is the person Matilde had been in contact with via text messages. Perhaps she's an accomplice in some way?'

'An old woman? That's all you've got?'

'She's the only one people have mentioned that we haven't been able to find,' said Mark.

'We think the abduction was carefully planned,' Henrik added. 'Maybe for months. Someone who knew Stine and

Matilde's routine, who watched them, befriended Matilde, turned it into some big secret, perhaps some cock-and-bull story about surprising Stine. They knew every inch of the park.'

'Where the CCTV cameras are,' said Mark.

'And where they're not,' said Henrik.

'Why?' said Wiese.

'We don't know that yet. But there was a plan. It wasn't just some random act. I'd like to stage a reconstruction on Sunday. Known facts only. We'd invite the press but keep them controlled. See what we get.'

Wiese refused to be drawn. 'We'll decide tomorrow.'

Henrik weighed his next words carefully. 'The other thing we could try is to look into the Lea Høgh case again.'

Wiese looked at him angrily. 'I said no, didn't I?'

'There might be knowledge from that time to draw on, certain parallels, we could . . .'

Wiese was shaking his head.

'For Christ's sake,' Henrik shouted, making Mark jump in his seat. 'Will you just listen to me?'

Wiese jabbed a finger at him. 'I'm warning you, Henrik. I said you were behaving erratically, showing signs of burn-out, and I haven't changed my mind about that. If you continue to get distracted like this, I'm going to have to replace you with another lead investigator.'

'You don't *have* anyone else,' Henrik roared. He wanted to tip Wiese's desk into his face, rip the reflective glasses off him and crush them under his boot.

'I'll get someone in from another force if I have to,' said Wiese. He sat back in his chair, looking smug. 'I had a call last night from a cop by the name of Hannemann. Said you've been asking questions about a reported assault that he responded to a week ago. He was wondering if we were now investigating the case. Care to explain to me what that was all about? He said that the woman who called it in is a friend of your stepmother's?'

Henrik stared at Wiese. 'She is.'

'I thought your stepmother had Alzheimer's.'

'She does.'

'But she asked you to check for her friend?'

'It was her friend who asked me.'

'So you found out Hannemann and Olsen were the first responders, and looked them up, in the middle of a major investigation, to exert pressure on them?'

'It wasn't like that,' said Henrik. 'I think I saw the alleged incident mentioned in some report. Then I happened to be passing the café and saw the pair of them inside.'

'Jungersen,' said Wiese, holding up both hands. 'Enough lies. If I find you looking into anything other than the Matilde case, I'll take you off duty. Now get out of my office, both of you.'

36

'Frank, what are you doing here?'

Frank, wearing his green parka, lumberjack shirt, old jeans and braces, got up from the red-leather sofa in the lobby at the third attempt. He threw a copy of today's news-paper on the table, shaking his head. 'The Swedish owners are having their pound of flesh, I see. *Dagbladet* has become tabloid trash if you ask me.'

In his right hand were two battered bags-for-life from the Co-op. As he handed them to Jensen, she caught a stale smell. 'I thought you might like these,' he said.

'What are they?' The bags seemed to be full of A4 note pads and photocopies.

Behind the reception desk, seated with his TV-star microphone headset, Marcus was pretending not to listen. She lowered her voice, led Frank towards the stairs, past the big Christmas tree circled by fake parcels. 'We can talk about it in my office. I've still got one, just about,' she said.

'He'll have to sign in,' Marcus piped up behind them.

'Come on, Frank worked here for more than thirty years. You know him,' said Jensen.

But Marcus was immovable. 'Rules are rules.'

Frank took a step back, held up his large hands. 'Calm down both of you. I've no desire to go upstairs, believe me. This place is clearly not what it was.'

The glass doors slid open, and a postman came in, his arms stacked high with parcels. Jensen used the opportunity to manoeuvre Frank outside.

Standing on the wet pavement, cars and buses splashing by, he looked lost, out of place. She realised what it must have taken for him to travel all the way here. To swallow his pride and ask for her.

'I'm glad you came,' she said, wrapping her arms around her jumper. 'I wanted to apologise for yesterday. I upset you. Not my intention, I'm sorry.'

Frank shrugged. 'You were just doing your job. I can't hold that against you. I'd have done the same. We're not that different when it comes down to it,' he said. 'No, don't say anything. It's the truth.'

She bit her tongue.

She had always found Frank irritating and awkward, as if he was deliberately misunderstanding her. She knew the feeling was mutual.

Margrethe always said that awkward people made the most interesting journalists.

Hear the man out.

'I overreacted yesterday. The truth is that the Lea case was one of the worst stories I ever worked on. It really got to me. The way she just disappeared out of the blue.'

'You don't believe she drowned?'

'No. I think it was a convenient explanation. It made some people feel better about the meaninglessness of what had happened.'

'Jan Loft had an alibi.'

'Yes, I know. He was with Lea's older brother and a few other boys that afternoon. It was a hot day. They were swimming in the pool, and Lea couldn't persuade Sebastian to come home with her, but . . .'

'But?'

Frank looked around him. A woman in a quilted onesie was approaching with a pram, having a loud conversation with someone on her air pods. He waited till she had passed them, though she scarcely noticed her surroundings, let alone the two of them.

'I think Loft had connections,' said Frank. 'He was never tried for having aided Lea's abduction, but I believe he absolutely could have played a part. There was an important character witness in his sex-abuse trial, someone called Kim Jespersen who had worked for Loft as a builder and testified that he was deeply manipulative and frequently lied in his business dealings. I tried to approach Kim for an interview afterwards, to find out what else he knew about Loft, but he had moved away from the Dragør area by then. I never succeeded in tracking him down.'

'What do you mean when you say that Loft had connections?' Jensen asked.

Frank glanced over his shoulder again.

'It's all in those bags, my notes from that time. After you'd left, I went and found them in the garage. I won't have room for them where I'm moving to.' He smiled. 'My handwriting isn't great, but you should be able to decipher it. If you can make something of it, well, that would only be a good thing.'

'Thank you,' she said. 'I'll look after them. It was good to see you, Frank.'

He hesitated. Christmas hits from the nineteen-eighties

streamed out from the open entrance of the 7-Eleven next door.

'Was there something else?' she said.

Frank looked around him again. He seemed nervous, distracted. He stepped closer to her and spoke in a low voice. 'Jon Høgh told me that he thought Lea's disappearance was linked to a paedophile ring that Jan Loft belonged to at the time. Høgh reckoned that's where Loft shared his videos and images of Sebastian and his friends in return for material from other producers. I understood from the police that Loft was found in possession of a vast quantity of material, which suggests that Høgh might have a point.'

'Did the paedophile ring have a name?'

'Not one that I knew for certain. You'll find some options in my notes. I asked around, did some research myself. It became something of an obsession for a while. If my wife were still alive, she'd tell you.'

'But you weren't successful?'

'It wasn't so much that,' said Frank, studying his shoes. 'I stopped looking after a while.'

'Why?'

'I got scared. My daughter was fourteen at the time. One day she came home from school terrified. Someone in a car had driven up alongside her, and started saying things to her.'

'What kind of things?'

'Commenting on her looks, asking her if she had ever had sex with a grown man. They clearly knew who she was. I was going to report it to the police, but then I started receiving all these messages. Pornographic images of children. I tried to delete them, but then I worried that maybe they weren't properly wiped, and that the police would somehow manage to find them and think that I was a paedophile. So I decided to stop writing about it. The messages ceased almost immediately. Later I destroyed the phone.'

'You think it was them who came for your daughter?'

'Who else would it have been? And those messages as well. It was terrifying.'

'Oh Frank, I'm so sorry. And there I was, trampling all over that old ground.'

'I'm not saying that you shouldn't look into the story, but I do want you to promise me something.'

'Anything,' she said.

He looked her straight in the eye. 'Be very careful, Jensen.'

37

'*Hej.*' Henrik dropped his keys in the bowl by the front door, recoiling at his own pallid reflection in the mirror.

His knees creaked as he sat down on the bottom of the stairs to undo his boots. He could have fallen asleep there and then.

'Anyone home?' he shouted.

No reply came, but he could hear a hairdryer going upstairs, and the TV was on loudly in the living room. He followed the smell of perfume up the stairs to the main bedroom, finding his wife in her underwear, leaning over with her hair hanging upside down as she blow-dried it.

She jumped when he laid a cold hand on her back.

'Shit, Henrik, don't do that!'

'Sorry,' he said, sitting on the edge of the bed.

'You look terrible,' she said.

'Thanks.'

He sat for a while in silence, then put a hand on her thigh and leaned over to kiss her on the cheek.

'Don't,' she said, recoiling. 'I just did my make-up.' She rolled up a strand of her hair on a round brush and pulled at it with quick, practised movements, holding the hairdryer close. 'There's no dinner for you. The kids have all eaten.'

'I'll find something,' he said, reaching for her bra strap, but stopping himself at the last minute, his hand frozen in mid-air. 'Where are you going anyway?'

She switched off the hairdryer. 'I can't believe you've forgotten. It's the Christmas party tonight. I must have reminded you fifteen times.'

He nodded, a vague sensation of jealousy passing through him at the sight of the slinky red dress hanging on the back of the cupboard door, the strappy black heels on the floor.

The annual staff dinner at the school where his wife was a head teacher didn't include partners. She always looked forward to it, a rare opportunity to let her hair down, without being on show for the pupils and parents.

Without him.

'It's the one chance I get,' she would say.

He had never liked the sound of that.

A chance for what?

'The babysitter will be here in ten minutes. You could have told me you were going to be home. I'd have cancelled him,' she said.

'I won't be,' he said. 'I just . . . wanted to see you all. I'll be off again in a minute.'

Her face softened, as she switched the hair dryer back on. 'Still no news about Matilde?' she shouted above the din, pulling at her hair with no mercy.

He shook his head.

'I can't bear it,' she said. 'Those poor parents. What if it was one of ours?'

He looked at his hands. He hadn't told her about the picture of Lea yet, wasn't sure he was going to. The investigation into her disappearance six years ago had been a nightmare.

For both of them.

He had been unable to sleep, unable to function, hardly spent any time at home for months.

Of the few cases of missing children he had dealt with in the past two decades, Lea was the only one who had never been found.

No body, no trace.

Would Matilde be the second? Was it about to start all over again?

The hairdryer fell quiet again. He looked up to find his wife had turned to face him. 'Hey, are you OK?' she said, lifting his chin.

Her sudden kindness threw him. He said nothing but leaned into her with his eyes closed, and she held his head to her chest, stroking him gently, and for a moment it was like the old days.

Before the children.

Before Jensen.

Not long ago she had thrown him out of the house, asking for a divorce. That she had taken him back was as much of a mystery to him as the fact that she had chosen him in the first place, when she could have had anyone.

Ostensibly, it was because their children needed him, but he wondered if there wasn't more to it: a desire to hang on to their shared history, perhaps even a core of love deep down inside of her.

If so, she kept it well hidden, only lowering her guard in rare moments such as these.

They broke the spell simultaneously. He rose to his feet, and she continued getting ready for a party he wasn't invited to.

*

When his wife had left, her heels clacking all the way to the front door, Henrik showered for the longest time, the water almost burning his skin. Then he put on a fresh pair of black jeans and a white shirt and tiptoed down the hall.

Mikkel and Karla barely looked up from their devices in their separate bedrooms, their faces bathed in blue light.

Oliver was breathing steadily, curled up in his pyjamas with innocent abandon. Henrik switched off the bedside lamp and lay down beside him, inhaling the boyish scent of his hair. It was Oliver who had saved their marriage, time and time again, through his very existence.

Oliver, their unexpected afterthought, who from birth had attached himself to his dad like a limpet. No matter how bad things got, he would never be able to leave Oliver.

Jensen would understand when she became a parent: the loss of control that parenthood taught you, the groundswell of love that made you endure it.

He put his arms around the boy and closed his eyes.

Sleep now.

Just for five minutes.

38

'I don't understand,' said Jensen, standing on the doormat outside Bodil's flat. 'I spoke to her at lunchtime and she seemed fine. I told her we'd be coming.'

'Maybe she's asleep,' said Gustav, hammering on the door.

Jensen kneeled and opened the letterbox. 'Bodil, are you there?'

No sound came from inside the flat. The lights were off. Gustav started pummelling the door again.

Far below them, they heard Palle's voice. 'Hey, what's going on up there?'

The lift began to go back down, clanging as it passed through the floors.

'It's just us,' Jensen shouted.

He came up regardless. 'I've just about had it with you two snooping around,' he said as he stepped out of the lift. 'You need to leave. Now.'

Jensen held up the bag with the boxes of open sandwiches from the covered market at Torvehallerne. 'Bodil was expecting us. I brought food, but now she's not answering. I think something might have happened to her.'

Palle frowned. He knelt, opened the letter box and shouted inside the flat. 'Bodil? Are you there?'

Still no reply.

'I saw her step into a car in Wesselsgade earlier, about half past four,' said Palle, scratching his chin. 'I'd have thought she'd be back by now.'

'Did she say where she was going?' said Jensen.

'To see her solicitor. He sent his driver for her. She didn't mention anything about going out afterwards. The arrangement was that the driver was going to bring her back.'

'A solicitor with his own chauffeur?' said Gustav. 'Who is he?'

Palle shrugged. 'I don't know.'

'Do you have the key?' said Jensen, gesturing at the door.

'Yes,' he said. From the pocket of his overalls, he pulled the keyring she had seen in his hallway.

He fumbled for a bit, finding the right one, then unlocked the door. Jensen and Gustav piled inside, moving quickly from room to room, calling Bodil's name.

The flat was cold and dark.

In the bedroom, Wolfgang the cat stared at them from a cushion.

'Anything?' said Jensen as they met up in the hallway.

Gustav shook his head. He held up a mobile phone. 'And she forgot this.'

'She told me she didn't know how to use it,' said Jensen.

Palle looked at them both. He seemed uncomfortable all of a sudden. 'We shouldn't be here,' he said. 'Not when Bodil isn't at home. I think we should leave.'

'I think we should call the police,' said Gustav, looking straight at him.

Jensen held up her hands. 'Wait a minute. Let's think. Maybe the driver took her home as planned, but she decided to go for a walk instead of heading straight up here?'

She turned to Palle. 'Go look for her by the Lakes. Gustav and I will see if we can find the name of the solicitor. We'll join your search as soon as we've called them. Let's exchange numbers,' she said.

Palle reluctantly did as he was told. In the doorway, he hesitated again, but left when she waved her hand at him impatiently.

'I don't like him,' said Gustav when he had gone. 'Always hanging around the place.'

He had a point. Palle's clinginess was curious, weird even, but not necessarily sinister. 'He's just trying to help,' she said.

'Oh yeah? Who told him to?'

'Gustav, shut up and focus. We have to find out where Bodil went. If only we had an address book or something.'

Gustav went to the hall table where the telephone was and held up a slim notebook. 'You mean this one?'

She snapped it out of his hand, leafed through the pages. There weren't many names. Some were crossed out. She found the number for 'dentist', one for 'doctor' and another for 'hair', but nothing was listed under solicitor.

Going through the names one by one, she got to E. And stopped.

Ernst Brøgger.

Also known as Deep Throat.

Solicitor, among other things.

She had never discovered where his office was, but he

201

had come in useful as a source of information on a number of occasions. Brøgger knew everyone, had a finger in a thousand pies, but preferred a quiet life.

Bodil had crossed out eight previous numbers for him.

'I don't believe it,' she said to herself. 'Of all the people in Copenhagen ...'

'Who is it?' said Gustav.

'Deep Throat. Remember when you tried to film him in Assistens Cemetery?'

'Yeah, he kept his face turned, the sly bastard.'

She dialled the only number that wasn't crossed out.

A gravelly, posh Copenhagen voice. 'Jensen. It's been a while.'

She pictured his compact form, his slacks and yellow V-neck jumpers, his horn-rimmed spectacles, his neatly contained, discreetly perfumed presence.

'How did you know it was me?' she said.

'I know everything,' he said. 'Speaking of which, you must be around seven months gone by now?'

'I'm calling about Bodil,' Jensen said, not quite succeeding in keeping the annoyance out of her voice.

'I guessed. She told me that you two have met, and that you've been trying to help her. I'm glad.'

'So it was *you* who suggested she call me.'

'Might have been.'

It wasn't the first time this had happened. Brøgger had claimed to have followed her career for a while, sought her out as a useful contact. She had always wondered how many other journalists he had at his beck and call.

'Well, she's missing. We were supposed to meet at her flat now, and she isn't at home.'

'I don't understand. I saw her not two hours ago. My own driver collected her and took her back afterwards.'

'I thought you said you knew everything?'

Brøgger was quiet.

'What did she want to see you about?'

'Jensen, you know perfectly well I can't disclose that.'

'It might explain why she's disappeared.'

'Trust me, it doesn't.'

'Did she seem all right to you? All there?'

'Why shouldn't she be?'

'Apparently, the report she made to the police a week ago wasn't the first time she'd called them. She'd previously reported a burglary but when the police came, there were no signs of a break-in.'

'I know that. Just because the police didn't find anything doesn't mean it never happened. Bodil owns several priceless first editions. I should know. It was I who got them insured for her, at great expense.'

'Her neighbours believe she's been showing signs of dementia.'

'Did Palle Dybdal tell you that?'

'Yes, as it happens.'

'I don't mind saying that I have my eye on him. I don't like the way he's inveigled himself into her affairs; but of course, Bodil never listens to me,' he said. 'She refused to have an alarm fitted. I can vouch for the fact that she's as lucid as ever. Her parents were the same. Bright as buttons until the day they died.'

Jensen sighed.

Brøgger wasn't helping. 'Gustav and I are going to look for her around the neighbourhood. If we don't find her, we'll call the police.'

'You do that,' said Brøgger. 'I'll speak to my driver, find out if he definitely dropped her off at home. And Jensen?'

'What?'

'Take care. I know it's anathema to you, but a woman in your condition needs to be careful. You're no longer just responsible for yourself.'

39

Henrik sat up with a jolt when his phone rang. For a second he couldn't remember where he was. Then he noticed Oliver beside him.

The boy was sound asleep, lying in a star shape, one arm flung across Henrik's chest.

How long had he been asleep for? He wiped saliva off his cheek and got out of bed on wobbly legs.

Jensen.

What did she want?

He tiptoed into the hall, squinting at the bright overhead lights. The TV was still on downstairs. 'Yes?' he whispered.

'Henrik? Is that you?'

'What do you want?' he said, letting himself into the bathroom and locking the door.

'You sound strange. Where are you?'

He coughed, rubbed his face hard with cold water from the tap. He would have to get back to the station immediately. Anything could have happened by now. 'Home, but not for much longer,' he said. 'Look, I'm in a bit of a rush. Whatever it is, can it wait?'

'No,' she said.

Suddenly, he was awake. She sounded upset, out of breath.

'What is it?' he said. 'Has something happened to you?'

'No,' she replied irritably. 'It's Bodil La Cour.'

'Ah. Her.'

'Yes, her. The woman whose witness statement you decided to ignore.'

'We didn't ignore it. Just . . .' he began, but he didn't have the energy to continue the argument and let the sentence peter out.

'She's gone missing,' said Jensen. 'I've just reported it to the police. They said they'd get on to it, given Bodil's advanced age and poor mobility, but to be honest, they didn't seem all that concerned.'

'It's probably nothing,' Henrik said.

'I'm really worried something bad has happened to her. Her neighbours think she has dementia, but her solicitor disagrees.'

'Her solicitor?'

'Yes. Bodil went to see him earlier. The solicitor had his driver pick her up and take her back. He checked, and the driver insisted that he dropped her in Wesselsgade behind her building, and that she stood on the kerb waving as he drove off. We've searched for her everywhere.'

'We?'

'Me and Gustav. And Palle, the caretaker.'

'I see.'

'I think that under the circumstances, I'd better cancel the interview with Jan Loft tomorrow. I'm supposed to be catching the train at six a.m.'

Henrik sat up straight. 'No,' he said quickly, leaving the bathroom and heading downstairs. 'Please don't do that. I need you to go.'

'But what about Bodil?'

'I'll get someone on it right now,' he said. 'We'll find her, I promise you. My stepmother has dementia. She used to go missing all the time before she went into a home. She always turned up, sooner or later. Please don't worry.'

'But, like I said, Bodil doesn't necessarily have dementia. Maybe this is all linked to the story I wrote about her, about the assault she witnessed. Maybe someone didn't like her talking to me.'

He pressed the phone under his chin and put on his battered Timberlands, lacing them up one by one, while looking around for his leather jacket. 'Jensen, listen to me. You need to calm down. Stay in the flat, I'll send someone to speak to you. I promise you, we'll find her. Get some sleep tonight, and make sure you're on that six o'clock train in the morning.'

He hung up and went into the living room to wave hello and goodbye to the babysitter.

It was Frederik, the pasty-faced boy from next door, barely sixteen. His eyes were glued to his game of FIFA. 'I'll call you later,' Henrik said. 'See how everything is going. Don't put your phone on silent.'

Frederik lifted his thumb in acknowledgement, still with his eyes on the screen.

Henrik hesitated in the doorway.

He wanted to tell the boy to sit up straight, to look at him when he was talking, to check on the kids every five minutes and to not, under pain of death, let anyone into the house.

Instead, he tapped his palm on the doorframe twice for goodbye and left the room.

He made two calls from the car, driving to the station through streets glassy with rain. The first was to arrange for a patrol to visit Jensen and take a report.

The second was to Mark. 'I'm on my way back,' he said. 'Any news?'

'Looks like the black Audi headed east towards Amager.'

'The airport?' Henrik said.

'Could be.'

'Any responses to our tweet about the potential witness? The old woman with the shopping trolley?'

'Plenty. But none of them have checked out so far.'

Wait a minute.

A shopping trolley?

Matilde was small. Could this be how she had been transported out of the park?

Jensen answered him on the first ring. 'Yes?' she said breathlessly. 'Have you found her?'

'No,' he said. 'But listen, does Bodil own a shopping trolley?'

'What?'

'Just go and look, Jensen, please, and if you find it, don't touch it.'

He heard her walking through the flat, opening and closing cupboards. 'There's something here,' she said at length. 'This big red thing. It's got four wheels, but Bodil told me that Palle always does her shopping for her. Why do you want to know, anyway?'

'I'm not in a position to tell you.'

'Henrik, you can't just ask me something like that without explaining.'

'Just trust me.'

'Can you understand why I might find that hard?' she said. 'Fool me once, and all that?'

He tried to think of a witty reply but came up with nothing.

'Wait,' she said. 'The police were looking for an old

woman with a red shopping trolley. I saw the tweet. You don't think Bodil . . .? Oh my God.'

She trailed off.

'Look,' Henrik said. 'I'm on my way. Stay where you are and remember, don't touch anything.'

He pointed the car at the Lakes and pressed the accelerator down as far as it would go.

40

'You have to leave this to us now,' said Henrik, virtually pushing Jensen out of Bodil's flat.

Gustav was sitting on the stairs with his head in his hands, cross because he had been told off for vaping.

'I would strongly advise you to keep what's happening here tonight to yourself for the time being. You've already messed up my investigation once,' Henrik said.

The team of technicians had arrived and set to work promptly, after taking DNA swabs and prints from the two of them.

'So we can eliminate you from whatever we find,' Henrik had explained.

'Can't you at least tell us what you're thinking?' Jensen said. 'Do you believe Bodil knows something about Matilde's disappearance?'

'I don't know,' he said, truthfully.

'Because I'm pretty sure she doesn't. We never talked about Matilde, and she didn't mention going for walks in Ørstedsparken. In fact, she uses a walking stick. I can't see her pushing a trolley around.'

'She might not have been watching the news or thought it was relevant,' he said.

It had occurred to him that the whole thing was a mix-up, another dead end.

Still, Bodil was missing. Perhaps she had seen something in Ørstedsparken that she shouldn't have.

He thought again about the red shopping trolley. It was big enough to have held Matilde.

Jensen read his mind.

As she had a habit of doing.

'You don't actually think – and I can't even believe that I'm saying this – that Bodil abducted Matilde?'

'We don't know anything yet,' he said.

'Why would Bodil do that? It makes no sense.'

'Look, just go home,' he said. 'Get some sleep, and then go and see Jan Loft in the morning. Meanwhile, I promise you we'll do anything we can to find Bodil.'

She finally left with Gustav, who sent him a death stare from the lift before closing the door.

Henrik went in search of the head technician, finding her in the bedroom. 'I want you to take prints, go through Bodil's things, and tell me about anything that stands out.'

He walked through the flat. It was dark, stuffy and full of furniture and ornaments.

It seemed Bodil led a very simple life, moving between her bedroom, the kitchen and the living room. The rest of the rooms had been unoccupied for years, judging by the thick layer of dust on everything.

The place reminded him of something out of a fairy tale, Sleeping Beauty's castle. He went into the bedroom and stood by the window, looking down at the dark courtyard and the red building on the other side of it. There was a light on in a few of the flats, people moving behind the windows.

As a child, people's night-time windows had been endlessly fascinating to him, their private lives in the golden glow behind glass seeming so much more enticing than his own in the terraced house in Brøndby. These days, he had come across enough misery behind the city's closed doors to know that this was an illusion.

He had watched the video Jensen had created with Gustav. Bodil had spoken with conviction.

Henrik felt as though the floor under him was moving. He put out a gloved hand to stop himself from swaying. His thoughts were swirling, colliding: Matilde, missing as though a giant hand had reached down through the clouds and snatched her off the face of the earth. Her biological father, a paedophile. A picture of Lea, missing for six years, found on a hidden hard drive.

The mysterious old woman with the red shopping trolley, seen by several independent witnesses in Ørstedsparken.

Had it been Bodil?

Why?

He went into the hall, donning his gloves before lifting the red trolley out carefully. Some mud had stuck to the wheels. He opened the cover and looked inside. Nothing visible.

The technician sauntered over to him. 'What's that?' she said.

'I want this looked at very carefully. Compare the soil to the samples found in Ørstedsparken. Full analysis of any DNA from the inside. I need to know if Matilde Clausen was ever inside this bag.'

'Why would—'

'Just do it,' he said.

He would need to ask Bodil's solicitor why she had met with him. It could be critical to their investigation.

He heard voices at the door.

A uniformed officer was standing next to a wild-haired man in blue overalls who was stretching his neck to look into the flat. 'I told you, you can't go in,' said the officer. He noticed Henrik and blushed. 'He insisted on coming up.'

'I'm Palle Dybdal,' the man said. 'As the caretaker, I have a right to know what's going on.'

'Actually, you don't,' said Henrik. 'This is a police investigation. You need to leave. We'll come and take a witness statement from you in due course.'

'Police investigation?' said Palle. 'Have you found Bodil? I've been out looking for her for ages. That *Dagbladet* reporter and her apprentice were supposed to come and help, but they never showed.'

He looked bewildered as Henrik led him out into the stairwell.

'They reported Bodil missing to the police. That's why we're here,' Henrik said. 'There is something you can do to help, though. Did Bodil ever mention going to Ørstedsparken of a Sunday?'

Day Six

41

Jensen took a seat on one of the two chairs by the table in the prison visiting room.

At first, she had sat on the sofa, then decided against it, afraid it would signal a friendliness she didn't feel towards the man she was about to meet.

She had spent the train journey to Jutland reading Frank's notes from the court case against Jan Loft, having to put them down several times to stare out of the window as Denmark passed by in a misty blur.

It was hard to concentrate for worry about Bodil. There had been no message from Henrik when she woke up, and nothing on the news. She forced herself now to look at her notes and try to frame the right questions for Jan Loft in her mind.

Frank had remarked that Loft had shown no signs of remorse, even smiling at times when the prosecutor had read the charges against him.

She was surprised that he had agreed to see her, rather than slipping away quietly somewhere far from Dragør where no one knew who he was, perhaps changing his name and appearance.

The room was bright and clean, swept of anything that might make it look homely: cushions, pictures on the walls, plants. She had been asked to leave her phone outside and felt naked without it.

It had been two in the morning by the time she and Gustav had stopped looking for Bodil. They had spoken to dozens of people, but no one recalled seeing an elderly woman with a walking stick. She had managed to sleep for little more than an hour, checking her phone for news every five minutes. Gustav had been asleep when she left Margrethe's flat, under strict instructions to phone her at the slightest news.

She had agreed to interview Jan Loft because she had been curious about Lea. Now she just wanted to get out of there and back to Copenhagen.

To Bodil and to Matilde.

The trip to Jutland seemed like an enormous distraction, a mistake. As soon as she had asked the questions Henrik had given her, she would be on her way. There was a train in an hour.

The door opened and Jan Loft stepped in, wearing a navy track suit, white socks and black crocs. He was smaller than she had expected, but carrying a few extra kilos, cleanshaven, with a thick mane of dull brown hair.

'Jensen?' He stretched out his hand. She hesitated for a second before shaking it, and he noticed, looking disappointed, before recovering his composure.

He sat down, folding his hands on the table in front of him, smiling sadly. 'You don't have to say anything,' he said. 'I'm a convicted paedophile. I can imagine it must be difficult for you to be here. Especially seeing as you ...' He pointed to her bump.

She pulled the cardigan closer and leaned into the table. 'Let's leave me out of it, shall we?'

'If it makes you feel any better about what happened ...
there won't be a repeat.'

'How can you be sure?'

'Chemical castration.'

'Didn't fancy the real thing?'

'It wasn't offered to me,' he said, deadpan. 'The drugs seem
effective enough. I've gained weight, though,' he said, slap-
ping his belly. 'And don't get me started on the hot flushes.'

'Why did you agree to the drugs?'

'This thing,' he said, pointing to his brain.

'Paedophilia?'

'Yes. It won't stop. Talking about it doesn't help. I tried
talking, but my body was stronger. I realised that the urges
would never go away.'

'You had a choice. You didn't have to act on the urges.'

'That's not true.'

'Then you should have sought help.'

'I was ashamed.' He looked at her calmly. 'Would it make
a difference to you if I told you that I was abused myself as a
boy?'

'I'm sorry to hear it, but that doesn't give you the right to
do the same thing to others.'

'Of course it doesn't, but maybe it makes it easier to understand. The shame is crippling. You carry that thing inside you
until it bursts out.'

Jensen looked out of the window at the tree in the courtyard. It was bending in the wind, its branches thrown here
and there. The window was spattered with rain.

'Do you regret what you did?'

'Yes.'

'You didn't when you were convicted. You were seen
smiling in court.'

'I was ill.'

'And that makes it OK? You were ill. You couldn't help it. Tell that to the boys whose lives you ruined. Those pictures you took, the videos, they're still out there.'

He smiled sadly again, still utterly calm, his folded hands not betraying the slightest tremble. 'None of us can turn back time, Miss Jensen.'

'It's just Jensen.'

'Sorry. Jensen. You seem ... on edge. Can I get you something? A glass of water? Some tea?'

'No thank you. I want to ask you something.'

'Of course. I understand that's why you came.'

'Lea Høgh. Sebastian Høgh's sister.'

Jan Loft's smile faded. 'I remember her. She disappeared walking home from my house. They never found her.'

'Did you abuse Lea, like you abused Sebastian and his friends?'

'Absolutely not. I wasn't interested in girls. Not ever.'

'I don't believe you.'

'I helped to look for Lea, same as everyone else. I didn't stop for days.'

'That doesn't prove anything.'

'I had an alibi for that afternoon.'

'Because you were with Sebastian?'

'Yes, I think that does prove something. Why are you asking me about Lea? It was six years ago. Has something happened?'

Jensen pulled from her pocket the picture that Henrik had given her. Lea's nakedness had been airbrushed away. She was asleep on a bed in a messy room. She passed him the picture. 'You said that you never abused Lea, so how do you explain this?'

Loft studied the photo in silence. 'Where did you get it?' he said quietly.

'You've never seen it before?'

He shook his head, holding her gaze, as he handed the picture back to her.

'You never introduced any of your friends to Lea?'

'What friends? I didn't have any friends.'

'Anyone working for you then?'

'Never.'

'You ran a building firm.'

'My father's before mine.'

'You must have had a lot of people working for you over the years.'

'Yes. I gave the police a list. After I got arrested for . . . the other thing. They became convinced I must have something to do with what happened to Lea after all.'

'Can you blame them?'

'I suppose not.' He scratched his nose. 'As it happened, no one on the list was ever prosecuted.'

'One of the builders, who worked for you for longer than most, testified against you.'

'Kim Jespersen. What about him?'

'He told the court that you lied. Frequently. He said you were devious and manipulative.'

Jan Loft shifted in his seat. For the first time he looked uncomfortable. 'I lied to get my own way, to place myself in situations where I would be alone with the boys. I didn't lie about Lea.'

'You sure about that?'

'Yes.'

'Look at the picture,' said Jensen, holding it up in front of him.

'I don't have to. I had nothing to do with what happened to her.'

Jensen put the picture into her bag along with her

notebook and pen. Her chair made a loud noise as she pushed it back.

Loft had obviously made peace with himself. He was as smooth as glass; it was impossible to tell whether he truly recognised the consequences of his actions. Whether he cared about anyone but himself.

She suspected not.

She had done as Henrik asked. He would be disappointed with the result, but that wasn't her problem.

'You going already?' he said. 'We've another thirty minutes.'

'I'm afraid so.'

'No time for a repentant sinner?'

'I'm not sure you really are repentant.'

'Not even if I were to offer you a tip?'

She sat back down again. Looked at him straight with an expression that said, 'This had better be good.'

He sat back in his chair, satisfied with finally having found something she wanted and obviously wanting to enjoy his moment.

She let him, staying silent.

'What I'm about to tell you didn't come up in court. The police knew about it, though.'

'What?'

'There was this online forum I used, dark web stuff.'

'A paedophile ring? Yes, I heard that.'

'Who told you?'

'Not important. What about it?'

'They called it Playland.'

Jensen remembered seeing the name in Frank's notes. She hadn't known what it meant. Nor had he, judging by their conversation in the street outside *Dagbladet*.

Loft continued. 'You got access to videos by sharing your

own, or you paid big bucks. In crypto currency. That's how it worked. There was an admin calling himself the Ugly Duckling.'

Only the sickest mind could have thought of subverting a children's fairy tale into a nightmare, thought Jensen.

'Why are you telling me this? What's it got to do with Lea?'

'I didn't tell the police at the time, but I always had the feeling that the Ugly Duckling knew everything about me.'

'They probably wanted you to think that.'

'No, there was more to it. Things they said that only I could understand; it was like they were watching me. In real life. Like they knew who I was, who the boys were.'

Jensen felt her skin begin to tingle. She became conscious of how quiet it was in the room.

'You could ask Kim Jespersen about it,' Loft said. 'He might have noticed something odd at the time.'

I would if I knew where he was, she thought. 'You think that the people who were watching you took Lea?'

'I think someone should look into it.'

'How?'

'You'd have to find them first.'

'How did you?'

'Different chat rooms, one led to another. Someone mentioned Playland. There was a vetting procedure. If you wanted in, you had to barter, and to prove that the material you offered was real, you had to film the kid holding a certain object.'

'Which was?'

'One of those colourful paper windmills that you see in sandcastles on the beach.'

'And you never told anyone else this before?'

223

'About the windmill? No one. You're the first. The question is, what will you do with it?'

Jensen took her notebook and pen back out of her bag and made herself comfortable. 'Tell me again, and this time leave out none of the detail.'

Jensen was trembling when she left the room. Had Loft been telling the truth? What reason would he have for lying?

As soon as they gave her back her mobile, she would call Henrik, make him promise to give her an exclusive in exchange for the information she now held.

Above all, she would ask him for news of Bodil.

The officer handed back her phone. She thanked him and turned to leave, almost falling over her own feet in the rush.

And stopped.

There was no message on her phone from Gustav or Henrik, but a bright yellow and black 'Breaking' alert. The words froze her to the spot.

WOMAN FOUND DEAD IN SAINT JØRGEN'S LAKE

42

Fuck, fuck, fuck.

Henrik ignored the phone buzzing repeatedly in his pocket and looked at the dead woman on the bank of the lake, trying to think straight.

Thankfully, someone had erected a screen to prevent the public from satisfying its morbid curiosity.

The story was already all over the media.

He had known as soon as the call had come in that the woman found by the dog walker was Bodil La Cour. He could feel it in his blood: the heavy, nauseating sense of failure.

Again.

The dead woman in front of him was wearing a blue coat. Sunglasses and a brown hat had been found nearby.

He was looking at the person in the drawing he had found in Matilde's room. Most likely the same person as had been spotted in Ørstedsparken last Sunday by a number of witnesses.

Saint Jørgen's Lake, the deepest of the Lakes and surrounded by more greenery, meaning that it offered more privacy, was under a mile from Bodil's apartment.

He struggled to piece together what had happened.

Jensen had called him ten times already. No point in answering. He knew what she was going to say. Especially when she found out that he had learned of Bodil's death while she had been on the train on her way to Jutland to interview Jan Loft.

He knew she would have turned around and come back if he had called her.

And he had needed her to speak to Loft.

'What can you tell me?' he said to the pathologist who had risen to her feet and was removing her latex gloves while a photographer snapped away at the body.

'The cause of death was almost certainly drowning,' she said.

'What about the gash on the back of her head?' said Henrik, trying not to look at the wound.

'I'd say the water got to her first. It's possible she was unconscious when she fell in.'

'And could the gash have been sustained in the fall? Was this a natural death? An accident?'

'I can't tell you before we've checked her out properly.'

'Time of death?'

'I'd say around twelve hours, but it's purely a guess,' she said.

There was a shout from the water. One of the divers was holding a dark object aloft. Henrik felt icy lake water seep into his boots as he reached for it with gloved hands.

It was a black handbag with a gold clasp. He opened it carefully: lipstick, compact powder, a pair of glasses and a red leather purse. He opened it and found a number of plastic cards, all in the name of Bodil La Cour.

What had she been doing in Ørstedsparken? And what had she done with Matilde, if indeed she had taken her?

Too late to ask her.

About Matilde or anything else.

Out of the corner of his eye, he saw a uniformed officer approach. 'I've got a man outside the cordon insisting on talking to you,' said the officer. 'He's causing a disturbance. Shall I arrest him?'

'Who is it?'

'Says his name is Dybdal.'

'What does he want?'

'Insists he knows the victim.'

Henrik sighed. Dybdal might come in handy when it came to the formal identification of the old lady.

He walked the short distance along the blocked path to the main road.

Dybdal looked dishevelled as he remonstrated with the officer guarding the cordon. 'Is it Bodil?' he shouted as Henrik approached.

'Probably.'

'Did she drown?'

'What makes you think that?' said Henrik.

Palle seemed agitated. *Too agitated*, Henrik thought.

Of course, this could be down to him having been up all night, but Henrik sensed that Palle was worried in some other way.

'Does Bodil have any next of kin?' he said.

Palle shook his head. 'None.'

'Give me your number,' Henrik said. 'Then go home and take a few deep breaths. We'll need you to help us verify her identity later.'

Palle walked away reluctantly, his shoulders slumped.

Henrik turned back to the scene where the body of the old woman was being lifted into a zip-up bag.

He needed to speak to Jensen.

He didn't want to speak to Jensen.

She was going to rip his head from his body.

43

Jensen had considered taking a taxi all the way from Jutland but, with her bank account already overdrawn, she had made do with the train, willing it to move faster across the leaden water of Storebælt towards Copenhagen.

She had called and left Henrik multiple messages, to no avail.

Ernst Brøgger, on the other hand, had answered his phone straightaway. He was as perplexed as her. 'I saw it on the news.'

'What do you think happened to Bodil?'

'I haven't been able to get anything out of the police as yet. Can't see her accidentally falling into the water, and what was she doing all the way over by Saint Jørgen's Lake anyway?'

'Someone killed her,' said Jensen.

'But who on earth would want to kill poor old Bodil?'

'Because she wouldn't go away quietly about what she had seen,' said Jensen. 'If *Dagbladet* hadn't published my video, then maybe none of this would have happened.'

When, finally, the train had pulled into Copenhagen

Central Station, she had cycled straight to Saint Jørgen's Lake, but the cops by the cordon had told her that Henrik had left. The path was taped off, and they were resistant to her pleading.

She had kept her promise and interviewed Loft, and now Henrik was avoiding her. Enraged, she had taken the S-train and sprinted the last kilometre to Teglholmen.

She left her bike outside the police building and rang the bell. The receptionist spoke to her via the intercom. 'Yes?'

'I need to speak to Henrik Jungersen. It's urgent.'

'Do you have an appointment?'

'Just call him. Tell him Jensen is here.'

Ten minutes passed before he showed, looking sheepish. 'I was just about to call you,' he said, marching her outside and around the corner, towards the car park.

'Liar,' she said. 'I read the press release. It said the body was spotted in the lake just after seven o'clock this morning. Why didn't you call me? You knew I was going out of my mind with worry.'

'We didn't know it was her,' said Henrik. 'Not at first.'

'Come on.' She folded her arms across her chest. 'Tell me, how many other women in their eighties have been reported missing within a mile of Saint Jørgen's Lake?'

'Jensen, I can't share police business with you. We've been over that.'

'But when you need something, like an interview with a convicted paedophile, then you *can* speak to me?'

'Don't be like that.'

A sudden cramp deep in her pelvis made her double over. It was stronger than the last few times. 'Ouch.'

'What is it?' he said, alarmed.

'I don't know.' She tried to breathe deeply. 'It's happened before, but not like this.'

Henrik manoeuvred her to a low wall. 'Are you having contractions?'

'No,' she said. The pain was lessening. 'I've got two months to go. I must just have been cycling too quickly.'

'For God's sake, Jensen, you need to take it easy.'

'Don't lecture me,' she said, holding up her hand. 'So, was Bodil murdered?'

'We don't know yet,' said Henrik. 'We'll need to wait for the post-mortem.'

'That means she might have been,' she said, covering her mouth with her hands. 'Oh my God, I got her killed.'

'What?'

'If I hadn't written about what she saw, she would still be alive. It's obvious. Whoever it was who strangled that young woman didn't want Bodil to talk about it. Perhaps they didn't even know that she'd witnessed it all, until they read it in my newspaper.'

It wouldn't have taken much for someone to work out where Bodil lived from the video Gustav had made.

She felt Henrik's hands on her arms, his face close to her ear. 'Listen Jensen, you need to breathe. I don't want to have to deliver your baby here on the pavement. We don't know for certain what happened to Bodil. It might have nothing whatsoever to do with the story you wrote.'

'Matilde then?'

'We don't know that either.'

A couple walked past laden with supermarket bags. She waited till they were out of earshot. 'Why were you asking about Bodil's shopping trolley last night?'

He glanced around nervously, making sure they weren't being overheard. 'OK, I'm going to tell you something, but you have to promise me to keep it to yourself.'

'Why?'

'Just do it.'

She made a scout's three-fingered salute. 'I promise.'

'We found a drawing in Matilde's bedroom of a woman matching Bodil's description. Messages uncovered from Matilde's phone suggest she was meeting someone in the park on the day she disappeared. It could have been the same person.'

'I'm telling you it wasn't Bodil. She definitely didn't know Matilde.' She frowned. 'Wait a minute, you're saying she was killed to make it look as if she was guilty?'

'I don't know, but I sincerely doubt it has anything to do with what she claimed to have seen in the courtyard in the middle of the night.'

'What she definitely saw,' said Jensen. 'I believed her.'

'And the times when she claimed that her flat had been broken into?'

'I think that happened too. Bodil had a lot of valuables. Maybe that's when someone stole her clothes and the red shopping trolley to disguise themselves as her.'

Henrik looked away.

'I don't have time for this,' she said, getting up and beginning to walk away. She needed to get back to *Dagbladet*, write the story, work out what had happened.

'Wait,' Henrik shouted. 'Did Loft say anything, about Lea?'

She sighed loudly, turned back. 'He denied knowing anything about her. He said he hadn't seen the photo before. I think he was being genuine.'

Henrik looked crestfallen.

'He did tell me something else, though,' she said. 'He told me that he had felt like he was being watched in the weeks leading up to Lea's disappearance.'

'Watched? How?'

'He said that he was part of this paedophile ring online, a forum on the dark web called "Playland". He would supply images and videos of his abuse of Lea's brother and his friends in exchange for other material.'

'I know that,' said Henrik. 'When he was caught, his PC was open. We tried for a while to access the forum through Loft's profile, but after his arrest made it into the news, the whole thing was shut down abruptly.'

'So you also know that there was an admin called the Ugly Duckling?'

'Yep.'

'Well, Loft said this admin appeared to know all about him, where he lived, and what he had done.'

'What made him think that?' said Henrik.

'Through the things they said. He felt like he was being watched in real life. He didn't think about it at the time, he said, but later on he developed the theory that Lea going missing had something to do with the paedophile ring. Perhaps it might explain how her photo ended up with Rasmus Nordby?'

'I'm not too sure,' Henrik said. 'That photo could have been taken by anyone before Lea disappeared.'

He looked pensive all of a sudden.

'What is it?' she said.

'It's funny, Loft never mentioned his suspicions to us. Why come out with it now?'

'Perhaps because he's had a chance to reflect on his actions.'

'I sincerely doubt Loft reflects much.'

'Did he tell you that to gain access to the forum for free, you had to create your own child sexual-abuse material, and to prove that it was genuine, the victim had to be holding a rainbow windmill?'

He looked at her sharply, and she could tell it was news to him.

'Since he told me that, I've been seeing them everywhere. Three alone on the way here.'

She thought again of the evil brain that had turned a child's plaything into a symbol of pain and distress.

'I didn't know that,' Henrik said. 'But it's not an unusual MO for paedophile rings to choose an everyday object like that as their secret code. I think I might even remember seeing images of Sebastian with one of those things.' He stood up abruptly, hands on his scalp. 'Why didn't Loft tell us at the time? It could have made a huge difference to our investigation.'

'Maybe because he didn't want to get any deeper into the shit he found himself in,' she said. 'There's something else too. I spoke to my predecessor, Frank Buhl. He covered the Lea case for *Dagbladet* back in the day.'

'I remember him well. Stubborn bugger.'

'Yep, him,' said Jensen, considering for a moment whether she ought to tell Henrik about how Frank had become too scared to investigate, that he had felt threatened, and made her promise to be careful. She decided against, suspecting it would only trigger his protective mode. The last thing she needed was another lecture about how she should and shouldn't conduct herself.

'What about him?' said Henrik.

'Do you remember Kim Jespersen? The guy who testified against Jan Loft in court?'

'Yes. Not the sharpest tool in the box, but reliable enough. Said he had seen Sebastian wearing nothing but underpants at Loft's a couple of times when he came to collect his pay.'

'Well, Jan Loft reckons he might have noticed if someone

was staking him out back then. I think it's at least worth asking the question.'

'Might be.'

'Only, Frank discovered that he disappeared shortly after the trial. His neighbours in Dragør believed he had moved to Copenhagen, but Frank never succeeded in finding him.'

'I'll check it out,' said Henrik.

His eyes widened. He looked at her desperately. 'Matilde's dad had tons of material in his possession. That's where we found the photo I gave you to show Loft. What if all of this is linked, Jensen? Bodil, Matilde, Lea?'

44

Henrik had never been more grateful to see David Goldschmidt, his favourite pathologist at Copenhagen's Forensic Institute.

Palle Dybdal had formally identified the dead woman from Saint Jørgen's Lake as his neighbour Bodil La Cour.

He had broken down over the body, sobbing so hard that Henrik had been forced to sit with him afterwards as the man gathered himself.

Guilty tears?

Now, Goldschmidt had finished the post-mortem and sewn up the Y-shaped incision.

The woman's body had been covered up with a sheet, and Goldschmidt had removed his gloves and was washing his hands. His dark eyes were smiling above the facemask.

'Well?' said Henrik, trying to breathe without drawing air through his nose. Post-mortems, with their raw, iodine smell of offal and disinfectant – like no other smell in the world – turned his stomach.

'I can confirm that the cause of death was drowning. The rigor mortis observed suggest that death occurred between eight and eighteen hours before the body was discovered.'

'So the head wound didn't kill her?'

'No,' said Goldschmidt, drying his hands. He removed his face mask, revealing a thick moustache. 'The bleeding might have killed her eventually, but the water got to her first. There's a good chance that she was unconscious by the time she went in the lake.'

'Could she have had hit her head in the fall and sustained the injury that way?'

'I'd say that was unlikely,' said Goldschmidt. 'The damage to the back of her head indicated that she was hit with a flat object, probably metal.'

'A pipe of some sort?'

'Potentially,' Goldschmidt said.

'In other words, someone hit her over the head, causing her to fall in.'

'That's certainly how it looks.'

'So, murder?'

'That's the most likely scenario,' said Goldschmidt, refusing as usual to be drawn into definitive statements. He frowned. 'You look pale, Henrik, are you OK?'

'Just a headache,' he said. 'I haven't slept much this week.'

'I can believe that,' said Goldschmidt. 'Come.' He turned off the overhead lights and led Henrik out of the white-tile and stainless-steel pathology lab. 'I'll give you something for the pain.' He made Henrik sit in the brown-leather armchair in his office and gave him a large glass of water and a couple of tablets, watching him knock them back. 'Do you suffer a lot from headaches?' he said.

All of a sudden, Henrik felt worried. His head was almost always hurting these days. 'Do you think there could be something seriously wrong with me?' he said.

What if he had a brain tumour? One of his colleagues had been taken out that way. By the time the cancer had been diagnosed, the poor bastard was dead within four weeks.

'I doubt it,' said Goldschmidt. 'More likely to be stress. I'd say you've been working too hard.'

I've done nothing but work, Henrik thought. 'Always,' he said. 'You know what it's like.'

'Saw it on the news. Matilde Clausen. Tough case,' said Goldschmidt. 'To be honest, I've been fearing the worst for the poor girl all week.' He looked intensely at Henrik, his voice gentle and warm. 'Maybe it's your body telling you that you need a break? I don't believe you took any time off after the thing in the summer. Perhaps that was unwise?'

The thing.

The incident.

Henrik dismissed the lucid memories that crowded his brain. Blood pumping from a gunshot wound. The paramedics shoving him aside. All sound disappearing around him.

'Thanks for the water,' he said, getting up. 'Need to find out who bashed our victim over the head and left her to drown.'

Goldschmidt put a warm hand on his shoulder. 'Always here, Henrik. Whenever you need to talk.'

His kindness almost made him crumple. Goldschmidt had always had a sixth sense as far as his mood was concerned.

On the way out, he remembered what Jensen had said about Kim Jespersen, and sent a text message to Mark, asking him to find the man.

He had just got into his car when his phone rang.

'Jungersen.'

'It's Olsen, sorry to disturb.'

238

'Now isn't a good time,' he said to the conscientious young police officer. 'Can we speak later?'

'The body in Saint Jørgen's Lake, it's Bodil La Cour, isn't it? I feel so awful.'

'You couldn't have done any more,' said Henrik, reversing out of his parking space and heading for the road back to Teglholmen. 'Don't feel bad.'

'Oh, but I could,' she said.

'What do you mean?'

'I finally found some CCTV, from a café in Wesselsgade, just yards from Bodil's block. They shouldn't have been pointing the camera at the street, but they've had a spate of burglaries lately. I promised them they won't be prosecuted. I hope that wasn't wrong of me. The quality is terrible, but the time fits.'

'What does it show?' he said.

'I'm pretty sure it's the same couple Bodil reported seeing in her courtyard.'

Henrik mouthed an obscenity, slamming his hand hard against the steering wheel as he overtook a yellow bus.

Jensen had been right after all.

'Good work, Olsen. Meet me in my office in fifteen minutes.'

239

45

Jensen shuddered in her thin coat. The picnic table bench felt like a block of ice under her damp trouser legs.

Gustav had pulled up his hood. His hands were buried deep in his pockets. 'Who killed Bodil?' he said.

'I don't know,' said Jensen. 'But I reckon it could be someone who didn't like her talking to us.'

'So it's our fault?' said Gustav.

Jensen looked away.

Yes, she thought. *It's our fault. And ours to put right.*

Palle had told them that he had identified Bodil at the morgue. He had looked startled to find them in the court-yard on his return. 'What are you doing here?'

'Talking about what happened to Bodil,' Gustav had said.

Palle had looked at him sternly. 'It's not up to us to speculate. We must let the police do their work. You should both go.'

'We offered to tell them what we know. They said to wait here, and they'll come and speak to us,' Jensen had said.

Palle had left, shaking his head. He was watching them from his windows now, moving back and forth in his living room.

'Such a weirdo,' said Gustav.

Jensen looked at the flat below Palle's. The lights were on. They still hadn't spoken to Thomas and Katja. If they were quick, they could make it before the police were ready to talk to them.

Thomas opened the door.

'Just us again. Is now a better time?'

'Not really,' he said, 'My wife and daughter are both napping.'

'Could you come out and talk to us?' said Gustav. 'Please?'

Thomas glanced over his shoulder. Then, finally, he nodded. 'Wait in the courtyard,' he said, shutting the door.

After a couple of minutes, he joined them at the picnic table, wearing a dark-blue puffer jacket and a black beanie. He lit a cigarette.

'You heard what happened to Bodil?' said Jensen.

'Yes,' he said. 'Why?'

He spoke with a strong Copenhagen accent, slowly, as though he was searching for the words.

'We're trying to find out if her death was related to the assault she reported last week.'

Thomas looked surprised. 'Related how? It was an accident, wasn't it?'

'We don't know yet,' said Jensen.

'That's why we want to talk to you,' Gustav added.

'I can't stay long,' he said. 'My daughter might wake up any minute. My wife's so tired all the time, now that the baby is almost here. I don't want her to be disturbed.'

'We'll make it quick,' said Jensen. 'We've asked every-one who lives here the same questions. You're the last on our list. Were you and your wife at home last Saturday between three and four in the morning when the alleged assault happened?'

'Yes. I mean no. Katja was at work. It was her last shift before going on maternity leave,' said Thomas. 'I would have been asleep with my daughter in the flat. Why?'

'So you didn't see or hear anything?'

Thomas shook his head, drawing hard on his cigarette and blowing the smoke out between pursed lips.

Jensen noticed that his hands were rough and calloused, and covered with scratches. She remembered Palle telling them that he worked part time as a builder.

'To be honest, I don't think it ever happened. Bodil was a bit . . . you know, doddery.'

'Ever see any of your neighbours acting strangely?'

He stared at her. 'Apart from Bodil, you mean? Do you know that she also thought her flat had been broken into? More than once?'

'Yes,' said Jensen. 'Are you saying that didn't happen either?'

'What do you think?' he said.

'Palle is always acting strangely,' said a female voice behind them.

Jensen looked up to find a heavily pregnant woman with wavy blonde hair and heavy eye make-up standing in the doorway to the red building. She was carrying a small child on her arm and smiled as she approached them.

'I'm Katja,' she said, looking at the child. 'And this is Emily, our three-year-old.'

The child observed them silently. Katja put her down,

but the girl stayed where she was, staring. She was so pale you could see the veins beneath her skin.

Gustav kneeled down in front of her, making a face.

She kept her eyes on him.

'She's shy,' said Katja.

'I didn't want to wake you, love,' said Thomas.

Katja pointed to her daughter. 'This one had other ideas,' she said. 'Besides, it's getting harder to sleep. You must know what I'm talking about?' she said to Jensen.

'I do,' said Jensen, smiling. 'When are you due?'

'In three weeks,' said Katja patting her bump. 'But Emily was early, so you never know.' She looked at Jensen more closely. 'Where are you having yours?'

'At Riget,' said Jensen. She knew Katja worked there and prayed she wouldn't ask for the name of her midwife, or the projected weight of her baby.

'Home birth for me, like last time,' said Katja. 'I'm a nurse.'

'Yes, I heard.' Jensen was keen to change the subject. 'Palle told us you thought Bodil was suffering from dementia,' she said.

'I didn't say she definitely did. Merely that she had all the signs. You heard about the alleged burglary?'

'Yes. Apparently, Bodil said she felt like someone had been in her flat.'

'Paranoia is quite common when the mind starts to go, poor woman.'

Jensen smiled. 'What if Bodil was telling the truth about everything? What if she really did see something here? Maybe her death wasn't accidental. Maybe someone saw the story I did for *Dagbladet* and decided to get rid of her?'

'That would be terrible. She was such a sweet old lady.'

Those words wouldn't have suited Bodil, Jensen thought. She would rather have been believed.

Strange how her neighbours were so willing to dismiss her as unreliable.

She noticed that Katja's face was red and seemed swollen on one side with scratches that she had attempted to cover with make-up. Katja saw her looking. 'Toddler tantrum,' she said. 'You'll get there.'

Jensen looked at the girl, who didn't seem capable of hurting a fly, let alone scratching her mother's face.

'You mentioned Palle earlier. You said he's always behaving strangely?' Jensen said, keeping her voice low. Palle was still inside his flat, watching them all. She wondered if he could hear them.

Katja didn't seem to care. 'You don't think so?' she said.

'Oh, we do,' said Gustav. 'Always hanging around Bodil. Seems very reluctant to help *us*, though.'

'Claims he only has her best interest at heart,' said Katja, doing quotation marks in the air with her fingers. 'I always wondered what was in it for him.'

Jensen frowned at her. 'What do you mean?'

'I mean that, if we accept that anyone was worried enough about Bodil talking to the press to actually want to kill her, then my money would be on Palle. You wonder why he's been so reluctant to speak to you?' Katja turned and looked deliberately at Palle's flat. It seemed to Jensen that she *wanted* Palle to hear her. 'He's worried about what you might find, sniffing around the place, that's why. I'd suggest the police take a closer look at his bank account.'

'Are you saying Palle was stealing from Bodil, that he killed her because he was worried about being found out?' Jensen said quietly.

Katja began to say something but stopped when they all looked up to see a couple of investigators approaching across the courtyard. They had their warrant cards open.

'If you think that, then you should tell the police,' said Jensen, nodding at the detectives.

Katja smiled. 'Don't worry, I will.'

46

'Play it again,' said Henrik, leaning in so close that his nose was almost touching the monitor.

Olsen pressed the button. 'Stop!' he told her when the woman appeared in the far left of the screen.

She was running, her pale limbs shining like bone, but her movements were sluggish and she almost stumbled over her own feet. Her hair was short and blonde, her white dress shapeless. She was wearing nothing on her feet, and no coat.

A man could be seen reaching into the frame and grabbing her arm, pulling her back.

Just two seconds of the couple could be seen. It was lucky that Olsen had spotted them at all.

'From the way the security camera was pointed, you can tell that the woman definitely came from the direction of Bodil's block,' said Olsen. 'And the man was pulling her back in that direction.'

'We don't know that they definitely came *from* the block,' Henrik pointed out. He tried to couple together the CCTV footage with Bodil's witness statement. What

Bodil saw must have happened in the seconds immediately afterwards. The woman must have managed to escape the man's grasp. Desperate, she had opened the door to the red building, which had been left unlocked, and had run inside the courtyard, perhaps intending to run across it and back out through the yellow building onto the lakeside path. He guessed the man had caught up with her again, strangling her until she lay lifeless on the ground. Then he had begun to drag her away.

Where had the couple come from?

The woman's naked arms suggested that she had run out of a nearby property, in a desperate, and ultimately doomed, attempt to escape her attacker.

They would need to go door-to-door.

Olsen turned to him, a look of remorse on her face. 'Bodil was right all along. And now she's dead, and we can no longer ask her about it.'

At least they had Jensen's video recording of her testimony, thought Henrik.

He had watched it several times in the past few minutes.

He composed a text message to Jensen.

Bodil was right. We need to talk.

He ignored the multiple pings that came back almost immediately.

Jensen would just have to wait.

'Thank you, Olsen,' he said. 'You're going to make a brilliant detective one day.'

She was about to say something when his phone rang.

Bagger.

Henrik felt his pulse rise.

'Jungersen, you've got to see this,' Bagger said.

For the second time in two days, Henrik sprinted across the lift lobby.

'It was Brian who saw it,' said Bagger, always eager to give credit to his team.

Wiese could learn a lot from him.

They crossed the hot and stuffy office, filled with the smell of overheated electronics, to a tidy desk in the corner.

Henrik recognised the lanky, forty-something officer with thinning dark hair seated in front of three large screens. There was a lunch box on the desk, topped with an apple, next to a water bottle and a framed picture of a black Labrador carrying a stick.

Brian brought up the picture of Lea, naked and asleep on the bed in the messy dark room. He pointed to the screen.

'I looked at each of the items in the room. It looks like junk, just a bunch of old boxes, discarded clothes and furniture. Except for this area here, with the bed and this upturned box that's being used as a table for water bottles and the TV.'

Henrik was inwardly willing the man to get on with it, but knew he had to stay quiet.

The work of Bagger's team required patience and dogged persistence.

The willingness to sit for hours in front of a screen getting nowhere. Henrik knew he could never do what Brian did.

'I realised that I have the exact same model of TV, so I thought I'd just check when it was released, and that's when I got the surprise. The manufacturer confirmed it. This model didn't come onto the market until five months after Lea disappeared. In Denmark or elsewhere.'

'We compared the photos of Lea from before she disappeared to this one. She's thinner here, and her hair is longer, but she doesn't look much older. We think no more than six months,' said Bagger.

Henrik felt dizzy. Though the investigation had never formally closed, the search for Lea had eventually fizzled out, the general assumption being that she had drowned.

They had waited for weeks for her body to wash ashore somewhere along the coast. It never had, but the assumption hadn't changed.

Her body could have been carried further out, got stuck on something, fallen apart and been consumed by sea life.

And now, here he was looking at Lea, alive six months after she was supposed to have died.

They had let her down.

They had stopped looking.

'Whoever took this must have bought the TV almost as soon as it was released for sale,' said Brian.

'This turns everything on its head,' said Henrik. 'I need to know if you're absolutely sure?'

'As sure as we can be,' said Bagger, a Mona Lisa smile on his weathered features.

Henrik pushed his knuckles onto the desk. 'What does it mean?' he said.

'It means that someone took her that day when she was walking home from Loft's house, and that she was still alive at least six months later.'

Henrik massaged his chin. 'Could she have been smuggled out of Denmark? I mean, could the picture have been taken overseas?'

'Possible, but unlikely,' said Brian and zoomed in on a corner of the picture. 'The label on that cardboard box is in Danish. See?'

'So she was somewhere in Denmark, we think,' said Bagger. 'At least at the time this photo was taken.'

'And since then?' said Henrik.

'Anybody's guess,' Bagger said. 'We're almost through Nordby's photos. This is the only one of Lea.'

The questions ricocheted around Henrik's brain. Why had someone taken the photo? And how had it ended up online, only to surface years later?

They would have to interview Nordby again. Find out if he knew anything about the photo, and, failing that, look closely at his browsing history. Could it really be a coincidence that a picture of Lea, another lost girl, had been found on the laptop belonging to Matilde Clausen's father?

Jensen had said that Loft had felt like he was being watched after he joined Playland, the online paedophile forum.

Had Rasmus Nordby accessed Playland too? Had they deliberately targeted him as a means of getting to Matilde?

He stared at the screen as if hoping that Lea would sit up and give them the answer.

'There's something else,' said Bagger. 'We reckon, from the relatively poor quality of the photo, that it's a screengrab from a video.'

'Some sort of live feed?' said Henrik, feeling the room spin around him.

'Could very well have been,' said Bagger.

Henrik knew that they were looking at ancient history, and that Lea might no longer be alive. It had been more than five years.

Still, Wiese would have to let him reopen the case now. It was a Saturday. Wiese would be at home, off-duty, preferring not to be called.

Never mind.

Henrik got out his phone and walked into the lift lobby.

'Jungersen, has something happened?'

'Yes. You know the photo we found of Lea?'

Wiese immediately sounded weary. 'What about it?'

'Bagger's guys did some further analysis on it. Turns out it was definitely taken after Lea disappeared.'

'How do they know that?'

'I'll explain later, but surely this changes everything?'

'In what way?' said Wiese.

'Can't you see it? It means Lea didn't drown. Someone abducted her.'

'And Bagger will need to look into that, of course,' said Wiese, 'But what's it got to do with Matilde?'

'We don't know that yet.' Henrik trailed off. He couldn't tell Wiese about Jensen's interview with Jan Loft, or Playland, or Kim Jespersen, not without revealing that he had been working on the case when he had been told explicitly not to. 'I would like some time and resources,' he said. 'To investigate whether there could be a link between the two cases.'

'No,' Wiese said. 'You're not going to do that. This is your final warning, Jungersen. I want you to focus on finding Matilde. Exclusively. Understood?'

He hung up, leaving Henrik to scream silently at his phone.

47

'The coast is clear,' said Jensen.

Gustav got up from the back stairs where he had been waiting in the musty darkness for her signal. 'At last,' he said, making a face. 'I'm famished, and it's bloody freezing in here.'

The top floor of *Dagbladet* was empty as usual for a Saturday evening. Margrethe was attending a premiere at the Royal Theatre, but they couldn't afford to take any chances.

Jensen had checked downstairs to make sure that Google Me wasn't around.

So far they had managed to avoid each other, but she knew it was only a temporary truce, not the end of the war.

She glanced at her phone as she led Gustav into her office and closed the door.

The police had issued a press release about Bodil's murder and said that they were appealing for witnesses.

Jensen needed to focus on writing the story. She was already wondering how much she could and couldn't say. She would need to speak to Henrik, but he still hadn't responded to her messages.

Bodil was right, his text had said. It was typical of him, to throw a hand grenade like that and run away.

The sight of the cardboard boxes leaning against the bookshelf pricked at her guilty conscience. She hadn't even started to think about clearing her office.

Gustav didn't hesitate before diving into the bag of take-away food they had picked up on the way back from Bodil's, busying himself with opening foil trays and snapping plastic lids off tubs of colourful sauces.

A smell of curry filled the room, making Jensen's heart ache for London. When all this was over, she would think seriously about moving back there and starting again.

They sat on opposite sides of the desk, just like the old days, eating straight out of the foil containers, as slowly their frozen limbs thawed.

'I can't stop thinking about Bodil,' she said. 'She cared enough to tell the police, to tell me. Yet no one believed her, not even her own neighbours.'

'We believed her,' said Gustav.

'Didn't do her much good,' she said. 'If Brøgger's driver really did drop her off in Wesselsgade behind the flats, then why did she decide to walk on to Saint Jørgen's Lake?'

'Maybe she fancied a walk.'

'The weather was horrible.'

'Maybe she met someone, and went with them,' said Gustav.

They ate in silence for a while.

'It's all so complicated. What Bodil saw, her death, Matilde, the shopping trolley. How do all those random pieces fit together?' said Jensen.

Gustav dropped his fork into the remains of his matar paneer and wiped his mouth with the back of his hand. 'That's what we have to find out,' he said.

'There's more,' she said. 'Stuff you don't know about yet.'

She told him about Loft, watching his eyes widen when she got to the bit about Playland, and the picture of Lea that the police had found on a hard drive belonging to Matilde's biological father.

'I told you some paedophile creep took Matilde,' Gustav said when she had finished.

'We don't know for sure yet that there's a link between Lea and Matilde. Or how Bodil comes into it, if she does at all.'

'I bet it's all to do with that paedophile ring. We need to get access to it, find the Ugly Duckling,' said Gustav.

'But how?' said Jensen.

Gustav picked up his foil tray again. 'Fie will know,' he said, mouth full of rice and paneer.

'Fie? Are you two still in touch?'

'Most days,' he said. 'She just moved into this cool new flat.'

'On her own?'

'Secure accommodation. Four flats in the block, carers checking in twice a day.'

Last time Jensen had seen the schoolgirl hacker from Roskilde, she had still been living at Skovhøj, a home for vulnerable young people.

Fie could find virtually anything online, get past encryptions, access all areas. It had landed her in trouble with the police before, but she had learned to be careful.

The online world didn't scare her; it was the real world she couldn't handle.

Fie and Gustav had initially bonded over gaming. Jensen was touched that their friendship had lasted and grown over the months.

'Maybe,' she said.

'Do you think Palle killed Bodil?' said Gustav.

'With what motive?'

'Perhaps because he was afraid of what she might tell us? Katja seemed to think he's got something to hide.'

Jensen thought about it. Katja's comments had struck a chord. Palle had always seemed reluctant to have her and Gustav around. She had assumed that he was simply being protective.

'He wouldn't let us look in the basement,' said Gustav.

'I saw a big keyring in his hallway,' said Jensen. 'If only we could get it, we could have a look for ourselves. See if he's hiding something.'

'Not while the police are still there,' said Gustav. 'Although ...' He pointed at her with an onion bhaji, dipped in bright-green coriander yogurt.

'What?'

'The basement is under the red building where Palle's flat is. If we enter through Wesselsgade, then the police won't even know we're there. We'll go in the early hours, just to be on the safe side.'

'And the keys?'

'Leave that to me.'

'You're a devious little bugger,' said Jensen. 'Did anyone ever tell you that?'

Gustav smiled broadly, onion and coriander stuck in his teeth.

They didn't hear the whirring of the lift on its ancient cables; they didn't even hear the footsteps approaching down the hall.

The first they knew of Google Me was when he pushed open the door, a terrifying, snarling vision in black, backlit by the light from the corridor. His hair and coat were glistening with rain. 'Well, isn't this cosy?' he said.

'It's not what it looks like,' said Jensen.

'Aw, the two old partners back together,' said Google Me. He turned to Gustav. 'I take it your auntie knows you're here?'

'It's Saturday night. He's not doing anything he's not supposed to. Chill out,' said Jensen.

'Oh, I don't know about that,' said Google Me, looking at Gustav, who had put down his food and was busy staring out of the window.

'Gustav?' said Jensen.

'Ah,' said Google Me. 'The boy is shy. Understandable under the circumstances. Anyway, I can't stay. I'm working on my next top story.'

'More child drug addicts?' said Jensen.

'Wouldn't you like to know,' he said, smiling and waving. 'You two have a lovely evening.'

'Now, are you going to tell me what this is all about?' said Jensen when Google Me had left. 'What's he got on you?'

'I said it before, it's nothing. He's just being all macho,' said Gustav. He began to clear up the half-empty food containers, with no sign of his usual voracious appetite. 'Let's get out of this dump,' he said. 'If we're going to be up in the early hours, we should get some kip.'

48

Henrik felt fury surge like a fire through his body as he looked at Rasmus Nordby.

Seated on the black chair against the wall in the interview room, the man was breaking down once again, wailing in a high-pitched tone as tears and snot ran down his face.

In the past hour, he had asked for tissues, water, the bathroom, a vaping break and painkillers, all of which had been granted.

Now, Henrik's patience was running out. It had already been sapped by his futile conversation with Wiese.

Not that Wiese's refusal to listen was going to stop him from asking Nordby about the picture of Lea again.

Not in a million years.

The only problem was Nordby's lawyer, a woman who looked far too young for her greyish-white hair. She had already asked once how the picture of Lea was related to the charges against her client. 'It's a category C asset,' the lawyer had pointed out, referring to the least offensive rung on the child sexual-abuse material ladder. 'Is my client under suspicion for a different charge in relation to Lea Høgh?'

Henrik had to admit that this wasn't the case.

The picture of Lea was tame in comparison to some on Nordby's hard drive.

'Remember that you don't have to answer any of this,' said the lawyer to Nordby.

Regardless, Henrik posed the same question for the fourth time, tapping his index finger on the picture of Lea. 'Look at it,' he said, pushing the picture onto Nordby's half of the table. 'Where did you get it from?'

'I told you, I don't remember,' Nordby wailed.

'I don't believe you,' Henrik said. 'I think you remember very well.'

'I can't take any more of this,' Nordby cried.

'I'll let you go as soon as I have an answer to my question.'

'I don't understand what any of this has to do with Matilde. I know I shouldn't have downloaded all that stuff. It was wrong, I'm sick in the head, I admit it.'

'We're aware that you knew it was wrong, because you deleted the photographs,' said Henrik. 'But we found them anyway, didn't we, and in amongst all of the sick photos and videos that you hadn't quite managed to get rid of, there was this one. And you recall why we're so interested?'

'I've said over and over again that I don't know anything about Lea Høgh. Why won't you believe me?' Nordby dropped his head on his forearms and sobbed.

'Was it a Danish site? Or an international one?'

'I don't know who runs them. They're just there.'

'Give me some names of sites you visited. Chatrooms, forums, live stuff.'

'I don't remember any,' said Nordby. 'You still haven't told me what this has to do with Matilde. If I knew, then maybe ...' He had recovered his composure somewhat, sniffling and wiping his puffy eyes and swollen, pink face.

His tone became firmer. 'I want an explanation. My daughter is missing and you're spending your time on some photo from six years ago?'

Wiese had made much the same point earlier. Henrik didn't have an answer for it. Just something deep inside his being telling him that they were onto something.

'Tell me,' he said. 'While you were accessing the forums or chatrooms, did you ever have the feeling that you were being watched?'

'They're hard to get into,' said Nordby. 'You have to prove yourself over and over.'

'I don't mean online.'

Nordby glanced up at him. It only lasted a second, but Henrik could tell that his words had hit home.

'What are you getting at?' said the lawyer. 'I repeat, if my client is under suspicion for something specific, I'd like you to do us the courtesy of saying so. I think we can all appreciate that Rasmus is very tired, and also anxious about his daughter. Now isn't the time for fishing expeditions.'

Henrik kept his gaze on Nordby. 'Did you ever feel like someone online knew stuff about you in real life? That perhaps they knew that you have a daughter, where she goes to school, and where she lives?'

That frightened look in Nordby's eyes again.

'Could it be that some of your online connections had threatened you in some way to reveal stuff about Matilde, or maybe to take photos of her?'

The lawyer folded her arms across her chest and sighed deeply.

But Nordby clearly wasn't taking any notice. He was holding his ears now, rocking back and forth on his chair.

'It could be important,' Henrik said, sensing that he was

finally getting somewhere. 'Someone that you know may be holding Matilde. You want her back, don't you?'

'STOP!' Nordby screamed, his voice breaking and dissolving into sobs. 'I thought she would be safer with Stine. God knows, I would never touch my own daughter. Never. That's why I gave her up,' he cried.

'Because someone was after her?' said Henrik.

'It was just a feeling. I can't explain it. They made some comments. It was like they knew where I live.'

'They who?' said Henrik. 'When did it start? What forum was it? The more you can tell us, the greater the chance that you will see your daughter again.'

Nordby mumbled something.

'Speak up,' said Henrik. 'I can't hear you.'

'Playland,' he said. 'There's an admin who calls themselves the Ugly Duckling.'

Bingo.

Henrik could scarcely believe it. Nordby was looking terrified. 'You can't tell anyone. If they have Matilde, they might hurt her if they find out.'

'Is the Ugly Duckling Danish?' said Henrik.

'I don't know,' said Nordby. 'Everything is in English. But it's just . . . the name, the Ugly Duckling . . . and sometimes how they put the words together. I think they could be Danish.'

'Why didn't you tell us sooner?'

'I didn't know for sure that it was them.'

'Or you were scared that we'd find out about you. And now all this time has been wasted,' Henrik said, exasperated.

The Playland admin had never gone away. He had just got smarter.

Wiese wouldn't be able to stop Henrik joining up the two cases now.

The admin had singled out Nordby, followed him and Matilde, and continued to follow her when he had sent her back to her mother.

And now they had taken Matilde.

Like they had taken Lea.

What had happened to the two girls?

Day Seven

49

Jensen shook her head at Gustav as he tiptoed down the stairs from Palle's flat, brandishing the promised keyring.

'How did you get it?' she whispered.

'Ignorance is bliss,' said Gustav.

At the basement door, he fumbled with the key, dropping it on the floor with a loud noise.

They froze, making scared faces at each other while they waited for the reaction. An open door above them, Palle's angry voice, police sirens.

Nothing.

Gustav finally managed to unlock the door. 'Let's get this over with,' he said.

It was three in the morning.

They had travelled from Margrethe's flat through the quiet city, Gustav on his e-scooter and Jensen following on her bicycle, their breath steaming behind them.

The basement smelled of dust, damp and decay. Once, people had washed their clothes down there, hanging them up outside in the courtyard when the weather was dry.

It was too risky to switch on the lights. Instead, Jensen

and Gustav shone their mobile torches into the darkness. The basement ran the length of the building, with storage lockups at one end and a laundry and drying room at the other. The ceiling was low and criss-crossed with ancient-looking pipes.

Running along the top of the wall facing the courtyard were high-set dirty windows protected with rusty bars. Jensen hoped no one was awake to see the pale, flickering light from their torches.

They looked through Palle's lockup first, finding an old suitcase, a bicycle, an empty mahogany chest and a heavy cardboard box.

'What are we looking for?' Gustav whispered as they opened the cardboard box.

'Anything weird,' she said.

The box was full of old Donald Duck comics, some of them more than forty years old.

'Like this, you mean?' said Gustav.

'They're collector's items now. He probably intends to sell them one day and make a mint.'

'Like I said, weird.'

'Let's look in his workshop,' Jensen said.

The door whined on its hinges as Gustav slowly pushed it open.

They tiptoed in, shining their torches into the space. There was a smell of paint and oil. Gustav cursed as he tripped over a pipe sawn in half.

Jensen let her torch glide over the workbench. The place was as neat and tidy as Palle's flat. Shelves with paints in different colours, pipes arranged into lengths, bottles of white spirit, an assortment of wood offcuts, a bag full of rags.

'You look through all this stuff, and I'll search the other end,' she said to Gustav.

She pointed her torch at a shallow cupboard. It opened out into a triptych of tools. Palle had drawn an outline around each of them in bold black pen: saws, hammers, Allen keys, screwdrivers, spanners, all arranged according to size.

Wait a minute.

The largest spanner was missing.

Palle might be using it somewhere, or he had forgotten to put it back.

This seemed unlikely for a man as organised as Palle. She took a picture.

A shout came from Gustav at the other end of the room. 'Jensen, I've got something.'

'Be quiet,' she whispered. 'Do you actually want us to be found out?'

'Look at these,' he whispered.

Jensen pointed her torch. Books. Leather-bound with gilt-edged pages. Jensen recognised some of the names of the authors.

'Bodil's priceless first editions,' she said.

'What?'

'Deep Throat mentioned these. Bodil might not even have known they were missing.'

So that was what Palle had been so worried about.

Gustav was rattling the paint tins and bottles of turps.

'Shush,' she said.

'There's something here ... I can't ...'

Whatever it was came loose and he almost fell on his backside.

Jensen caught the object in his hand with her torch.

It was a green glove.

A child's glove.

50

'Goldschmidt,' said Henrik. 'Thank God I caught you.'

'You're lucky,' said the pathologist, his voice rising above the cry of a restless toddler. 'I was up with Max. He's teething – you know what it's like.'

Actually I don't, thought Henrik guiltily. His children's teething, like their feeding and nappy changes, was something his wife had always dealt with. He wondered now where he had been during all those early mornings and late nights. It seemed the baby stage had happened while he had been elsewhere; though he tried, he couldn't recall it now.

'I'm sorry it's so early,' he said. 'But I need to know something urgently.'

'Shoot.'

'The head wound sustained by Bodil La Cour. Could it have been made by a forty-millimetre spanner?'

'Easily,' said Goldschmidt. 'Why?'

'I think we have our murder weapon, or at least we now know what we're looking for. It's most likely in the lake, near to where the body was found.'

'Good luck,' said Goldschmidt, as his son's crying reached a deafening climax. 'When you find it, bring it to me.' He hung up.

The divers had just wrapped up in the lake in Ørstedsparken ahead of the park reopening later today. Now they could start again in Saint Jørgen's Lake.

Had Palle Dybdal lured Bodil over there, with some excuse, only to hit her on the head and cause her to fall in and drown?

Why had it been necessary to kill her? What role had she played in the abduction of Matilde, and, if the little girl was still alive, where was she now?

They would need to take Palle in for questioning, but first Henrik had to deal with a more immediate issue: Jensen and Gustav.

Jensen had texted him photos of the leather-bound books they had found in the basement, along with Matilde's glove and the empty space on the tool board in Dybdal's workshop.

He already knew about Dybdal's interest in Bodil from the interview his team had conducted with his downstairs neighbours, Katja and Thomas. The couple had been most helpful with their enquiries.

Apparently, when Dybdal had told Katja and Thomas that Bodil had reported an assault, he had discredited her statement to such a degree that they hadn't believed the incident had happened.

In hindsight, Dybdal's eagerness to describe Bodil as unreliable and suffering from dementia had seemed suspicious to them.

The man was odd, they said. He hadn't been formally appointed caretaker but had bestowed the role on himself and proceeded to lord it about the place as if he owned it.

'Luckily, Thomas is good with his hands, so we don't need any help with our flat,' Katja had said.

She had told them that she had caught Palle looking strangely at her daughter once or twice and wouldn't be surprised if he had paedophile tendencies.

Henrik had told Jensen and Gustav to put down the glove immediately and stay where they were. A squad car had arrived shortly afterwards, sealing off the basement and securing the evidence.

Now, Jensen and Gustav were waiting in one of the interview rooms down the corridor, sipping tea.

The situation was uncomfortable to say the least.

Good job it was a Sunday and quiet in the office. Even better that Wiese wasn't around.

'Well, did you arrest him?' said Jensen, jumping out of her chair as soon as he opened the door to the room.

'Sit down,' he said.

Jensen opened her mouth to speak. But he cut her off with a raised hand. 'I want to know,' he said. 'Exactly how did you gain access to the basement?'

Gustav mumbled something.

'Speak up, lad.'

'I picked the lock to Palle's flat. Very poor security if you ask me,' he said. 'And keeping his keys right next to his front door is just plain silly.'

'Where did you learn to pick the lock?'

'Saw it on YouTube.'

'You sure that's all? Because, if I find out later that you've been using your new skill to break into places where you have no business, then—'

'Then what?' said Jensen. 'You should be grateful for what we did. You wouldn't have had a clue if we hadn't shared those photos with you.'

'I would have got there, sooner or later,' Henrik said. 'Dybdal's downstairs neighbours were very helpful. They don't think much of him.'

'We know,' said Jensen. 'We spoke to them too. Well, are you going to arrest him?'

He ignored her. 'How did you get the idea to search his workshop?'

'Because Palle is weird,' said Gustav.

'He was cagey about showing it to us,' said Jensen.

'Right.'

'And now we know why.'

'Thank you, Miss Marple.'

'By the way, you said Bodil was right about what she saw that night. Does that mean you have CCTV?'

Henrik sighed. 'Yes, but it's inconclusive. As in, we know it happened, but still not exactly how, or who the couple were.'

'Can we see it?' said Gustav.

'No,' said Henrik. 'In fact, if you could leave the investigations to us from now on, we'd all be a lot better off.'

'After the massive favour we've just done you?' said Jensen.

'What you found in Palle's workshop is compromised by the means of access. You broke in. That might make things tricky in court.'

'Why?'

'He could argue that you took the spanner and placed the books and the glove there.'

'But that's ridiculous,' said Gustav.

And that wasn't all of it, Henrik thought. There was something highly peculiar in Palle's actions that didn't sit right with him.

If the evidence were to be believed, he had both

271

defrauded Bodil and abducted a nine-year-old girl, fooling the police into the bargain.

Could that really be the same man who had left such obvious clues in his own workshop?

They would have to go through his background with a fine-tooth comb, request access to his bank accounts, search his laptop and phone records.

His mobile lit up with a text message from Mark.

They've got Palle Dybdal. On his way in.

He would have to wait to interview him when a defence lawyer could be found.

Enough time for him to catch an hour's sleep on the couch in his office, read through his emails and prepare for the reconstruction in Ørstedsparken that afternoon.

He looked at Jensen and Gustav and sighed.

What was he going to do with them?

He would have to think about it later when his brain was functioning again.

'I want you to go home now and stop meddling,' he said. 'If I catch you doing anything like this again, you'll be in extremely serious trouble. You've been warned. Now go, before I change my mind.'

51

'I'm asking you again. What was the nature of your relationship with Bodil La Cour?' said Henrik, leaning back in his seat and folding his arms across his chest.

To say that the interview with Palle Dybdal was going badly would be an understatement.

The man was putting up a fight.

Henrik's mood was volatile. He hadn't managed to get more than about twenty minutes' sleep before Mark had knocked on his door. Getting up had felt like pulling himself out of the grave.

Before collapsing onto his couch, he had received two interesting pieces of information:

Matilde's DNA matched that found in the red shopping trolley. Palle's prints were on it, as well as Bodil's. And her solicitor was none other than Ernst Brøgger, one of Denmark's most elusive personalities, friend to the rich and powerful, and occasional supplier of stories to Jensen.

Brøgger was also the brother of the career criminal Leif Kofoed, an evil specimen who had left chaos and destruction in his wake for decades.

Henrik had sworn to himself that if he ever got the opportunity, he would hunt Kofoed down and throttle him with his bare hands.

Kofoed was the only man he knew whose murder would be worth going to prison for.

According to Brøgger himself, he was as straight as his brother was crooked and hadn't seen his sibling in years. Henrik had always wondered if that were true.

Had he not been so exhausted, with a murder and child abduction on his hands, he would have forced Brøgger to explain himself face to face.

The man's email had been succinct, explaining why Bodil had met with him just a few hours before someone had killed her. The purpose of the visit had made Henrik raise his eyebrows in surprise, though he had dismissed it quickly as irrelevant to the case.

Brøgger said his driver was available for an interview immediately, should they wish to speak to him about anything he had noticed while driving Bodil to and from their meeting.

Henrik would have to wait longer for Dybdal's phone records and bank statements. They had confiscated his laptop, and Bagger's team were going through it, but nothing had turned up yet.

'I told you already. I helped Bodil around the house, went shopping for her, fixed things. She was elderly and alone, and I was glad to do it.'

'You helped her with her laptop and mobile phone, is that right?'

'Who told you that?'

'Just answer the question,' said Henrik. 'Is it true?'

'She asked for help. She found it hard. It's virtually impossible to live in Denmark these days if you're not digitally able.'

Henrik nodded. He often had to help his own father access the internet, losing his patience repeatedly in the process. 'That's very neighbourly of you,' he said, smiling. 'Does that mean you know Bodil's passwords?'

'Are you accusing my client of something?' said the solicitor.

'Just asking questions,' said Henrik.

'She asked me to pick the passwords for her. Said she hadn't the imagination for it, and couldn't remember them anyway, so I did it. I also wrote them down for her. I know that I shouldn't have done that, but I was trying to help.'

'Admirable,' said Henrik.

'I don't like your tone,' Dybdal said.

'I'm just thinking that it's not often you see someone so selfless nowadays. Putting in the hours without receiving any kind of compensation. It's really ... quite something.'

Dybdal scowled at him.

'Let's talk about the report Bodil made a little over a week ago,' Henrik said.

Dybdal was instantly suspicious. 'What about it?'

'You didn't believe her, did you?'

'I helped the police officers search the property.'

'From what I understand from my friends in uniform, the search didn't go on for very long.'

'Long enough,' said Dybdal. 'There was nothing there.'

'Or maybe you weren't keen on them looking too hard?'

Another scowl.

'You told my colleagues that Bodil had previously reported burglaries that didn't happen.'

'It's the truth,' said Dybdal.

'How do you know that?' Henrik pretended to consult his notes. 'She reported two break-ins, one as late as a month ago.'

'It was the same story as the report she made last week. When the police got there, there was nothing to show for it.'

'Yet, Bodil was under the clear impression that someone had been in her flat,' said Henrik.

'She was elderly and anxious with plenty of time to worry about things like that.'

Henrik smiled. 'You have a key, don't you?'

'She gave it to me herself,' said Palle, blushing. 'In case something happened.'

'Must have been quite the temptation. Have a good nosey around, whenever an opportunity presented itself?'

'It's for emergencies. I'd never just let myself in.'

'You sure about that?'

The lawyer flashed Henrik an angry look, and he held up his hands in surrender. 'The thing is, Bodil wasn't mistaken about what happened last week,' he said.

Dybdal's eyes widened. 'She wasn't?'

Henrik shook his head. 'We found some CCTV, and a woman is clearly seen running out of your building into Wesselsgade on the Saturday morning in question, exactly at the time Bodil claimed. She's then stopped and pulled back by a man.'

Dybdal glanced at his lawyer.

'Were you that man?' Henrik said.

'No,' Dybdal shouted.

'Because I find it curious that you were up and about when the police got there in response to Bodil's report. No one else was.'

'I heard the commotion, so I came out to see what it was all about.'

'But you didn't hear the assault itself.'

'No, I told you that. What is this?'

'Where were you last Sunday afternoon?'

'At home.'

'Can anyone verify that?'

'I live alone, so no.'

'Did you dress up as Bodil and take her red shopping trolley to Ørstedsparken last Sunday, and the Sundays before that?'

'No.'

'Then how do you explain that your prints were found on the trolley?'

'Easily. I often helped her into the lift when she came back with her shopping and happened to see her.'

'I think that's enough for now,' said the lawyer. 'First you insinuate that my client abused Bodil's trust in him. Next, it's an assault on Friday night, and now you want to know if he's got an alibi for last Sunday? What exactly are you accusing him of?'

'Do you like little girls, Palle?' said Henrik. 'What will we find on your computer?'

'That's it,' said the lawyer, standing up.

'Wait a minute,' said Henrik. 'I do have something. I'm not sure if your client has been entirely honest with you.'

The lawyer glanced at Dybdal, who shrugged at him.

Henrik chose his words carefully. 'A child's glove was found in your workshop. We've conducted some tests, and it belongs to Matilde Clausen. What do you say to that?'

'What?' said Dybdal. 'I don't even know her. Someone must have put it there. I couldn't find my keys this morning.'

'Who would have put the glove there?'

'No idea, isn't that your job?' Dybdal tore at his wild grey hair. 'This is a nightmare.'

'Any idea where your forty-millimetre spanner is?'

'My spanner?' said Dybdal, laughing in disbelief.

Henrik looked at him deadpan. 'I have divers out search-ing Saint Jørgen's Lake as we speak,' he said. 'Will they find your spanner at the bottom, Palle? Did you throw it in the lake after you hit Bodil over the head with it, so she fell in the water and drowned?'

'No, I never—'

'We know that you stole from her. First editions make a change from peddling Donald Duck comics, don't they?'

Finally, the man was quiet.

'Nice old lady, not all there, probably doesn't know the value of those dusty old books. Besides, she's got so many. Probably won't even know they're gone.'

Stunned silence. 'You lied to us, and you lied to Bodil,' said Henrik. 'Why should I believe a word you say about her murder? About Matilde's abduction? Where is Matilde, Palle? What have you done with her? We found her DNA in the shopping trolley, along with your prints. Did you enter her flat and help yourself to Bodil's things whenever you wanted, disguising yourself as her to satisfy your sick cravings for small children?'

The lawyer frowned at Dybdal, who looked out of the window.

Not so cocky now, are you? thought Henrik.

'I'd like a word with my client,' said the lawyer.

Henrik was glad of it.

They would keep Dybdal in overnight and hopefully the custody hearing in the morning would go their way.

He needed more time to think.

And Bagger needed more time to dig into Dybdal's online history.

Time they didn't have.

52

'Where have you been?' Margrethe's voice was quieter than usual.

Worryingly quiet.

Cold, almost.

Jensen and Gustav had chatted excitedly all the way home from Teglholmen, discussing possible explanations for what they had found in Palle's workshop.

They had stopped at a bakery to pick up breakfast; the bag with the poppyseed rolls was still warm in Jensen's hands. She had been looking forward to wolfing them down with butter and cheese and a pot of tea, then crawling back into bed for a few more hours' sleep.

Margrethe was sitting in the kitchen with the Sunday papers spread out in front of her. The golden light from the Poul Henningsen lamp above the table lit up only the bottom half of her face, leaving the rest in obscurity.

Jensen sensed her glaring at them. 'Is something wrong?' she said. 'We were just ... you must have seen there's been a murder. It's that woman I interviewed over by the Lakes who had witnessed an assault. I thought, seeing as it's the weekend, you wouldn't mind Gustav tagging along.' She glared at him, imploring him to join in his own defence.

He was studying his big toe; it was poking through a hole in his sock.

Margrethe sent him a hard stare. 'Jensen wants to know what's wrong. Why don't you explain?' she said.

'What's going on, Gustav?' said Jensen. 'Say something.' She nudged him with her elbow, but he turned away from her.

'Jannik told me everything,' Margrethe said.

I might have known, Jensen thought.

Google Me had been quiet since he burst in on her and Gustav having the Indian takeaway in her office.

Naively, she had thought that he wouldn't really go ahead and grass them up. It was an infantile move, playground stuff.

'He's lying,' she said. 'He's angry because I didn't ask him to come along to the interview with Bodil, but I honestly wasn't planning to film her. It just happened. And of course, now that she's been murdered, he's interested all of a sudden.'

Margrethe turned to her. 'You think this is about Gustav shooting a video and you pretending it was yours?'

'Isn't it?' said Jensen.

'Jannik told me that Gustav has been skiving off school. I didn't believe him, so I phoned the head teacher this morning. She's a friend of a friend. And guess what?'

Jensen looked at her blankly, thinking, *What have you done now, Gustav?*

'He never even bothered turning up at the start of term,' said Margrethe.

'Is this true?' said Jensen, looking at him as he studied the ceiling with intense interest.

'It gets worse,' said Margrethe. 'You know how hopeless I am with anything technical, and how Gustav always sorts it out for me?'

Jensen nodded miserably, afraid of what was coming.

'I assumed that my nephew – a boy I have done so much for – was merely being helpful,' said Margrethe. 'Goes to show how gullible I am. The school emailed me on numerous occasions, but each time Gustav intervened, then deleted his tracks.'

Jensen's mouth fell open. She had known something was up, but this was extreme, even for Gustav.

'Yes, it's as bad as it sounds,' said Margrethe. 'The head teacher was surprised to hear from me, as, apparently, back in August I confirmed by email that he'd changed his mind and wouldn't be going to high school after all.' She sighed deeply, her shoulders sinking lower. 'So, here's the deal, Gustav. I'm taking the train to Malmö later today for meetings with the Swedes. I'll pop back for Henning's funeral on Wednesday, but I won't be back here till after work on Thursday. I expect you to be gone by then.'

'Where?' said Gustav.

'Not my problem,' said Margrethe. 'Back to your father I suppose, or maybe one of your nice new drug-addict friends has a sofa you can stay on.'

'Drug addict?' said Jensen.

'Yes, Jannik has been most enlightening on all accounts,' said Margrethe.

'It was just a bit of weed,' Gustav mumbled.

Margrethe turned to him with a devastating look of disappointment. 'You betrayed my trust. I thought you had promise, that you'd make a good journalist. You certainly seemed to have all the right instincts. Instead, you chose to deceive me. No integrity. It's a mystery how you and I are related. Now get out of my sight.'

Gustav turned on his heel and stormed off. They heard the door to his bedroom slam so hard that the fine crystal glasses that had once belonged to his grandmother clinked in the kitchen cupboards.

It felt like an earthquake in more ways than one. Margrethe's ability to detect bullshit was legendary, but when it came to her teenage nephew, she had always been curiously soft. Jensen suspected she had secretly considered him her son and heir.

Now, he was cast out of her circle.

Jensen felt like running after him, but Margrethe was looking at her strangely, as though the whole thing was her fault. 'I swear, I didn't know,' she said. 'I suspected something was up, I tried to tell you, but I could never have imagined this.'

'Oh, I don't know,' said Margrethe, beginning to gather up her newspapers and stacking them in a pile. 'From where I'm standing, you didn't try that hard.'

'I didn't want to be a snitch.'

Margrethe looked at her with the same diamond stare that she had directed at Gustav at minute ago. 'Don't insult my intelligence, Jensen.'

'I beg your pardon?'

'You encouraged him.'

'I did not.'

'I told you to leave Gustav to his studies, to not indulge his fantasies about following in your footsteps by dropping out of school and becoming a reporter.' She rose to her feet. 'Yet, here the two of you are, working together again.'

'We're not, I swear, it was just this one story. Gustav insisted. He—'

'Do you know what I've come to think?' said Margrethe, interrupting her. 'I think you've actually been a bad influence on my nephew. And after everything I've done for you, giving you a job, a roof over your head, defending you to all and sundry. You have a couple of days to sort yourself out, collect your stuff from the office. You can post your keys through my letterbox. I hear your mum's got a nice cottage on the west coast.'

'You're firing me?'

Margrethe shook her head. 'I'm sending you on early maternity leave, on full pay. Others would be delighted in your place.' She headed for the door. 'I've said what I needed to say. Goodbye Jensen, and good luck.'

53

The police tape and barriers had been removed and Ørstedsparken reopened, but the visitors were still thin on the ground.

Henrik wasn't surprised. No one would be rushing back, knowing what had happened here. The weather didn't help. The air was wet, leaving a thin film of moisture on his aching scalp as he entered the playground where the reconstruction was about to take place.

Whenever he thought about his headache, anxiety took hold of him. He hated going to the doctor, and what if this was something really serious?

He forced himself to think of the job at hand. Known facts only. Those were the rules of police reconstructions. Which gave them precious little to go on.

Until he could make Dybdal confess, or Bagger found more evidence, there was still so much they didn't know.

Was Dybdal the Ugly Duckling? If he was, how had he managed to evade detection for so long, only to make a schoolboy error and leave evidence in his workshop? Where was Matilde, and did Dybdal have accomplices?

The media had played ball so far, promoting the reconstruction along with the invitation to those who had been in the park last Sunday afternoon between 3 and 4.30 p.m.

Henrik noticed *Dagbladet*'s unsavoury cameraman among the reporters who had turned up and were being corralled by uniformed officers.

Jensen was nowhere to be seen.

Did this mean she had finally heeded his advice and stopped sticking her nose in where it wasn't wanted?

Oh sure, Jungersen.

The reconstruction was set to begin at the opposite end of the park from the playground.

A friend of Stine Clausen, and her nine-year-old daughter who was at school with Matilde, had volunteered to play the main parts, dressed in replicas of the clothes that Stine and Matilde had been wearing exactly one week ago.

At five minutes past three, the two of them entered the park at the corner of Nørre Farimagsgade and Gyldenløvesgade. The mother was pushing the pram and the little girl's eyes were flickering left and right as she held her mother's hand. Her red coat stood out like a beacon against the decaying vegetation.

Little Red Riding Hood.

A shiver ran through Henrik. It was as though the entire city was holding its breath.

The reporters had been warned that they would be asked to leave, and the reconstruction halted, if they attempted to interfere in any way. They moved silently with their cameras alongside the mother and daughter, on the path, over the grass and around the trees.

The woman pretending to be Stine parked the pram by the picnic table with the graffiti and sat down, getting out her phone.

A small gaggle of parents had turned up, no kids. They stood around the climbing frame and behind the swings, looking terrified, as though they were about to witness a real-life child abduction.

The little girl made her way into the bushes, almost but not quite disappearing behind the evergreen branches.

Wiese had argued that the woman in the blue coat with the brown hat, sunglasses and red shopping trolley should not be included in the reconstruction. 'She's not a known fact,' he had said.

'Independent of one another, three witnesses said they saw the woman sitting on one of the benches that back onto the shrubbery between the playground and the lake-side path. Matilde's DNA was in the shopping trolley. That makes it a known fact,' Henrik had said.

Wiese had caved in the end.

A female police officer had agreed to play the part of the old woman and was seated on the bench. Henrik couldn't see her from the playground. That was an interesting fact. She might have been talking to Matilde, without Stine being aware that she was even there.

The reconstruction ended at five minutes to four, the time Stine reckoned she had looked up to find Matilde gone and the search for her had begun. By now, it was almost dark and hard to see.

'What happens now?' shouted one of the reporters in the general atmosphere of anti-climax that followed.

'Now we wait,' said Henrik.

He had told his team to take the rest of the day off, go home, eat something and spend time with their families. His own had barely seen him for the past week.

He was leaving the park, with Mark in hot pursuit, when a man came up to him, dressed in chef's trousers and a black puffer jacket. Henrik had noticed him earlier, smoking by a tree in front of the café next to the playground.

He spoke Danish with an Eastern European accent. 'Are you in charge of the investigation?' he said.

Nominally, Henrik thought. 'Do you have information?' he asked.

'Maybe,' said the man.

'Did you see Matilde last Sunday?'

'No,' said the man. 'Not the girl, the old woman. I was outside smoking. She was pulling the red trolley up the hill. It looked heavy, so I offered to help her, but she sort of waved me off before I could get anywhere near her. She seemed to be in a hurry.'

Did she now? Henrik thought.

'Do you recall if she was carrying a walking stick?'

'She definitely wasn't, and from the way she moved, she didn't look like she needed one.'

Henrik smiled at the man. 'What's your name?'

'Bartek.'

'Listen, Bartek. Mark here will take down your details. We'll need you to make a statement, but before you do, tell me exactly what the woman looked like. Perhaps she wasn't even a woman?'

He was distracted by something in his peripheral vision, a slim figure in black, moving towards him at pace.

Wiese.

Looking unhappy.

'Come with me, now,' said Wiese when he'd caught up.

They went behind a tree. 'What is it?' Henrik said. 'I'm a little busy.'

'Not anymore.'

'Excuse me?'

'I received an interesting phone call from Rasmus

287

Nordby's lawyer. Said you questioned him yesterday, about the photo of Lea Høgh. Which means that you deliberately ignored an official order. I'll be reporting you for a disciplinary.'

Henrik tried to remonstrate, to explain.

He hadn't slept in a week.

Hardly eaten.

The pressure was getting to him.

His head hurt.

But Wiese didn't care. 'I'm sending you home with immediate effect.'

Day Eight

54

'What did you imagine was going to happen?' said Jensen. 'Your aunt is one of the sharpest journalists in the country and you thought you'd run rings around her?'

Gustav looked down into his orange juice, face resting in his hands. 'I tried to tell her, but she wouldn't listen. You know what she's like, so determined . . . so stubborn.'

'Clearly runs in your family,' said Jensen.

Margrethe had been true to her word, refusing to speak to either of them about what had happened. She had left in a taxi without saying goodbye.

'So you just decided not to turn up?' said Jensen.

'It wasn't like that.'

'Then what was it like?'

'I got almost as far as the school gates, but when I saw the other kids, I just panicked and ran the other way. There were too many of them, all smiling and happy,' he said. 'I thought I'd go back the next day, make up some excuse for what had happened, but I was embarrassed. The longer I delayed going there, the more impossible it became. Then, at the end of the first week, the school wrote to Margrethe. I know her password, so I caught the email and wrote back.'

The waiter arrived with their breakfasts. Toasted rye bread with soft-boiled eggs, sliced avocado and a ramekin of yogurt topped with raspberries and toasted seeds and nuts.

Gustav pushed his plate to one side. Unlike him. 'That bastard Google Me,' he said.

'How did he find out about you?'

'I guess he must have followed me,' Gustav said. 'Proper creepy.'

'We should probably take it as a compliment,' said Jensen, cracking the shell on her egg with a teaspoon.

'How do you make that out?' said Gustav, picking the seeds off his yogurt.

'He really must have seen us as a serious threat to go through all that trouble just to prove a point.'

Gustav picked up a fork and spiked a piece of avocado. Then he grabbed a slice of rye bread and buttered it thickly. 'I'll get my own back,' he said with his mouth full.

'Don't do anything stupid,' said Jensen.

Gustav had a temper. Last year, he had been expelled by his school in Aalborg after he had exacted revenge on his bullies. They were never going to forget it.

'Wait,' she said, dipping rye bread into her egg and watching the micro volcano of yolk spilling over the side. 'I've seen you a few times in the morning, getting up and leaving for school. What did you do with yourself all day?'

'Sometimes I went back home to bed when I was certain that you and Margrethe had left. Or I just stayed out all day, hung around.'

'And the drugs?'

'I'm not really into them. People offered me some. It

would have been rude not to.' Gustav looked at her. 'I want to work with you again,' he said.

'At *Dagbladet*?'

'Yes,' he said.

'That won't be happening. Margrethe sent me on maternity leave two months early. She said I led you astray.'

'But that's not fair.'

'It's my own fault,' said Jensen, mouth full of rye bread.

'We could set up on our own. It would be fun.'

'Look at me, Gustav. I'm seven months pregnant and don't even have a place to live, let alone the money to set up my own business.'

He bent over on the table and rested his head on his forearms.

'So,' she said. 'Will you be going back to your dad's in Aalborg?'

'I'd rather stick pins in my eyes,' he said, his voice muffled.

'Then what are you going to do?'

'I'll ask Fie. She has a spare bedroom at her new place. I can stay there for a while.' He sat up abruptly. 'We could go and see her now, ask her to help us find Playland?'

Jensen thought about it as she sipped from her orange juice. Gustav's suggestion was as good as any.

She wasn't ready to go on maternity leave.

Henrik wasn't responding to her messages, and he had told them to stop meddling.

As if.

'All right,' she said. 'You're on.'

55

You've gone and done it now, Jungersen, thought Henrik, as he rolled over in his marital bed and stared at the bedroom ceiling.

'Are you ill?' his wife had said as she had woken up to find him still beside her.

He hadn't felt like telling her that he had been sent home, not yet. 'Just a late start,' he had said.

He had pretended to be asleep as he lay in bed and listened to the sounds of his household waking up and getting ready for the day. Packed lunches, lost socks, tangled hair. His wife ran the whole thing like a military drill.

Now the house was quiet.

Everyone in the street had left for work or school, carrying on with their lives, bar the odd pensioner walking their dog.

He had to hold a hand up in front of himself to make sure that he was really there and not dreaming the whole thing.

Wiese's behaviour had been odd. Did he really have a right to send him home? Wasn't it Henrik's job as investigator to uncover the truth, wherever it might be found, regardless of case boundaries?

He could challenge the decision. There was a good chance a grievance would fall out in his favour, but that would take weeks, and Matilde was still out there.

If she wasn't already dead.

It was hard not to let his thoughts go there after this long.

Monsen was in Rome. He wouldn't want to be disturbed, couldn't focus on the ins and outs of office politics while he was on holiday.

Or when he wasn't.

Office politics. Was that all this was?

Wiese's objection to merging the two investigations – claiming that this would create a distraction – seemed illogical when it was highly likely that Playland held the key to the whole mystery.

He sat up, planted his feet on the wooden floor. He couldn't just stay home and do nothing. What had been driving him to find Matilde, to determine once and for all what had happened to Lea, had nothing to do with office hours and salary.

Policing wasn't an occupation to him, it was a calling, always had been. The warrant card around his neck was merely a reminder that he was operating within certain rules and boundaries.

It was access and authority.

It was licence.

Without those things, he would have to be extremely careful. If Wiese found out that he was still at it, a disciplinary might not be the end of it. He could get thrown out of the force altogether.

Not something he wanted to contemplate.

Right now, to make any progress, he needed information. He got out his mobile, pressed Mark's number.

'Hello Jungersen,' Mark said cautiously. 'Are you OK?'

'Wiese sent me home.'

'I heard. Hold on.' When Mark spoke next, Henrik recognised the echo of the men's toilets at Teglholmen. 'I'm not supposed to be talking to you. Wiese called us all in. He's put Lotte in charge of the Matilde case.'

'What did he say?'

'That you needed some time out for personal reasons. He said you must have complete calm and that no one is to contact you.'

'That's rubbish, and you know it.'

Mark didn't say anything, clearly caught between wanting to be loyal and needing to keep his job.

This got Henrik's hackles up. Being sent home hardly warranted him being treated as a pariah. 'So, what's been happening?' he said, irritably. 'Any news?'

'Jungersen, you know I can't tell you that.'

'Right. So you agree with Wiese?'

'No, I . . . it just . . . you can't put pressure on me like this.'

'I'm still me, Mark. You trusted me five minutes ago. Why not now?'

The question went unanswered. Henrik knew he was being unfair, but he wished, and not for the first time, that Mark would show just a little more willingness to break the rules.

'There is *something* I can tell you,' said Mark, after a pause.

'Yes?'

'Do you remember Kim Jespersen? You asked me to find out where he moved to after leaving Dragør?'

Henrik's mood lifted.

If he could have a chat with Jespersen, he might be able to make some progress.

'Did you find him?'

'Yes. It's a really strange coincidence. I couldn't believe

it at first. I mean, of all the places ... but I doublechecked it, and there's no mistake.'

'Tell me.'

'He now lives by the Lakes.'

'He does?'

'Same block as our murder victim Bodil La Cour. You know that red building across her courtyard?'

My God, Henrik thought. Was this the link they had been looking for?

He remembered reading somewhere that Palle Dybdal, the caretaker, was a structural engineer, which meant he was in the building trade just like Loft had been. 'Is it Palle Dybdal? Did he change his name?'

'What?' said Mark. 'No. It's Thomas Jespersen. Lives with his wife Katja. Changed his first name from Kim to Thomas for some reason. Why did you want to know anyway?'

There was a noise in the background. Mark came back. 'I've got to go,' he whispered. 'Maybe, we can talk some more ... another time. I'm sorry.'

Henrik tossed the phone on the bed and rubbed his face in his hands.

Kim Jespersen living in Bodil's block, under a mile from where Matilde had been abducted, six years after Lea had disappeared?

He hadn't dealt with Jespersen himself during the Lea Høgh case. He had been brought in as a witness by the prosecution, and an extremely helpful one at that.

Henrik was a strong believer in coincidences. Just because something was unlikely, didn't mean it was impossible.

Nevertheless, he needed to speak to Jespersen, urgently.

But first he needed to know what was going on with the investigation. Someone had to be prepared to tell him.

He picked up the phone again and pressed Bagger's number.

'It's me,' he said.

'I thought you might be calling,' said Bagger.

'Are you too scared to talk to me too?' His voice came out more angrily than he had intended. 'Sorry,' he added quickly.

'It's all right, Jungersen. I did try to warn you, though.'

'I know.'

'For what it's worth,' Bagger said, 'I don't know what Wiese was thinking. And in the middle of a major investigation. It's madness.'

'Yeah, well,' Henrik said.

'In case you're wondering, there will be no let-up in our efforts to find out where that picture of Lea originated.'

'That's good,' Henrik said. 'But Bagger, please just tell me one thing. Was there anything of interest on Palle Dybdal's laptop?'

'He's been looking up the prices of rare books. Seems he was intending to make himself a nice little nest egg from that poor woman's library. Other than that, clean as a whistle.'

'Too clean? Didn't you once say that we all have some dirt lurking?'

'Yes.'

'So if there's nothing, isn't that suspicious in and of itself? Perhaps there's more to be found in his flat? Hard drives? USBs? Another laptop?'

'We took his place apart.'

'I don't understand,' Henrik said. 'What about Bodil La Cour? Could he have been doing stuff in her name?'

'They're still going through it all, but from what I gather, there's nothing.'

'Matilde's DNA was found in Bodil's shopping trolley.'

'Yes, and the soil from the wheels was definitely from Ørstedsparken. It's a complete mystery,' said Bagger. 'If we find anything, I'll let you know.'

'I appreciate that,' Henrik said.

'Look,' Bagger said. 'We're on it. Why don't you just take a rest. It'll all be over soon enough. Before you know it, you'll be back here moaning about working too hard.'

Henrik attempted a laugh. It came out sounding false. 'Yes,' he said. 'Maybe I'll do that. See you around, Bagger.'

No way will I take a rest, he thought, as he headed for the shower.

There were things he could do. Things no one else needed to know about.

56

'This place is awesome,' said Gustav, throwing open the doors to the balcony overlooking a small garden with a lawn bordered by young birch trees.

They were on the outskirts of Roskilde in a small community centred around a row of shops. The building was brand new; it looked like an architect's model.

'I like it,' said Fie, smiling.

'It's good to see you,' said Jensen. 'I should have come sooner.' She pointed to her bump. 'I suppose you heard about this?'

'Gustav told me.'

If possible, Fie was even bigger than when they had last met, her smiling eyes buried yet deeper into her face.

Her new home was like her room at Skovhøj, warm and full of things: cushions, stuffed toys, tiny plants, fairy lights and posters.

A gaming chair stood pointed at a flatscreen TV. On a desk were three large monitors and a huge laptop.

'So you finally got your own place,' Jensen said.

'Tobias helped me move in,' said Fie.

Jensen nodded. She remembered the youth home manager from Skovhøj. He had been protective of Fie, warning Jensen and Gustav several times not to take advantage of her. To treat her as a friend and not just as a source of information whenever they needed it.

Only Gustav had heeded that advice, thought Jensen guiltily.

There was extra security on the entrance to the small group of flats, notices in the hallway to keep the noise down, lists of numbers to call in an emergency.

Had Fie merely swapped one kind of self-imposed prison for another?

You could hardly blame her for seeking safety and comfort. She was all alone: her mother had died from a drug overdose, and she was out of touch with her brother, who had been sent to a different foster home when they were children.

'Fie got a job,' said Gustav, throwing himself into the gaming chair and picking up the controller.

'I work in the Co-op a couple of days a week now,' said Fie, smiling.

She could have been a highly paid coder, an ethical hacker of the kind that corporations would pay millions for, but Fie wasn't interested in any of that.

'It's five minutes down the road, just stacking some shelves in the morning. No biggie,' said Fie, her smile slowly fading.

'Oh, but it is,' said Jensen. 'Congratulations! That's great news.'

'Do you think so?' She was smiling again.

Jensen nodded. 'It's good that you're getting out more. Hopefully it's just the beginning,' she said.

She considered how best to broach the subject of

Playland. They hadn't told Fie yet, and she wondered now if it had been a mistake to come at all.

'We need your help,' said Gustav, abruptly ending her deliberations. 'Did you read about Matilde, the missing girl from Copenhagen?'

'Yes,' said Fie. 'It's on the news all the time. Horrible.'

News stories weren't helpful to Fie, thought Jensen; they merely confirmed her understanding of the world as a bad place, full of bad people.

'Want to help us find her?' said Gustav. He had his eyes on the screen, putting together his character for a shoot-out game.

Fie raised her eyebrows. 'You think I can? How?'

'It's complicated,' said Jensen. 'You need to promise that it stays between us. And if at any point you're not comfortable, you must say so.'

Fie sat in silence as Jensen told the whole story, about Matilde, Lea, Jan Loft and Palle. About Playland and the picture of Lea that the police had found on Matilde's father's laptop.

When she had finished, Fie sat curled up on the sofa, hugging a cushion.

'We need to find the Ugly Duckling, which means finding Playland, which means accessing the dark web. Do you know how to do that?' Gustav said.

Fie nodded, biting her lip as she glanced at the screens on her desk. 'I'm not supposed to do stuff like that anymore. I could get into trouble,' she said.

'But you know how to make yourself invisible online, don't you?' said Gustav. 'Delete your tracks, stay anonymous?'

'I suppose,' said Fie.

'So what do you reckon?'

'I can have a look around, see what I can find,' she said. 'There are sites tracking down people like that.'

'Paedos,' said Gustav.

'Yes,' said Fie. 'I mean there are people who hunt down paedophiles and try to expose them. I could try to look there first, but it's not going to be easy.'

'If anyone can do it, it's you,' said Gustav, turning up the charm.

On the face of it, he and Fie were an odd pair. Slightly older than him, she was timid, while he oozed self-assurance. But Jensen knew Gustav's confidence was an act. She had never seen him with a friend his own age. He had been in love with a girl when he lived in Aalborg, but that had all come to nothing thanks to the bullies who had made his life a misery.

Gustav's revenge had been sophisticated and brutal, but his heart was broken. In Fie, he had found a fellow loner.

'OK,' Fie said. 'Let me try.'

'Great,' said Jensen. 'Takeaway pizzas for lunch. On me.'

57

Please don't ask me any questions, thought Henrik as Thomas Jespersen opened the door to the flat, glaring at him from behind the security chain.

Wearing a baseball cap, he had entered the building through Wesselsgade, relieved to have found the entrance unlocked.

He smiled, flashing his warrant card. 'Detective Inspector Jungersen, Copenhagen Police. Can I come in and speak to you for a moment?'

He heard a woman's voice in the background. Thomas's wife, presumably. 'Who is it?' she said.

'It's the police again,' said Thomas into the flat. The security chain stayed put.

'Well, don't just stand there, let them in,' she shouted.

The chain was snapped off, the door opened wide by a heavily pregnant woman with short blonde hair. Immediately, Henrik knew it wasn't her who had been caught on the security camera in Wesselsgade, running from a man. She was too tall and powerfully built. 'I'm Katja,' she said. 'And this is Thomas. You must excuse him. It's just that we already spoke to you guys a few times. We're just devastated about Bodil. And to think that Palle is involved in it all.'

He smiled. 'This isn't about your neighbour's murder. Can I . . .?' He pointed to a chair.

'Of course.' Katja swept clothes, toys and a laptop off the sofa.

Only then did Henrik notice the little girl in the corner of the room. She was sitting at a small plastic desk. Drawing materials were laid on in front of her, but she didn't seem interested. She looked silently at Henrik.

'That's our daughter Emily. She's just woken from her nap. Always a bit quiet after sleeping.' She pushed her hands out. 'Can I offer you anything, Detective Inspector? Tea? Coffee?'

'No thanks. There's just something I wanted to ask you. I'll be out of here in five minutes.'

He became conscious of Thomas's hands; the knuckles were white. A muscle was moving at his temple. Had he guessed why Henrik was there?

He tried to think of the best way to start.

In the end, he decided to go straight in with the excuse he had concocted. 'I'm here about Jan Loft,' he said, watching Thomas for his reaction.

The man stared at him wide-eyed.

'I believe you worked for him once, Thomas, or should I call you Kim?'

'It's Thomas now,' Katja cut in. 'Anyway, why are you looking into that old business with Loft?'

'It's just routine. He's due for release on Tuesday. I wanted to make you aware of that.'

'Thank you,' she said. 'That's considerate of you, but we knew that already, didn't we Thomas?' She rubbed her husband's back. He nodded silently.

Katja looked at Henrik. 'You don't think we're in any danger from Loft, do you?'

'No. But some people want to know, to prepare mentally. Kim ... I mean Thomas testified against Loft in the trial. That's why I'm here. It was me who ... led the investigation back then.' He looked at the couple. 'You moved away from the area after the trial. Tell me why that was?'

Katja put her hand on Thomas's thigh. 'What Loft did,' she said. 'It devastated the whole community. I mean, Thomas had worked for Loft. How do you think that made him feel?'

'But his evidence helped secure the conviction. He was an important character witness,' Henrik said.

'Didn't matter to some people. They looked at us in a funny way afterwards, like we were tainted,' said Katja. 'Some suggested that Thomas should have stopped Loft. But those things he saw at Loft's house ... it was only afterwards, when it all came out about Sebastian, that they made sense. If you've met Loft, you'll know that he's a despicable human being, manipulative and deceitful. Isn't that right, Thomas?'

'Yeah,' said Thomas, his jaw slack, mouth open. Henrik was reminded of his testimony against Loft during the court case. He had sounded slow-witted then.

Now, next to his articulate wife, he came across as positively thick.

'There was also the other side of it,' said Katja.

'What other side?'

'People who didn't like what Thomas said about Loft in court, people who didn't want to stop the horrific things they were up to and wanted to punish Thomas for speaking out.'

'Threaten him, you mean?' He glanced at Thomas, who was looking at his hands.

'Both of us,' she said. 'Stuff started to happen around the trial. A flat tyre, a smashed window in our garden shed, little nuisances like that. But the worst was the pictures. Hundreds of them, sick stuff featuring children, sent straight to Thomas's phone. They threatened to report him, said the pictures would be evidence.'

'Did you tell the police?'

'No,' she said. 'We couldn't take any more. We destroyed his phone, left the area. Thomas changed his name. Then it all stopped.'

He looked at Katja. 'Did you ever meet Loft yourself?'

'A couple of times when I went with Thomas to collect his pay. We lived close by. You wouldn't have known then what Loft was up to, he was always so charming. Makes me want to throw up, to think about it now.'

'So you moved.'

'Yes. I got the nursing job at Riget, so we bought this place.'

Henrik looked around. The living room faced the courtyard, raised above it and overlooking the picnic table with the plant pots and, further away, the yellow building facing the Lakes.

Through an open door, on the other side of the room, he could see the kitchen with windows facing Wesselsgade. Beyond the living room, he guessed there were two, maybe three bedrooms.

The decor was understated, not cheap, but not exactly expensive. A pretty typical Copenhagen home, though tidier perhaps than most with children under the roof. This was a Monday, and Thomas wasn't at work. Nurses didn't get paid a lot, nor did occasional builders. 'It's a lovely flat,' he said.

Katja immediately caught his meaning. 'Thomas's dad

died shortly before we moved. We sold his house, and our own in Dragør, to be able to afford it. Lucky Thomas is a builder. This place was a mess when we bought it. Then Emily came along.'

She smiled at her daughter. The child kept her worried eyes on Henrik.

'It's an odd coincidence,' he said. 'Lea Høgh, the sister of one of Loft's victims disappeared in Dragør the summer before Loft's conviction. And now you live here, and another girl has disappeared nearby.'

'I know,' said Katja, looking at her husband. 'That's why we're so worried. It's like it's happening all over again.'

'You think Palle Dybdal had something to do with Matilde?'

'Doesn't he? You found her glove in the lockup, didn't you?'

So this was public knowledge now. Perhaps Jensen had told the couple. He wouldn't put it past her.

'Bodil must have found out what he was up to. Poor woman. She was so confused.'

'You'll appreciate that I can't discuss details of the investigation with you,' said Henrik. He tried to keep his voice casual. 'You said you went to Loft's house a couple of times. Did either of you ever see Lea there? Thomas, did you?'

'The police asked him that before. He always said the same thing,' said Katja.

'I don't remember her. There were always so many kids around the place,' Thomas said.

'Did you ever see Loft with any other men?'

'Not that I recall,' Thomas said. He glanced at his wife, nervously.

'We think it was Loft who took Lea,' she said. 'He must have had associates.'

Henrik looked at her. He couldn't divulge what Loft had said to Jensen, about Playland and feeling like he was being watched in real life. Or what Rasmus Nordby, Matilde's father, had told them.

Katja studied him more closely. 'You seem very interested. I thought you were just here to let us know about Loft?' she said, still smiling.

'Lea wasn't found. I'll never stop thinking about her, never stop worrying,' he said. He rose to his feet before she could think of asking him anything else.

His time was up.

Out of the living-room window, he noticed some people entering the courtyard. His pulse rose when he saw that it was Lotte and Mark.

'I'd better go,' he said, jumping out of his seat and heading for the door. 'My colleagues will take over now. No need to mention I was here.'

As he left, running towards the Wesselsgade exit, he felt Katja's eyes on his back.

He wouldn't be able to get away with something like this a second time.

Day Nine

58

Jensen woke with a start, recoiling when she opened her eyes and saw Fie's smiling face leaning in close to hers. She remembered how quiet Fie was, how effortlessly she moved across a room. 'What's happened?' she said, sitting up.

She had been lying on the sofa in the Roskilde flat with her feet up. There was a blanket on top of her; Fie must have put it there.

At the other end of the sofa, Gustav was still asleep, mouth open, headphones on, lanky limbs spread out in all directions.

There were pizza boxes on the coffee table, half-drunk bottles of Coke. She remembered going to get the pizzas with Gustav from a takeaway in Roskilde. They had got lost on the way back; all the streets looked the same.

Now it was dark. How long had they been out for the count? Outside it was misty and quiet: no traffic, no people.

'You were sleeping so soundly, I didn't want to wake you,' said Fie. 'You must both have needed it.'

'Did you find Playland?' said Jensen.

'Not yet,' said Fie. 'But I think I've got something.'

Gustav mumbled something in his sleep and turned over, smacking his lips.

Jensen looked at her phone. It was past midnight. There was a message from Henrik.

I need your help. Can we meet?

'Give me a minute,' she said to Fie. 'Where's your bathroom?'

She splashed water on her face. Henrik's message had been sent hours ago. She composed a reply.

I thought you said no more meddling.

She was curious. She sent him a map pin for a Christianshavn café and suggested they meet there at nine o'clock.

When she returned, Gustav was awake, sitting next to Fie. He was yawning and scratching his midriff.

'I looked for a few hours on the dark web,' Fie said. 'Plenty of stuff there that will turn your stomach, but no Playland. I went to a few paedophile-hunter sites, spoke to some people who sent me on to other sites, but it didn't lead anywhere. No one seems to know anything about your paedophile ring.'

Jensen nodded. She remembered Fie once telling her that sites you could access with any browser, or the 'surface internet', was like the tiny tip of a giant iceberg. Most of the web, also known as the deep web, was inaccessible to regular users: banking transactions, for example, or anything that required users to access through layers of security. Stuff that wasn't indexed and couldn't be found by regular browsers.

And at the bottom of the iceberg, hidden in the deepest, murkiest waters, was the dark web, accessed with special browsers, mostly by people hiding behind untraceable VPN connections.

Not everything on the dark web was bad or illegal; it was a marketplace like any other, but criminals flourished among the buyers and sellers. One of the many goods and services for sale was child sexual-abuse material.

'So I thought I'd try to speak directly to someone who might have accessed different sites. I looked at loads of OnlyFans user profiles.'

'OnlyFans?' said Jensen.

'Yeah, you know, sites where you have to subscribe and pay for access to content. There's a direct messaging feature. So I found this guy who seems to be everywhere, including in some fairly innocuous chatrooms. I can tell it's the same user, though he has different aliases. Sometimes he says his name is Mattias, aged fifteen. I started chatting to Mattias on Messenger after we made friends on Facebook.'

'You made friends with him?'

'Not as myself,' said Fie.

'Look,' said Gustav, laughing. 'This is Fie's profile.'

It was a photo of a pouting blonde girl with very few clothes on. She looked to be about thirteen years old.

'Who's that?' said Jensen.

'Oh, she doesn't exist,' said Fie. 'It's AI. Quite realistic, isn't she? I called her Nanna. And look.' She pointed to the screen and a more than hour-long conversation between Mattias and Nanna.

'You can see that it's innocent at first. But then Mattias starts asking for photos. Nanna isn't keen. She asks him to send a photo of himself first. So he sends this.'

'That's a penis,' said Gustav.

'Yes, thank you,' said Jensen. 'I *have* seen one of those before.'

'Then Mattias says, "Now your turn." He's clearly putting pressure on, but his tone is still friendly and playful.'

'You didn't actually send him anything?' said Jensen.

Fie scrolled. Now Nanna was naked.

The conversation continued with three more suggestive pictures following from Nanna. Mattias was keen to meet tomorrow. 'And here it gets interesting,' said Fie. 'Can you see how suddenly he becomes much less nice? He's saying what he might do with the photos if she doesn't agree to meet. How he could share them with his friends. How her parents and friends might get to see them. He's keeping the tone light, but he's clearly coercing her. He says that if she agrees to meeting in person, he'll delete the photos. He tells her that he was only joking when he suggested that he could share them, and that she shouldn't be so touchy.'

Jensen felt sick. She found herself folding her hands protectively over her bump. 'You must tell us if this is too much,' she said to Fie.

'I'm fine,' said Fie. 'Actually, it makes me angry.'

'Good,' said Jensen.

'And I know I'm safe. This guy can't hurt me.'

'What a dick,' said Gustav.

'You can meet him if you want,' said Fie. 'I agreed to a meet-up tomorrow morning at eleven in Copenhagen.'

'Where?' said Jensen.

'He said he'll send me the exact location thirty minutes before, but that it'll be in the centre of Copenhagen.'

'He doesn't want you to do your research first,' said Jensen.

'I'd like to meet him,' Gustav said.

'He seems pretty prolific on the different sites,' said Fie.

'I'll keep looking at this end, but you could ask him for information. Once he gets over the shock that you're not Nanna. Though, it could be a waste of time. There's no guarantee it'll work.'

'Oh, I think it'll be worth it anyway,' Gustav said. 'Just to see his face.'

59

Henrik had taken a corner table in the back of the Christianshavn basement café and sat with his back to the wall where he had a full view of the room. Out of the high windows, half-obscured by parked bicycles, he could see the boats in the canal, and a row of pretty red and yellow houses on the other side of the water.

He had left home at a quarter to seven, pretending to his wife that he was going to work as usual.

If she found out what was really going on, she would only be asking questions that he couldn't answer.

She hadn't even opened her eyes when he had kissed her goodbye.

He had thought of making her a coffee and leaving it by the side of her bed as a show of affection, but decided against, lest the unusual gesture would come across as suspicious.

The early morning had passed at a snail's pace. He had felt like an outcast in his own city, roaming aimlessly around Copenhagen as he tried to avoid areas where he might be spotted.

He couldn't go to the gym in case someone saw him and wondered why he wasn't at work. Instead, he had found himself joining the sluggish traffic out of the city to Dragør.

There was no van in Jon Høgh's driveway this time. As expected, Høgh had been distraught when Henrik had shown him Lea's photo; he was no longer sure that it had been right to do so.

Bagger would have been back since then to speak to him. By now, Høgh would know that Lea had still been alive at least six months after she disappeared.

Henrik couldn't imagine what the man must be going through.

He knew that having a loved one go missing without trace could feel worse than knowing they were dead.

Loft's house stood empty, the front garden neglected and messy. At one time, the kitchen window had been broken by a brick, and the damage boarded up. Now there was a sign on the metal fence, warning that trespassers would be prosecuted.

Built in the nineteen-seventies, the property would be a tough sale for any estate agent, even if it wasn't known among the locals as the house of horror where a group of young boys had been abused.

If Loft did eventually manage to find a buyer, the new owner would probably want to bulldoze it to the ground.

If only Loft's crimes were as easy to erase.

Henrik had walked the footpath behind the houses. It ran between two hedges and led to another street, a set of traffic lights and a right turn before he found himself at Høgh's house.

It would have been a popular route for Lea and Sebastian. Anyone could have been watching them walking it numerous times. Perhaps they had befriended Lea over a long time, desensitising her to the danger.

Thomas and Katja's old house was a few streets away from Loft's in the other direction.

The waitress came over to his table. She had pierced eyebrows, he noticed, as she placed his latte in front of him along with the pastry he had ordered. The coffee was too strong. He had forgotten to ask for lots of milk.

As always, he marvelled at the strange places where Jensen liked to hang out. He liked his coffee single shot, bog standard beans, no frills.

Eventually, Jensen came rushing through the room like a wind, her dark hair tied into a messy ponytail, dark-blue eyes burning.

A couple of guys at a nearby table checked her out but turned their gaze away when they noticed she was pregnant.

Perhaps they would think that he was the father. The thought thrilled and terrified him in equal measure.

Jensen herself seemed oblivious.

He made a point of checking his watch. 'You're late.'

'What's up?' she said. 'You don't look too good.'

'Thanks,' said Henrik, looking around to make sure they weren't being overheard. 'My bastard boss sent me home.'

'Why?'

'Apparently, I wasn't looking hard enough for Matilde.'

'That's not true.'

'Tell me about it,' Henrik said, pushing his coffee to one side. 'I never got a chance to tell you, but we discovered that the picture of Lea that I asked you to show Loft was definitely taken after she was supposed to have drowned. We think six months later, somewhere in Denmark.'

'My God, Henrik, that's huge.'

'Shush, for God's sake, do you want the whole of Copenhagen to know about it?'

'Sorry,' she said, in an almost-whisper. 'But that would still make it a long time ago. You think Lea could be alive?'

'I don't know,' he said. He looked at her, decided that he might as well share everything with her now that he was off the case. 'There's something else. Remember Kim Jespersen, the guy your colleague couldn't track down?'

'The witness for the prosecution?' said Jensen. 'You found him?'

'Yep.'

'Where?'

'In Bodil's block by the Lakes. Goes by the name of Thomas these days. Thomas Jespersen. His wife's name is Katja.'

'Shit,' said Jensen. 'But how ... I don't understand.'

'They reckon all the things happening right on their doorstep is no coincidence. They think they're being targeted because of Thomas's court testimony in the Lea case.'

Jensen fell quiet.

'What is it?' he said, knowing there was something on her mind.

'I thought Thomas was being odd when we interviewed him. He didn't seem all that keen to talk to us,' she said. 'Katja yes, but not him. Are you sure he doesn't have anything to do with it?'

'His alibi checked out for the day Lea disappeared. We checked the alibi of everyone Loft had even a passing acquaintance with, and Thomas's was rock solid. He was in Helsingør that day, ironically on a job for Loft. His online history was also looked at. Nothing there.'

'OK,' said Jensen. 'What they said about being targeted – it does seem that Playland operates through coercion and threats. Remember that Loft said he had the feeling he was being watched in real life whenever he accessed the network? Like the administrator knew where he was and where he lived.'

'The Ugly Duckling,' he said.

'Yes.'

'Rasmus Nordby said the same.'

'Really?'

'Yes. I don't know what to do,' he said. 'I can't work it out.'

'You don't think Palle is behind it?'

'Thomas and Katja certainly do. By the way, you shouldn't have told them about the glove you found in his workshop.'

'Did I?' she said, frowning.

He shrugged. She had probably let it slip without thinking. Or one of his team had.

'Is someone looking into where the picture of Lea came from?'

'Yes, but it's not being prioritised, and it's not being linked to the Matilde case.'

They fell silent as the waitress with the pierced eyebrows approached with a pot of tea for Jensen.

'Jan Loft is being released today,' said Henrik when she had left, and Jensen had poured her tea. It looked like dirty dish water.

'Where will he go?'

Henrik shrugged. 'I can't see him staying in Dragør. He'll change his name, try to slip into obscurity, maybe even emigrate somewhere. Some people like him end up in Southeast Asia.'

'I might be able to help,' Jensen said. 'I've got someone looking for Playland right now,' she said.

'Who?'

'I can't tell you that. They're a friend. An exceptionally gifted one.'

He sat back and stared at her, incredulous.

She shrugged, sipping her tea. 'If you didn't want me to look into it, then you shouldn't have asked me to speak to Loft.'

He narrowed his eyes. 'I didn't see you at the reconstruction in Ørstedsparken on Sunday, only that idiot colleague of yours.'

'He's not my colleague anymore.'

'He's been sacked?' said Henrik. 'Finally, your boss has seen sense.'

'No. It's me who has left. Margrethe sent me on early maternity leave.'

'Jesus,' said Henrik. 'So we're both out.'

'Looks like it.'

'I thought Margrethe was your biggest fan,' he said.

'Not after she found out that Gustav is working with me again. Plus, he was supposed to have started school in the summer, but never turned up. He got access to Margrethe's mailbox and communicated with the school in her name.'

'Ah. That's identity fraud.'

'Thanks, I had no idea,' she said sarcastically. 'Anyway, she's furious, threw him out, told him she doesn't want to see him again.'

'Want me to have a word with him?'

'Like that's going to help,' she said. 'Anyway, Margrethe blames me. She threw me out too.'

'You?'

'Yes. Pregnant and homeless. Not pretty, is it?'

'Looks all right from where I'm sitting,' he said, smiling at her suggestively.

It was true: pregnancy suited her. Her cheeks were flushed pink, she had even grown breasts. A shame that she seemed to have lost her sense of humour. 'Where will you go?' he said.

'Back to my mum's in Jutland, I guess.'

He laughed.

'What's so funny?' she said.

'Look at us, a right pair of down-and-outs.'

'Speak for yourself,' she said. 'I intend to go on working on this. You could help if you want? Unless you'd rather feel sorry for yourself?'

'Let's say, just to humour you, that I agreed to help. Where would we work? What would be our base? We'd need somewhere private.'

'Margrethe's place is huge, and she's away at the moment,' Jensen said, sipping her tea. 'We'll be all right there, at least until Thursday morning. We could meet later today, say at lunchtime, after eleven, if that works?'

'What happens at eleven?'

'Gustav and I have an appointment with a paedophile who thinks he's meeting a thirteen-year-old girl.'

She looked at his pastry. It sat untouched, next to his coffee. He could tell that she was practically salivating at the sight.

'If you're not having that,' she said, 'can I eat it?'

60

Henrik had insisted they check whether Margrethe was definitely out before he agreed to come up, and even then he had taken the back stairs.

He had looked into every room in the flat before settling, refusing to remove his leather jacket or take off his boots.

They sat in the kitchen, eating chicken sandwiches from Lagkagehuset and warming their hands on the tea Gustav had made: something herbal that had languished in the cupboards for so long that it had lost its flavour.

Henrik grimaced at it and pushed it away, the fussiest man on the planet. 'I don't want either of you to try a stunt like that again,' he said.

'Yes Dad,' said Gustav, with his mouth full of chicken, lettuce and curry mayonnaise.

'It worked, though, didn't it?' said Jensen.

'It could have been extremely dangerous,' Henrik said. 'What if there had been more than one of him? I thought he was going to hit you at one point.'

Jensen shrugged and took a giant bite of her sandwich.

The man who had pretended to be a fifteen-year-old boy

had been nearer forty-five. As promised, he had provided a map pin for the meeting place, a dingy and empty corner of Fælledparken.

They had watched him from behind a tree for a while, as he paced up and down, checking his watch every few seconds.

When a dog walker passed him, he pretended to be on the phone to someone, hurrying quickly in the opposite direction, before turning back and beginning to pace again.

The most extraordinary thing about him was how ordinary he looked. He was slim, in dark jeans and a tight-fitting puffer jacket, not bad looking. On his head, a black baseball cap. He could have been anyone: the guy behind the counter in a clothes shop, a driving instructor, an insurance salesman.

'Mattias?' Jensen had said, walking towards him. 'I wouldn't run if I were you. We've hundreds of pictures, plus a complete dossier of your online history, ready to hand over to the police. Or, if you prefer, we could share it online. There would be a kind of poetic justice in that. Oh, and by the way, we're also being filmed now.'

The man looked around him wildly. 'Who the hell are you?' he said.

'Let's just say that I'm not Nanna, and not thirteen years old, Mattias. Can I call you Mattias? I know your real name by the way, but you seem to prefer your alias.'

'Just tell me what you want,' he said through gritted teeth.

'I want names,' she said. 'Ever heard of an online paedophile ring called Playland?'

'No. Is this a joke?'

Jensen took out a notepad and a pen and handed it to

him. 'I want you to write down the names of as many paedophile chatrooms, forums and websites as you can think
of. You've got half an hour. If I find out that you've kept
stuff back, or made names up, you know what's going to
happen.'

'That's all you want, names?'

'You're actually smarter than you look.'

'How do I know that you're not going to report me
anyway?'

'You don't,' she said. 'You have to take it on trust. Like
Nanna. Feels uncomfortable, doesn't it?'

He snatched the pad out of her hand, then filled three
pages, printing aggressively with the paper pressed against
his thigh.

'Thanks,' she said. 'Oh, and there's one more condition
you need to know about. If you ever, and I mean as long
as you live, try to meet up with someone under-age again,
there's going to be severe consequences.'

The man looked like he was going to attack her. She
placed her hands on the small of her back to make herself
look more pregnant. Henrik and Gustav were close by,
but not close enough to prevent some damage if he went
for her.

Luckily, the man appeared to think better of it.

Henrik picked the salad leaves out of his sandwich and
took a careful bite. 'You went too far, Jensen. He could
have been nasty.'

'How could he possibly have been any nastier?' she said.
'Anyway, did you pass the details on to your colleague?'

'Yes,' said Henrik. 'They'll be paying him a visit.'

'I can't believe he was stupid enough to think you
were going to keep your side of the bargain,' said Gustav,
laughing.

Jensen had sent photographs of the handwritten sheets to Fie, who had responded with a thumbs-up emoji and a brief message.

I'm on it.

'So, what do we do now?' said Gustav.

'We consolidate the information we have. Find the gaps, then set about closing them,' said Henrik, dropping his sandwich on the table and wiping his hands on a napkin. 'Is there somewhere in this place we can work?'

'There's my room,' said Jensen. 'There's a notice board in there.'

'We should get Fie down here too,' said Gustav. 'Then we'd be a proper team.'

'Who's Fie?'

'She's the friend I was telling you about, the one with the exceptional computer skills,' said Jensen. 'She lives in Roskilde, but she might not want to come. She's vulnerable, you see, agoraphobic.'

Henrik buried his face in his hands. 'What the hell am I doing here,' he mumbled to himself.

Jensen and Gustav argued about how best to organise the wall of information, until Henrik exploded. 'Quiet. I can't hear myself think.' He pointed to the photo of Matilde. 'We start here. Give me some names.'

'Her dad,' Gustav said.

'Yes,' said Henrik, moving across the photo of Rasmus Nordby.

'Her stepdad,' said Jensen. 'Simon Clausen, married to her mum, Stine Clausen.'

'Bodil,' said Gustav. 'Someone who looked like her was

328

seen in Ørstedsparken by witnesses on the day Matilde disappeared.'

Henrik pinned up the photos. 'It wasn't just a resemblance,' he said. 'According to the witnesses, whoever they saw that day – and it could have been a man or a woman, but not Bodil as the person was younger and fit – was wearing the clothes we found Bodil dead in.'

'Murdered in,' said Jensen.

'And there's the shopping trolley,' said Henrik. 'Before I continue, I want you to promise that what I'm about to say won't go any further than this. If people find out that I've been sharing this information with you, then I'll be finished in the police for good.'

'You can trust us,' said Jensen.

He pointed to Gustav. 'I want to hear him say it too.'

'I promise,' he said, holding a hand to his heart.

Henrik sighed. 'Matilde's DNA was found inside Bodil's shopping trolley.'

'So someone disguised themselves in her clothes and used her shopping trolley to abduct Matilde,' said Jensen. 'Someone who had access to her flat. Bodil said she'd been burgled. It fits.'

'It's possible,' said Henrik. 'Let's think it through. Bodil could have met Matilde and talked to her on previous occasions. Perhaps the abductor knew this?'

'No,' said Jensen. 'Bodil had heard about Matilde going missing, but she didn't have a clue who she was.'

'She could have had reasons to hide it from you.'

'If she wanted to hide it, why invite a journalist round to her flat the day after Matilde went missing?' said Jensen.

'Palle had her key,' said Gustav.

'Bodil was killed with Palle's spanner,' said Jensen. 'We also know that he had been stealing from Bodil.'

'What would be Palle's motive for abducting Matilde?' said Henrik.

'It's obvious, isn't it? He's a paedo,' said Gustav.

Henrik shook his head. 'So far, we've got no evidence for that. His flat has been split apart, his devices, online accounts, everything. There's no trace of anything of that sort.'

'Maybe someone else forced him to abduct Matilde,' Gustav said. 'As a kind of blackmail.'

'Or maybe he's just a lot better at hiding his sexual preferences than Nordby,' said Jensen. 'He could easily be behind everything. Maybe *he* is the Ugly Duckling.'

'Let's park that for a moment,' said Henrik, scratching his head. 'We also have the picture of Lea found on Rasmus Nordby's hard drive.'

'The picture showing that she was still alive at least six months after she disappeared,' said Jensen.

'Precisely,' Henrik said. 'Nordby told us that he'd accessed Playland and that he'd felt like he was being watched.'

'Loft told me the same thing,' said Jensen.

Henrik drew a bold line between the photos. 'That's a clear link between Matilde and Lea. Playland. So let's say that whoever is behind Playland took them, exploited a weakness in Loft and Nordby to get access and information on the victims.'

'But wait,' said Jensen. 'What about the couple Bodil saw in the courtyard?'

'I've been thinking about that. The door to Wesselsgade is constantly being left open. I found it open myself yesterday. Perhaps it's just a coincidence that it happened around the same time as everything else,' said Henrik. 'Palle didn't want the police looking around the place, so he made out as though Bodil had dementia. It suited him as he was helping himself to her things, coming and going as he pleased.'

'Only he hadn't reckoned with Bodil,' said Jensen. 'She wasn't going to take it lying down, so she called me.'

'It can't be right,' said Gustav. 'It's all too weird.'

'It's still possible,' Henrik said. 'A woman runs to escape her boyfriend during a heated argument. She finds the door to the red building open. Runs inside, but he's following her. He goes too far, she faints. He pulls her to her feet. They leave. Weirder things happen every day, trust me.'

'Bodil thought the man killed the woman.'

'Then show me the body,' Henrik said. 'Show me the missing person's report.'

'It doesn't make any sense,' said Jensen. 'We've spoken to everyone on the block. There's no one here who matches the description of the woman Bodil saw, no single man of an age and situation to have a girlfriend around.'

'No,' said Henrik. 'I think the couple must have come from somewhere else nearby.'

'So, all you need is to get Palle to confess?' said Gustav.

'And tell us what he did with Matilde?' said Jensen.

'Theoretically, yes,' said Henrik.

Jensen shook her head. 'None of this is getting us any closer to finding out what happened to the girls.'

Henrik's phone rang.

He walked into the hall. '*Nej, nej, nej, nej,*' they heard him say. 'When?'

When he came back into the kitchen, he was resting his hands on top of his head, staring at Jensen and Gustav.

'What is it?' said Jensen.

'It's Jon Høgh,' he said. 'Lea's dad. He just killed Jan Loft.'

61

'Jungersen, I told you not to come.' Incredibly, Bagger's eyes were still smiling as he edged himself out of the back door, looking left and right.

The ground was an unpaved mess of mud and gravel, littered with cigarette butts. It was the worst kept secret in the office that you could smoke here without being caught on the security cameras.

He had pinged Bagger from the car, asking him to meet him for a fag, their code for wanting a private chat.

'Then why tell me about Høgh?' he said.

'Out of courtesy. It was your case – I thought you'd want to know.'

'How did it happen?'

'Wait,' said Bagger, looking over his shoulder, then signalling for them to swap places, so that Henrik's back was against the door, and Bagger was able to spot anyone coming near them. 'Loft had barely got half a mile from the prison. He was waiting for a bus to the train station when Høgh walked up and stabbed him repeatedly in full view of witnesses. He then ... mutilated the corpse.'

'Mutilated?'

'I'll let you use your imagination on that one.'

'Oh,' said Henrik, involuntarily reaching for his crotch.

'Yeah. It was a bloodbath. Afterwards, he threw his knife into some bushes and waited calmly for the police to arrive.'

'Did he say anything?'

'Yes, that he wasn't sorry.'

Henrik mouthed an obscenity. 'I saw him only the other day.'

'I know,' said Bagger. 'He told me. You shouldn't have shown him the photo of Lea until we were sure it was her.'

'I *was* sure,' said Henrik. 'And as her father, he had a right to know. Do you think that's what sent him over the edge?'

'I think he went over years ago. When his only daughter vanished into thin air.'

'Yeah, and now he's gone ahead and ruined everything. We'll never get the truth from Loft now.'

'Unless, of course, what Loft told us *is* the truth.'

'I strongly doubt the man ever spoke a true word in his sorry life,' said Henrik.

Sebastian Høgh had lost his mother and little sister, but he still had a father. A father who would now be locked away in prison until he was an old man. 'Has Sebastian been informed?' he said.

'Yes. He didn't seem surprised,' said Bagger. 'Nor particularly delighted.'

'Doesn't change what happened to him six years ago, I suppose.'

Bagger was silent for a beat. 'I'm sorry that Wiese sent you home, Jungersen. I gather Monsen wasn't happy about it when he found out. He's flying back from Rome tomorrow, apparently. Wants Wiese to account for himself.'

'I'd like to hear him do so,' said Henrik. 'Any updates from this morning's briefing?'

'Dybdal's still the main suspect, both in Bodil's murder and Matilde's abduction,' said Bagger.

'I get it,' said Henrik. 'But still, something about him just isn't the right fit.'

'I know what you mean,' said Bagger. 'Only, it turns out that Dybdal wasn't as clean as we first thought. The guys found an iPad in his flat, hidden under the floorboards. The full gamut of nasty stuff.'

'I see.'

'Yeah,' said Bagger. 'He's denying all knowledge, of course, except he *has* admitted to stealing Bodil La Cour's first editions. I believe he thought he was entitled to some sort of compensation for everything he did for her. His bank statements suggest books weren't all he took. Seems he also helped himself to the odd allowance from her bank account. Too little to arouse any suspicion, but enough.'

'Any news on Matilde?' said Henrik.

Bagger beckoned him closer. 'Actually,' he said, 'there's been a new development on that front. We asked a few law enforcement agencies around the world for help. A few hours ago, we had something interesting come through from the US. A thirty-minute video of what we believe to be Matilde, shared from a Danish IP address.'

'User identified?'

'Yep. Guy over in Randers. No VPN, obviously an amateur,' said Bagger. 'Though not so amateur that he worked without a kill switch. His entire gear was destroyed as soon as we crossed the threshold to his apartment. Of course, he's refusing to talk now.'

'What's on the video?'

'Matilde, asleep in a room similar to the one we saw in

the picture of Lea. Again, we've reason to believe it was filmed somewhere in Denmark. But the really interesting bit is the soundtrack.'

'How do you mean?'

'Brian has cleaned it up. It's obviously near an airport, and we think it's Kastrup, judging by the frequency of planes coming into land.'

'Jesus,' said Henrik. 'If Dybdal took Matilde, maybe he handed her off to someone else.'

He thought of Playland, and the Ugly Duckling, and Jan Loft who said that he'd felt under surveillance when he accessed the paedophile network.

'There's a timer running in the bottom right corner, counting down.'

'What does it show?'

'At the end of the recording, four days, sixteen hours and fourteen seconds remain on the counter, but the trouble is that we don't know when it started, except it must have been sometime after four o'clock in the afternoon a week ago last Sunday.'

'Shit. So whatever it was counting down to might already have happened.'

'Or it might not,' said Bagger.

'We need to check out any empty premises in a radius of five hundred yards from Kastrup.'

'Yep, that's what we're doing. Brian is in there now with the others going through the possibilities. Talking of which, I'd better get back. It's mayhem in there.'

'Wait,' said Henrik, grabbing his arm. 'This means I was right. Wiese has to put me back on the case now.'

'We told him about the video earlier,' said Bagger. 'Since then, no one has seen him.'

'That's odd,' said Henrik.

'Someone said they saw him leave. He's not picking up his phone.'

'Has anyone tried him at home?'

Bagger's expression changed. Just the tiniest movement of his eyes as he looked over Henrik's shoulder.

'Don't look, but someone's coming,' he said, as he pushed Henrik towards the gate opening onto the street. 'I'll call you later when I know more. Don't do anything or go anywhere. Go straight home and wait.'

62

It had been Gustav's idea to bring Fie to Copenhagen. 'It'll be quicker if she's here with us,' he had said.

Fie had been reluctant. 'I don't know. I have all my stuff here.'

Gustav hadn't bought it. 'You only need a laptop,' he had said, but Jensen knew Fie wasn't talking about her IT equipment.

It had taken her years to leave Skovhøj and get her own place. She was probably just getting used to the relative freedom of it.

In the end, Gustav had promised to come to Roskilde to collect her. 'I promise, nothing will happen to you as long as you're with me,' he had said.

Wanting to take care of others than himself was a sign that Gustav was becoming an adult, Jensen reflected.

Not all adults met the same standards.

Gustav and Fie had arrived at Margrethe's flat with a large holdall and a sleeping bag.

'Just in case we don't make the last train back,' Gustav had said, winking at Jensen.

He had rigged Fie's laptop up to his giant monitor, and all three of them were now seated in a row by Margrethe's dining table, watching the screen.

'What's happening?' said Jensen.

'We're waiting for the Ugly Duckling,' said Fie.

'Who are you making out to be this time?' said Gustav.

'It doesn't matter,' said Fie. 'Everyone on here is pretending to be someone else. Nothing is real.'

'Except the child sexual abuse,' said Gustav.

'Except that,' Fie said.

She seemed in a low mood, slouched in her chair as she frowned at the screen.

Jensen still wasn't sure they had done the right thing by bringing her into this mess. 'Is it getting too much? Do you want to stop?' she said.

'No. I want to help you find this person. I think I can do it.'

'Maybe it's not one person. Could be a group of people,' said Gustav.

'What I don't understand is why they're doing it,' said Fie. 'What's in it for them?'

'Same as with any other crime,' said Jensen. 'Lust. Greed. Notoriety. A sense of power over other people.'

'It's horrible,' said Fie. 'Those poor kids.' She looked at Jensen. 'I think you're brave, having a baby.'

Actually, Jensen thought, she was the opposite of brave.

Inaction had got her where she was now.

'I mean, it's a hopeful thing to do, isn't it, to have a child?' Fie continued. 'It means you believe that the good people will win over the bad.'

'We have to win, Fie,' said Jensen. 'There are more of us than there are of them.'

Fie bit her lip. 'Sometimes that's not how it feels.'

'What's happening now?' said Gustav, yawning to the point of being in danger of dislocating his jaw.

'I'm not sure anything is going to happen,' said Fie. 'Not for a while. You have to be patient with these things.' She looked around. 'This is a nice place. You're lucky to have an aunt like this.'

'Are you kidding me?' said Gustav. 'She's just thrown me out.'

'Really?'

'Gustav isn't telling you the whole truth,' Jensen said. 'Margrethe found out that he never started high school in the summer. He was supposed to be retaking his first year, but he lied to her.'

'I know,' said Fie.

Jensen looked at Gustav, outraged. 'Fie knew and I didn't?'

Gustav shrugged.

'I hated school too,' said Fie.

'Nice that *someone* gets it,' said Gustav.

Jensen shook her head at him. 'Margrethe thinks I've been a bad influence on Gustav, so she's thrown me out too. I'm now officially on maternity leave.'

'So this isn't going in the newspaper?'

'Oh, it will if I've got something to do with it,' Jensen said. 'If *Dagbladet* doesn't want it, then I'm sure others will.'

'Where will you be staying?' said Fie.

'I'll head back to my mum's.' Jensen gestured at the screen. 'But not till this is done.'

'And you?' Fie looked at Gustav.

He sat up, put on his most angelic smile. 'I'm glad you asked, Fie,' said Gustav, hands folded in mock prayer. 'Any chance I could stay at yours? Just until I get myself sorted with new digs and a job?'

He made it sound so easy, Jensen thought, to start again, to reinvent yourself.

That was exactly what she had to do.

She didn't know if she could.

63

Superintendent Jens Wiese lived in a bijou villa in Hellerup, a home out of a magazine, which despite its petite size had cost a bomb.

Henrik knew how much because he had once looked it up online.

He had wondered how his boss had been able to afford a house like that, until he had found out that Wiese's wife was an executive of one of the country's biggest banks. No one on the force had ever seen her. Apparently, she was never at home and lived a virtually separate life from Wiese.

You couldn't blame her for that.

The couple had no children. You could tell from the way they lived, Henrik thought as he walked up the neat driveway lined with symmetrically spaced trees and low box hedges.

The lawn was pristine, not torn into a muddy mess by studded football boots. No lost balls in the bushes, no iridescent plastic toys ruining the perfect picture.

He rang the doorbell, listening to it chime inside the house.

Cupping his hands and looking through the tall, narrow glass panel to the hallway, he noticed an oak bench with shoes neatly stored below it, a wardrobe and a console table with a mirror in which he could see his own face.

'Hello, Wiese, are you in there?' he said, bending down and shouting through the letterbox.

Wiese cycled everywhere. Henrik thought he could see a pair of cleats under the bench and, if he stretched, the edge of what looked like a black cycling helmet.

It didn't mean that he was at home, of course. He could have a car that no one knew about.

He was surprised at how quiet it was. Barely a few streets away from the main road and shops, and all you could hear was the low and distant hum ever present on the outskirts of big cities.

He tiptoed through a flowerbed into the front garden. He walked around the house and looked inside the dark, sparsely furnished rooms with ugly modern art on the walls. It looked like no human had ever lived there.

Where had Wiese gone? Could he have a doctor's appointment? Or have gone to the gym? He wasn't the sort to be absent for so many hours without telling anyone.

Was he embarrassed because he, Henrik, had turned out to be right after all? Embarrassment wasn't an emotion you often saw from Wiese, but there was a first time for everything.

His phone interrupted the silence, startling him.

Monsen.

'Just landed?' Henrik said.

'Unfortunately.'

'How was Rome?'

'Preferable to Copenhagen in most ways I can think of. I should have stayed there, given this God-awful mess we're in,' said Monsen. 'Any idea where Wiese has got to?'

'You're asking the wrong person. He sent me home.'

'Yes, thank you, I'm aware of that.'

'He still hasn't turned up?'

'Nope. I rang his wife. She's in New York on business and was highly surprised to hear that her husband wasn't at work. He'd better have a damn good explanation.'

'Do you think something's happened to him?'

'To Wiese? I doubt it. Never known a man with a stronger self-preservation gene,' said Monsen.

Rich coming from you, thought Henrik. Monsen was famous for looking after his own interests.

On the other hand, Monsen had never left him in the lurch, like Wiese had. He knew how to lead people, to step in and take the flak for his team whenever the police commissioner lost her cool. The kind of leadership skills that Wiese didn't possess.

'I shall look forward to him explaining himself,' said Monsen.

'I'm outside his house,' said Henrik. 'No sign of life.'

'What on earth are you doing there?'

'Let's just say I had some time on my hands.'

'Not anymore. Get your arse here where you belong. We'll speak later.'

'But I've been taken off the case,' Henrik said.

'I'm putting you back on it,' said Monsen, ending the call.

On the way back to the city through the usual clogged-up Christmas traffic, Henrik called Jensen. She immediately bombarded him with questions about Jon Høgh and Jan Loft.

'Stop,' he said. 'I don't know any more than you do.'

This wasn't true, of course, but now that he was back at work, he couldn't afford to leak any more information from the investigation, including the new video that had surfaced of Matilde.

343

'Has your friend, the computer wizard, managed to make any progress?' he asked.

'As a matter of fact, she has,' said Jensen. 'She's right here next to me and not only has she managed to find Playland – she's also in touch with the Ugly Duckling.'

Henrik had to brake last-minute to avoid bumping the car in front as the lights changed to red.

'She's what?'

'We're waiting for a response.'

'Stay where you are, I'm coming.' he said. 'I'll need to bring you and your friend into the office.'

'I thought you'd been sent home?'

'Decision's been reversed. And Jensen?'

'Yes?'

'I'm taking a significant risk, working with you on this.'

'You told me that already.'

'I want you to promise me that when you meet my colleagues, ours is a strictly professional relationship, and always has been. We'll behave as if we don't know each other intimately. Understood?'

'Oh yes,' said Jensen. 'And that won't be a problem.'

64

Henrik's office at Teglholmen was nothing like Jensen had imagined. It could have been any corporate office outside of business hours, only less flash. The same went for the meeting room they were taken to. With the exception of a large map, showing the inner city and Nørrebro with Ørstedsparken and Matilde's home marked out in red, it was disappointingly dull.

A police jacket on a coat rack and the fact that everyone was wearing guns at the waist of their jeans were the only clues that this was where major crimes in the capital were being investigated.

Everyone seemed calm, not running around, shouting or panicking.

Henrik had arrived as promised to collect them. He had wanted just Jensen and Fie to come, but Fie had refused to leave without Gustav.

'This is highly unorthodox, I hope you realise,' Henrik had said as he led them up the stairs.

'You were the one who wanted us to come in,' Jensen said.

'We've been trying to penetrate this paedophile ring for years, and you've made contact. That's not something I can ignore.'

In the meeting room, Henrik introduced the three of them to a colleague he called Bagger.

'Is that a real gun?' Gustav said, pointing to the weapon on the man's belt.

Bagger promptly took it out and let Gustav hold it. He had friendly eyes, and was interested in Fie, asking her about her background, what she did for work. 'How did you learn to do this stuff?' he said.

Fie seemed embarrassed by the attention.

Badly bullied at school, she had found kindness and acceptance online, joining a virtual community of people who had shown her the back routes and deep plains of the internet.

Aged eleven, she had managed to book tickets to Florida for her family. Later, when her mother was sent to prison for an unrelated offence, she had hacked into the system in a bid to change her criminal record. Caught by the police, she had received a caution and ended up at an institution, eventually being transferred to Skovhøj, a home for vulnerable youth.

None of that was comfortable for her to discuss, least of all with strangers.

'Maybe Fie should just show you where she's up to with Playland,' Jensen said.

Fie looked at her gratefully. 'Where do you want me to set up?' she asked Bagger.

A space was cleared for her on the meeting table and soon a small audience had formed behind her. She showed them how she had finally found the paedophile ring. 'I've made some friends over the years who pointed me in the right direction. You just have to try lots of things, and give it time,' she said.

'We don't *have* time,' said Henrik. 'How long will it take before the Ugly Duckling responds?'

'I don't know,' said Fie. 'I told them that I want in. If I push too hard, they'll get suspicious.'

Jensen could tell how uncomfortable Henrik was with them being there, chatting to his colleagues. He kept rubbing his face the way he did when he was nervous. 'OK,' he said to Bagger after a few minutes. 'I'll be in my office. Come and get me the moment you hear anything.'

Day Ten

65

'Henrik?'

His first thought was that if he didn't get a proper night's sleep soon, he was going to die. Bagger's voice was like an angle grinder, splitting his head in two. 'I'm awake, for Christ's sake,' he mumbled.

He had been asleep for what felt like five minutes, and was shocked when his watch told him that it was almost four in the morning.

He jumped up from his couch. 'Why didn't you wake me sooner?'

'There was no material development, so I thought I'd let you rest,' said Bagger. He looked as fresh as though he had just woken from a ten-hour sleep, eyes still smiling benignly. 'Anyway, you'll want to know that the Ugly Duckling has just responded.'

They ran to the meeting room. Gustav was sleeping at the end of the table with his head on his forearms. Bagger's colleague Brian sat on one side of Fie with Jensen on the other.

Everyone else had left.

Outside the window, the cars across the road were covered in frost, mist hanging low around the streetlights.

Henrik slapped his cheeks hard a couple of times to wake himself up. It hurt to move. 'What's the story?' he said.

'Something's happening,' said Fie. 'Tonight.'

'What?'

'I don't know, but people are talking about a link. It's clearly a big deal.'

'Fits with the countdown on the video clip we received,' said Bagger. 'And probably means that whatever it's counting down to hasn't happened yet.'

'What video clip?' said Jensen, sitting up straight.

Henrik glanced at Bagger, who gave a slight nod. Having trusted Jensen and her strange companions this far, they might as well tell them everything. 'OK,' he said, weighing his words carefully. 'Given the extraordinary circumstances and the fact that *you* came to *us*, we'll tell you. In strictest confidence, mind.'

'But I get the exclusive once the story can be made public?' said Jensen.

'*If* that ever happens,' said Henrik.

'Simon and Stine Clausen have been informed of what I'm about to tell you, but it can't go any further.'

'What is it?'

'We're in possession of a film clip of Matilde, recorded in an unknown location. There's a countdown in the bottom corner of the clip. Matilde appears to be sleeping, or perhaps she's sedated. If the news leaks, then the whole operation could be jeopardised.'

'What operation?'

'Our attempt to find and free her. Before it's too late. She's obviously being billed as the star of some sort of live-streamed performance.'

The room fell quiet, as each of them struggled with the implications of this.

'How do we find her?' said Jensen after a while. 'I mean, do you have any idea where to look?'

'There's a faint sound on the recording that we believe to be of planes coming into land at Kastrup,' said Bagger. 'We're trying to make some headway from that, but it's a long shot.'

'Or we could try to find her by gaining access to the Playland link,' said Jensen.

'That's a risky strategy. Matilde might come to harm in the meantime,' said Bagger.

'And it won't be easy,' said Fie. 'The Ugly Duckling wants money. The equivalent of two hundred thousand euros, paid to a crypto wallet.'

'By when?' said Henrik.

'Midnight.'

'So that's when it's all kicking off?'

'Presumably,' said Fie. 'Do you want me to respond?'

'How are you supposed to get the money to them?' said Henrik.

'By transferring crypto currency from my wallet to theirs,' said Fie. 'The money is only released to the Ugly Duckling when the link is delivered. Theoretically we can track the payment. To extract the actual money, the Ugly Duckling will need to go through a crypto exchange. We might be able to identify them that way.'

'By the time we do that, it'll be too late for Matilde,' said Henrik.

Like they were years late for Lea.

He tried to think straight. His eyes fell on Gustav, sleeping at the end of the table. Jensen looked positively ill. This couldn't be good, in her condition.

They were all tired, running on empty.

He turned to her. 'There's nothing more you can do now. Why don't the two of you go home and try to sleep for a few hours?'

'And miss out on the action?' said Jensen. 'No way.'

'We'll call you the minute something happens.'

'What about Fie?'

'I'm fine,' said Fie. 'I'm not tired. Maybe I could take a look at that video clip you mentioned. See if I can help?'

When Henrik got back, after dropping Jensen and Gustav off at Margrethe Skov's flat in Østerbro, he could hear Bagger, Brian and Fie talking excitedly as he approached down the corridor.

'This girl is the best analyst I've ever met,' said Bagger, looking up as Henrik entered the meeting room.

Henrik couldn't remember the last time he had seen Bagger this animated.

'We've got a possible location near Kastrup. Going by the airport noise, this area is the most likely.' He pointed to the map.

'Stop,' said Henrik. 'That's Dragør.'

Jan Loft had lived in Dragør.

The building Bagger was pointing to was under a kilometre from Loft's house.

Now they were talking.

'Let's get this show on the road,' said Henrik.

66

Jensen had tried unsuccessfully to sleep for a couple of hours. When, finally, she had been about to drift off, Henrik had called.

'We think we know where they might be keeping her,' he said.

'Where?'

'I can't tell you that.'

'You only found out because I introduced you to Fie, so you owe me.'

'If you come along, the whole thing could end up going wrong.'

Afterwards, Jensen had tried to get Fie to talk to her, but she had refused. 'They said you'd call. They told me Matilde might get hurt if I tell you. Sorry.'

She had been too restless to sleep after that. Gustav was comatose and didn't even stir when she looked in on him.

Famished, she had gone out in search of a bakery, returning with enough bread, pastries and chocolate milk to feed an army.

A text message pinged as she headed up the stairs biting into a warm poppy-seed roll.

And another text message.

Her phone exploded in pings. She looked at the screen. Dropped the phone.

It was pictures of children. Dozens of them. Horrific, pornographic images.

Shaking, she picked up the phone and ran up the last few steps to the flat, while looking over her shoulder.

They must know that she had been helping the police, which meant that they had been following her.

This was what had happened to Frank. She shook Gustav awake. 'Please, wake up.'

'Let me sleep,' he mumbled, trying to bash away her hands.

'Come on, Gustav,' she shouted as loudly as she could.

Finally he woke up. 'What is it?' he said, with one eye open.

'Look what someone sent me,' she said, pushing the phone under his nose.

'Fuck,' he shouted, sitting up. 'Eww.'

'Frank Buhl warned me this might happen.'

Gustav pushed the phone away. 'Delete them,' he said. 'Block the number.'

'No,' said Jensen, trying to slow her breathing. 'We need to show them to Henrik. Perhaps the police can use them to find out who's behind all this.'

She texted him.

> *Something's happened. Call me as soon as you get this.*

While she waited for him to reply, Gustav got out of bed, scratching his hair.

She had lost her appetite, but Gustav launched himself

at the bread rolls, twisting open the chocolate milk and drinking thirstily straight from the bottle.

Palle had her number but, as he was still in custody, it couldn't have been him who had sent the images.

Didn't mean he had nothing to do with it.

There was no reply from Henrik, but then he would be in the middle of trying to rescue Matilde.

'Look,' said Gustav, mouth full of food. He held up his mobile phone showing *Dagbladet*'s front page. 'The bearded clown has done it again.'

'What?' said Jensen, feeling lightheaded and sweaty. 'Is it about Matilde? Has he got something?'

'Nope,' said Gustav. 'Just more interviews with child gang members.'

He turned up the sound and played a clip with people who had been burgled, talking about how violated they felt.

'These gangs, some with members as young as eight years old, represent a new low for Danish society,' said a child psychologist.

The story had pushed Matilde way down the page again.

An article written by one of Jensen's colleagues talked about the anguish of Matilde's parents.

She scrolled down the page to the coverage of Bodil's murder. 'They found the spanner in the lake, just as we thought,' she said.

'Hang on,' said Gustav.

She looked at him, still shaking, though her breathing had almost returned to normal.

Would they be coming for her?

Gustav was frowning at Google Me's latest video creation. 'I recognise some of these clips,' he said. 'Those kids, they're not talking about being in gangs; they're talking about bullying.'

357

Jensen frowned. 'What do you mean?'

'He faked the voice distortion, recorded the words himself and passed it off as coming from the kids. He must have done the same with the first video.'

'How do you know?' said Jensen.

'Because, believe me, I've done nothing but watch YouTube for four months. I think I watched the entire internet.' He jumped up. 'Those kids aren't even Danish, I swear to God.'

'You need to tell Margrethe immediately.'

'She won't listen to me.'

'She will if you can provide evidence. Margrethe likes nothing like she likes facts.'

Jensen checked her watch.

Henning's funeral was a couple of hours away. She had nothing suitable to wear that she could still fit into, except for a dark-blue summer dress. She would need to wear tracksuit bottoms underneath to stay warm.

It would have to do.

'Do you have anything smart to wear?' she said to Gustav.

'Why?' he said, still looking at his phone.

'It's Henning's funeral this morning. I think we should both go.'

'OK, but you can forget the smart clothes. I don't have any, and it's not like Henning's going to mind.' He looked up. 'Do you think Fie is OK?'

'She seemed to be,' said Jensen.

More than OK, she thought.

Perhaps she had finally found her vocation.

67

For the second time in a week, Henrik had his hopes up that a breakthrough was imminent.

And for the second time in a week, he told himself to manage his expectations.

It had taken longer than he wanted to assemble the rapid entry team and prepare the operation to free Matilde.

If she was there.

What if they were completely wrong about that?

He was waiting in the car with Bagger, parked outside an inconspicuous-looking storage building.

Mark and Lotte were parked behind them.

'How did you find this?' he said.

'We were looking for premises that have been standing empty for a while, but to be honest, that girl your journalist friend brought in . . .'

'She's not my friend,' said Henrik. 'She's *Dagbladet*'s chief crime reporter.'

Neither was a lie, he thought to himself. Just not the whole truth.

Bagger held up his hand defensively. 'Acquaintance then,' he said. 'Anyway, that girl.'

'Fie,' said Henrik.

'Yes, Fie; she works so fast I'm not exactly sure how she did it. But it was her who found this. My instinct says she's right.'

Henrik nodded.

Instinct.

Sometimes, even most of the time, it was all you had to rely on.

'Imagine if this was where Lea was kept all along, while we were looking for her by the coast and in the water,' he said.

'I've thought about that,' said Bagger. 'But we didn't know then what we know now. No video of Lea, for a start.'

Henrik turned in the car seat to face Bagger. 'Yes, and that really bothers me,' said Henrik. 'Six years ago, and the picture is only surfacing now?'

'I've seen that sort of thing happen before,' said Bagger. 'There's so much stuff out there that never gets caught in the net.'

'I think there's more to it,' said Henrik. 'It feels like we're being played with. Like none of this is a coincidence.'

He looked at his phone, noticing a message from Jensen, asking him to call her. It seemed urgent. What was she up to now?

She would have to wait.

The operation had started.

He and Bagger watched as the uniformed officers in full protective gear approached the building, signalling to each other, then disappearing inside in a burst of noise.

Henrik began to count. After eighty-four seconds, his radio burst into life. 'All clear,' said the team leader.

'What?' Henrik said. 'There's nothing?'

'I don't know. Could you come in here for a moment?'

Henrik and Bagger got out of the car and sprinted for the entrance.

They ran through the dark building. It stank of rot, and Henrik almost tripped over a barrel knocked on its side.

There was mess everywhere, years' worth of rat droppings and dust.

They found the team leader in a windowless room in the heart of the building.

A clean room.

Strangely clean.

Four black-painted walls.

Entirely empty.

'This is it, I know it,' said Henrik. 'This is where they kept her.' He addressed himself to Bagger. 'We need CCTV from all around the area.'

He thought of the black Audi. They had painstakingly tracked it half of the way to the airport, but the trail had gone cold somewhere west of Dragør.

They could easily have swapped cars somewhere, he thought. They needed to look for any vehicle approaching the storage building in the past two weeks. They would need to get an army of people on it.

Why had Matilde been moved?

There was only one answer. 'They knew we were coming,' he said.

'Looks that way,' said Bagger, hands at his waist. 'But how?'

They had kept it out of the press, included only the necessary people in the operation.

What would he say to Matilde's parents?

That his intuition told him their daughter was still alive?

That she was in grave danger, and he didn't know where to turn next?

Mark and Lotte had entered the room, her blonde pony-tail lighting up the darkness like a beacon. 'Looks like a stage,' she said, shuddering.

Henrik's thoughts had run in the same direction. He felt ill.

'Get the forensic guys out here,' he said to Mark. 'I want every inch of this room going over.'

As he and Bagger headed for the car, he got out his phone and pressed Jensen's number.

68

If Henning Würtzen had been invisible towards the end of his life, in death he was everyone's friend. Arriving late for the service in Skovshoved Kirke in Klampenborg, Jensen and Gustav had found all the pews taken and been forced to stand at the back.

Jensen had been unsettled on the short ride from the S-train station, through the quietly affluent residential streets with Christmas trees in the front gardens.

Were they being followed? She had left her phone in Margrethe's flat in case they were using that to trace her somehow but felt naked without it.

Whenever a car came too close, she had wobbled on her bicycle, at one point almost colliding with the kerb and coming off.

She kept thinking of Brøgger's warning that she wasn't just looking after herself now.

If they hurt her, they would hurt her baby too.

Like they might hurt Matilde.

Henrik and his team had discovered where they thought Matilde had been held for a while. This meant that the net was closing in; the Ugly Duckling would be getting desperate.

Henrik had immediately leapt to DEFCON 1 when she had told him about the images she had received. 'Don't delete anything, don't touch or use your phone. Switch it off. And stay in Margrethe's flat and double lock the doors.'

'I can't. I'm going to a funeral.'

'One day soon it'll be your own,' he had said. 'You saw what happened to your friend Bodil. Do you want to end up the same way?'

'Gustav is with me,' she had told him. 'We'll be careful.'

'Why doesn't that reassure me?'

Now it felt like she should have heeded his advice after all. She felt exposed, at a disadvantage to those who were after her.

They knew who *she* was.

She had passed the number of her anonymous correspondent to Henrik, but his team hadn't been able to trace it.

Now, as she watched the pallbearers carry Henning's coffin down the aisle, she wondered if she was even safe among the mourners. She recognised a couple of editors from Denmark's other broadsheets, and an ageing TV news anchor, but most were strangers to her.

Her former colleagues from *Dagbladet* had been stretching their necks to stare at her and Gustav through the service.

Google Me had turned and looked at them once, his eyes widening in surprise. Jensen had sent death stares at the back of his head.

Margrethe got up from the front pew and followed the coffin out, dressed in a sombre black coat. Google Me followed, a supportive arm behind her back. Gustav turned to Jensen, doing an impression of someone being violently sick.

In her eulogy, Margrethe had said that Henning's approach to journalism could be summed up in three little words: tell the truth. 'Henning never stopped looking for the truth. He was unafraid of it, knew its value,' she had said. 'It's a perpetual disappointment to me how many others don't.' Margrethe had looked up then, letting her eyes roam over the congregation, and it had felt to Jensen as if her words had been aimed at her and Gustav directly.

That morning, *Dagbladet* had printed the obituary Henning had written about himself: a dry-witted, self-effacing account of upwards of seven decades in Danish journalism – some of the best years, and the worst.

'You really need to speak to Margrethe,' Jensen whispered to Gustav as they followed everyone out. 'Tell her that she's got Google Me all wrong. If anyone is dishonest, it's him.'

Gustav shook his head. 'No,' he said. 'I sent her an email this morning. No message, just the evidence that he's a total fraud. The rest is up to her.'

There was a look of grim determination on his face; it reminded her of Margrethe.

Outside, people had assembled around the coffin as it was being loaded onto the hearse. Roses and lilies, in the colours of the Danish flag, next to a copy of the newspaper to which Henning had dedicated his life.

'Can we go now?' said Gustav.

He looked tired, dark rings around his eyes, his face pasty pale. It was as if, in Margrethe's presence, all the air had gone out of him, turning him back into a young boy.

Jensen shuddered in her thin summer dress, topped by

her inadequate coat, and steeled herself for the journey back to town.

What was she going to do now?

The sensible thing would be to go home and wait.

69

'But at least we've got our man,' said Monsen. 'Palle Dybdal had the means and the inclination to abduct Matilde.'

Henrik had been called in to give Monsen a comprehensive briefing.

Having turned over the evidence collected in the past week, his unease had grown. It seemed an extraordinary mess, a collection of odds and ends, but nothing conclusive.

No Matilde.

And time was running out.

'He's still denying everything.'

'His prints were on the iPad.'

'He says he lost the iPad and hasn't seen it in months. Is adamant that someone planted the child sexual-abuse material on it.'

This was entirely possible, Henrik thought, given what had just happened to Jensen.

He didn't like that she'd gone to the funeral despite his warning.

'Of course he is,' Monsen said.

'He denies dressing up in Bodil's clothes and abducting Matilde in the shopping trolley.'

'Yeah, sure.'

'He says his prints were on the trolley because he often helped Bodil with her shopping.'

'The man has a clever answer for everything.'

But is stupid enough to leave Matilde's glove in his workshop, thought Henrik.

'He also denies any knowledge of Playland, though we can see from his iPad that he's used the Tor browser.'

'Tor?' asked Monsen.

'Stands for The Onion Router. Tor lets users browse the web while staying anonymous. That's the whole point of it.'

'And you're sure Dybdal is not this Ugly Duckling administrator fellow?'

'Not unless he has accomplices, which is not impossible. As he's in custody, it can't be him our freelance web expert spoke to last night.'

'Ah yes, the web expert. Remind me who she is again?'

'Fie Pedersen. She's a friend of *Dagbladet*'s chief crime reporter, a hacker. She was in our sights a few years ago. No offences since, or none that we know of anyway. Bagger reckons she's an extraordinary talent. I think he wants to hire her.'

'We'll see about that,' Monsen said grumpily. 'And the Ugly Duckling has asked for money?'

'Yes. We're trying to keep the contact warm, to ask for more time.'

'While we look into who's behind it all. Yes, I see.'

'Trouble is, not even Fie Pedersen can uncover the real-life identity of the Ugly Duckling. He's hiding behind all sorts of layers of security.'

'And Matilde was held here in Copenhagen, right under our noses?'

'We think so, yes, or at least until recently. She might be outside of Denmark now. We're still collecting CCTV from the area.'

The fact that Matilde had been moved suggested that the Ugly Duckling knew they were onto him. Why hadn't he simply closed the paedophile ring down and cancelled the live show?

Perhaps there was too much at stake to stop now. Money flowing in from all over the globe. Money that would only be released to him once the show had been delivered as promised.

'Our best chance is getting Dybdal to tell us more,' said Henrik. 'I'm going to have another go at it after this. Though it's possible that his job was merely to hand Matilde over.'

There was a canyon-deep frown on Monsen's forehead.

'Still no sign of Wiese?' Henrik said.

'No,' said Monsen. 'Did anything happen while I was away, something that could have caused this?'

'Nothing that sticks in my mind,' said Henrik.

'His wife's flying home today,' said Monsen. 'She doesn't seem to think he's been depressed lately, but then she hasn't spoken to him properly in a while.'

'From what I hear, they're living separate lives,' said Henrik.

'Some people,' said Monsen. 'Why stay married at all, if that's your attitude?'

Henrik could think of a few good reasons, children for example, but he didn't want the conversation to turn onto his own failing marriage.

It was awkward enough having had to refer to Jensen in his conversation with Monsen.

Dagbladet's chief crime reporter.

As if he didn't know her better than he knew himself.

'We've got the intelligence guys involved now. In case Wiese has been the victim of some sort of targeted assault to do with his position,' said Monsen. 'And you're sure he didn't say anything odd to you in the past few days?'

Henrik shrugged. 'Wiese has never been my biggest fan. He'd rather I'd been found responsible for the ... incident in the summer. That way he would have got rid of me for good.'

Monsen said nothing, which Henrik took to mean that he was spot on. 'He wasn't keen on me linking the Matilde and Lea cases, but we now know for sure that there's a link,' he said.

'The paedophile ring,' said Monsen.

'Yes.'

Wiese had also thought Playland was a distraction during the investigation into Lea's disappearance six years ago.

He had thought it more likely that Lea had been abducted by a complete stranger. His reluctance had cost them valuable time.

Not that it had mattered in the end, as Playland had stopped operating almost immediately after Loft's arrest.

Henrik had always wondered why. The arrest hadn't been made public at first as his team had wanted to access the paedophile ring using Loft's profile.

Perhaps Loft had been telling the truth when he explained to Jensen that he thought he was being followed in real life.

It was the only possible explanation he could think of. Someone had watched Loft closely enough to know that the police were onto him.

'How much time did you say we have until this thing with Matilde happens?' said Monsen.

'Under twelve hours,' said Henrik.

It wasn't time enough.

Not by any stretch of the imagination.

70

Jensen had seen Gustav off the S-train at Østerport Station.
Fie had messaged him to say that she was being driven back
to Margrethe's flat for a rest, and Gustav had agreed to meet
her there. They were going to have some food, then try to
catch a few hours' sleep.

Jensen didn't feel like sleeping. Henning's funeral had
left her uneasy. She wanted to think, to breathe in the cold
winter air, to stay awake.

Getting off at Nørreport, she pushed her bike through
Ørstedsparken, looking intently at the few people she met.
They hurried past her, heads bent against the wind. No one
was sitting on the benches.

Passing through the walled park entrance at
Gyldenløvesgade, she turned right, crossing the Lakes and
walking down Peblinge Dossering to the yellow apartment
block she would always think of as Bodil's.

Had the police taken away Wolfgang the cat? Had they
fed him? Perhaps they didn't even know he existed.

She still had Palle's keyring in her pocket. He wasn't

around to tell her off for using it, or to creep up on her in that disturbing way of his.

Making sure no one was watching, she locked her bicycle to the white picket fence and walked quickly up the garden path, looking over her shoulder.

As the old lift clanged through the floors, she looked at her face in the mirror. Her hair was wet, her eyes huge and dark.

Now the sensation was back, deep in her abdomen, as if the muscles in her belly were tightening of their own accord.

The thought of going into labour, being subjected to an unstoppable force beyond her control, made her feel desperate.

She wasn't ready.

Nowhere near.

As she stepped out of the lift on the fourth floor, she saw a note on Bodil's front door, warning against unauthorised entry. She unlocked the door and stepped carefully over the crime-scene police tape.

It was a little over a week ago that she had first come here. Now, Bodil was dead, Jan Loft had been killed, and she was homeless and on enforced maternity leave.

She hadn't had a chance yet to tell her mother that she was about to move back in.

Traces of the police forensic team were everywhere in the flat: dust on the surfaces where prints had been collected, little signs with numbers left everywhere for the photographs, a pair of latex gloves and a facemask forgotten on an occasional table.

A bell tingled, sending her heart racing.

Wolfgang.

The cat looked at her with his strange pale-blue eyes,

then decided that she could be trusted and rubbed himself against her leg.

She found a tin of cat food in the kitchen, filled his bowl and replenished his water.

Perhaps she could bring Wolfgang along with her to Jutland, she thought, as she watched him eat. Her mother's cottage was full of mice. You could hear them in the night, running behind the skirting and under the floorboards.

There were still plenty of butter cookies left in the tin from La Glace. She ate them one by one, washing them down with a glass of water from the tap.

Bodil's bedroom was warm and smelled of her perfume. It was as though she had just left it, as though any minute now she would be calling from the living room.

Resisting the temptation to lie down on the pink silk bedspread for a nap, Jensen went up to the window, taking care to stay hidden behind the curtain as she looked down into the courtyard.

A flowerpot had been knocked over by the wind, leaving a trail of soil by the picnic table. The bicycles were rattling in the shed.

The lights were on in Katja and Thomas's flat; it looked cosy and warm inside. The couple would be busy preparing for the arrival of their second child. Above them, Palle's flat was dark, the curtains open.

She frowned.

Strange.

There were three windows facing the courtyard in Palle's flat, and the flats above his, but only two in Katja and Thomas's.

A builder, he must have refurbished the flat at some point, changing the layout, or perhaps it was just smaller than Palle's.

She and Gustav had never been in there. Everyone else had invited them in, but both times they had tried to visit Katja and Thomas, he had stood in the doorway behind the security chain, like a human boulder.

None shall pass.

He had behaved strangely with them. Not saying much, letting Katja speak for them both. It had felt like he was worried about something.

Had the police checked his alibi for the night Bodil saw the man assaulting the woman in the courtyard? Katja had been at work, so he had been alone in the flat with his daughter.

Had he been cheating on his pregnant wife? He could easily have had someone over while Katja was doing the night shift. Perhaps he had argued with his girlfriend, and she had run out of the flat and down Wesselsgade, but he had caught her, pulled her back and tried to strangle her.

She could see Katja and Thomas moving behind their windows.

Bodil kept binoculars on the windowsill in her living room. 'For the birds,' she had said. 'They belonged to my father.'

No one knew Jensen was there; it couldn't hurt to have a look.

Katja was sitting by the dining table, a laptop in front of her. Thomas was pacing up and down the floor behind her. He was wearing his coat and hat. There was no sign of their daughter.

It looked like the couple were arguing, Katja trying to reason with Thomas, gesticulating with her hands as she looked up at him with her back to the window.

Thomas stopped, pulled at his hair.

What were the couple arguing about? Something trivial,

like whose turn it was to take out the rubbish? Or something more serious? The girlfriend maybe?

Katja looked out of the window, and Jensen stepped further back behind the curtain.

Thomas was a big man, strong. Suddenly, he raised his hand and drew it back as if about to hit Katja. Jensen couldn't see Katja's face, but she must have pleaded with him, because Thomas stopped himself at the last moment.

She remembered Thomas's hands and the scratches on Katja's face, covered with make-up, that she claimed had been made by her daughter.

Her silent, frightened-looking daughter.

What if it had been Thomas all along?

Him Bodil had seen that night?

Him who had dressed up as her and abducted Matilde in the red shopping trolley?

Him who had walked Bodil to Saint Jørgen's Lake and killed her?

He was bending down now, shouting at Katja, who was doing her best to ignore him.

Jensen felt in the pocket for her phone, then remembered that she had left it at home.

Bodil had a phone. She went into the hall and looked at it. She didn't have Henrik's number in her head, or Gustav's. Bodil also had a laptop, but what was the password?

She could dial 112, report a domestic, but nothing had actually *happened*. It was just her intuition telling her that something was wrong, very wrong.

In the end, she called anyway, begged the man on the other end of the line to get a message through to Detective Inspector Henrik Jungersen. It took ages to get him to take down the address. 'Tell Jungersen to come as soon as he gets this.'

Anything could have happened to Katja by now, a defenceless pregnant woman. She hung up, ran down the stairs, no time to wait for the lift.

She could hear Thomas and Katja shouting. 'No,' Katja kept saying. 'No.'

She rang the doorbell, smiling at the spyhole, as if she didn't know what was going on inside the flat, as if she were just passing and dropping in on the off-chance.

The flat fell silent, the door was pulled wide open. No security chain. On the other side was Katja, and behind her Thomas.

'Hello, Jensen,' said Katja, smiling. 'What are *you* doing here?'

'I just . . . I was feeding Bodil's cat, so I thought I'd drop in, see how you're doing.'

'Come in, come in,' said Katja, pulling her inside and closing the door behind her.

Katja seemed fine. It was Thomas who was looking worried and upset.

There was something strange about Katja that Jensen couldn't immediately put a finger on.

Then she realised. The woman's heavily pregnant belly was gone. She opened her mouth. 'What . . .?'

The blinding pain came out of nowhere, a shadow swinging through the air.

Then darkness.

71

Henrik looked at his phone. He hadn't heard from Jensen in a while. She should be home from the funeral by now. His calls were going straight to voicemail. Then he remembered that he had asked her to switch her phone off.

He couldn't help worrying about her. She had done stupid things before.

Plenty of stupid things.

He was scrolling through his phone for Gustav Skov's number when Mark burst into his room. 'A white Ford transit van was caught on camera, leaving a car park adjacent to the storage building in Dragør last night,' he said.

'Got the number plates?' said Henrik.

Mark nodded. 'Yes. False again, but at least now we know what we're looking for. Should be faster to track them down.'

'Good work,' said Henrik, looking at his watch. 'Tell the team they need to work twice as fast. At most, we've less than nine hours left to find Matilde.'

Like most cities in the world, Copenhagen was awash

with white vans. And Matilde could be in Sweden by now, or halfway to Germany.

Matilde's mother Stine was in the family room, reunited with Simon. He was back in her good books, or at least tolerated for now.

Thankfully, he had stopped spouting his theories about Rasmus Nordby, who was still co-operating fully with the police enquiries.

Both men would receive their punishment for their poor life decisions. All in good time.

Updating Stine Clausen hadn't been easy. 'We think your daughter's abduction is linked to a paedophile ring run out of Denmark. She may not be its first victim. We believe Matilde was held right here in Copenhagen until just a few hours ago, and that her captors are preparing her for some sort of live-streamed performance tonight.'

Stine had screamed so hard that she had fainted. They had been forced to call in a medic to attend to her, and she was now sedated to a point of incoherence.

He ought to get some rest himself. To eat something.

No chance.

He was almost getting used to the feeling of the ground gently swaying beneath him as though he was on a boat, the sharp pain behind his eyes whenever he needed to read anything or look at someone's face.

He pressed his wife's number. 'Hello stranger,' she said. 'Everything OK?'

'Yes.'

'Only, you don't normally call me at work. I'm lucky if I get a text.'

'I know. It's just . . .'

'Yes?' she said. Then, 'Why are you being weird, Henrik? You were weird the other day too. What's going on?'

'I just . . . were the kids OK this morning?'

'That's why you're calling?'

'Please,' he said, his voice coming out strangled. He felt something rising in his throat, a sudden stinging inside his eyelids.

He swallowed, shook his head of the feeling.

If Matilde is found safe and well, I'll never cheat again. I'll be a decent husband, a decent father, and never ask for anything ever, he thought, bargaining with a God he didn't believe in.

'Did you take them to school?'

'I took Oliver because his tyre's still flat,' she said. 'Mikkel and Karla cycled. I don't have time for this, Henrik.'

'And you definitely saw Oliver go in through the school gate?'

'Yes!' she snapped.

He didn't reply.

'Look,' she said, her tone softened. 'I can understand why you're anxious, given what's going on with that girl, but we're fine, all of us. I'm in the middle of preparing for parents' evening. It's a bloody nightmare to organise. Why don't you just . . . focus on your work.'

'Sorry,' Henrik mumbled.

He didn't just mean to apologise for asking her about their children.

He meant for everything he had ever done to wrong her.

A lot there to pick from.

'I don't know when I'll be back tonight,' he said. 'Or if I'll be back.'

'So, what else is new?' she said and hung up.

He had begun scrolling for Gustav Skov's number again when he saw a call coming through from Monsen.

Not now, he thought. It was only an hour since they had last spoken.

But Monsen was persistent.

'No news,' Henrik said, finally picking up. 'Except we think they're now using a white transit van. Mark is—'

'That's not why I'm calling,' said Monsen. He sounded odd, not his usual bombastic self. 'Are you sitting down?'

'What?' he said. 'Tell me.'

'It's Wiese. His wife is back from the US. Found the poor man dead in the garden shed. He'd taken pills.'

Henrik's hands flew up to his mouth. 'I can't believe it. Wiese was always so ... sure of himself, so ...'

'Cocky?' said Monsen. 'Yes, just goes to show that you never know people, not really.'

'There must have been a reason,' Henrik said. 'Money troubles?'

'His wife's one of the country's top earners. Not likely.'

'What then? Was he ill, depressed, suffering from burnout?'

'His wife says not. We'll get to the bottom of it soon enough, but I wanted you to know as soon as. There'll be a message going out to staff tomorrow. The timing is not ideal ... not in the middle of this dreadful business with Matilde Clausen.'

Monsen ended the call.

Henrik stared at his phone, feeling numb. When a call came through from the switchboard he declined it and turned his face to the window. It was almost completely dark.

72

Jensen woke up, blinking. She waited for her eyes to get used to the black.

They didn't.

The darkness was total.

There was a sharp pain at her temple. It felt swollen; her fingers came away wet. She licked the side of her mouth and tasted blood.

Her hands went to her bump. She could feel the baby moving, but also that strange, deep pull inside of her, downwards and outwards.

She rose to her hands and knees, waited for the nausea and dizziness to pass. Then panic seized her. She screamed.

Eventually her hands collided with a wall. It was soft and spongy like fabric. She hammered on it, leaned her face into it and cried out at the top of her voice in fear and rage. 'Let me out. Let me out!'

She stopped and turned towards a sound she had heard.

A groan, a sigh, something.

She became conscious of a strong smell. Urine, sweat, faeces, blood.

'Hello?' she shouted, frantically. 'Is there anyone in here?'

More groaning, louder.

Could it be Matilde?

'Wait,' she said. 'I'm coming.'

Feeling her way, she walked the length of one wall, no more than three yards or so. On the next wall, after two steps her shin collided with something sharp, sending a searing pain up her leg. She ignored it and inched forwards until she came up against the sharp edge again. A raised bunk.

There was something. A bony leg. On the ankle there was a hard metal cuff with a chain attached. She followed it to the wall.

'Matilde?' she whispered into the dark. 'Is that you?'

No reply. Jensen ran her hand up the leg and further up past the hip. A girl, but not a child.

She withdrew her hand. There was a large bump there, naked skin stretched, belly button protruding. The bump was moving.

It was a movement she recognised.

She found the girl's face. Her hair was ragged and short, her breath fast under the tape that was fixed across her mouth.

Jensen pulled the tape off.

The girl said something inaudible.

'What?' said Jensen, leaning closer.

'They can't hear you,' said the girl. Her voice was weak. She seemed to be in pain, her breath fast and laboured.

'They who?' Jensen said.

'The man and the woman.'

'Katja and Thomas?'

'I don't know their names.'

'Did the man do this to you?'

'Yes, but the woman is the worst ... she ... she ...' The girl trailed off.

'I'm here to help you. Everything will be OK now.'

'It won't,' said the girl. Her crying morphed into a low, straining growl.

'Is it the baby?'

'Yes,' said the girl, breathing fast. 'It's coming. Like before.'

'You gave birth before?'

'Yes, twice. One of them lived, but they took it away, like they'll take this one. They're going to kill me when it comes,' said the girl. 'And they'll kill you.'

'Shh ...'

'They left the door open. Just once. I tried to escape. I made it as far as the street, but he caught me. I couldn't scream because of the tape over my mouth. I thought someone would have seen it and called the police, but nothing happened.

Someone did see it, thought Jensen. *But no one believed her.*

'It'll be OK,' she repeated.

The girl began to cry again.

Jensen thought of the message she had left for Henrik with the person who answered her 112 call. It seemed impossible now that it would ever find its way to him or that he would know what to make of it.

And even if he did, she wasn't even sure that she was still in Thomas and Katja's flat.

Thomas was muscular and tall. He could easily have carried her to a car and driven her somewhere. She might have been out for hours.

Katja and Thomas were in it together. They had broken into Bodil's flat, stolen her clothes and the red shopping trolley. It must have been Katja who had dressed up as Bodil and spent weeks befriending Matilde in Ørstedsparken, persuading her to hide in the trolley, then pushing her the short distance to the waiting car, driven by Thomas.

Where they were hiding Matilde now was anyone's guess.

'What's your name?' she asked the girl. But she already knew the answer.

'I'm Lea.'

73

Henrik had stepped out to splash water on his face. Bagger and his team were still tracking the white van, but piecing together its progress on CCTV was painfully slow and, in any case, left them several steps behind the perpetrators, who could easily have swapped cars again.

Bagger had gone to collect Fie Pedersen and bring her back to the office to see what she could do. He seemed convinced she might be able to pull off some sort of magic.

Henrik wasn't so sure.

He was still shaken by Monsen's news. Wiese had never exactly been a pal but still, the man was a colleague. He kept thinking back to their last conversation, wondering if he had missed some vital clue, but Wiese had been his usual sneering self, not behaving like a man who felt all was lost.

He glanced at his phone. There was a voicemail from the switchboard, and Gustav Skov had called.

His thoughts immediately went to Jensen. 'What's wrong?' he said, calling back.

'Have you spoken to Jensen?' said Gustav.

Henrik felt cold all over. 'Why?'

'She hasn't come home yet.'

'From the funeral? But that was hours ago.'

Henrik checked his watch. It was after eight o'clock. They had less than four hours left to find Matilde before the start of the live-streamed show touted by Playland.

'She said she needed some air afterwards.'

'And you let her go?' he shouted.

'I had to get home. You guys were dropping Fie off. We fell asleep. I've only just woken up,' said Gustav. 'What shall I do? She hasn't got her phone with her.'

'Fuck,' said Henrik, slamming his hands on the edge of the sink.

He remembered the voicemail from the switchboard. Could it have been Jensen? 'I'll call you back,' he said, cutting the phone dead over Gustav's protests.

He listened to the message. 'Journalist called Jensen called 112, asking them to get hold of you. They thought it was a prank, but she sounded desperate. Apparently, a guy named Thomas Jespersen is acting suspiciously. No idea what that means, but there's an address, and you're to go there immediately.'

Thomas and Katja's flat.

Behind the block at Peblinge Dossering.

Henrik ran. 'I can't stop,' he shouted to Bagger and Mark as he passed the door of the meeting room. 'I'll explain later.'

He rang Gustav from the car. 'It's Thomas Jespersen. Jensen's there. Or she was, hours ago.'

'What?' said Gustav.

'It must have been him all along. He took Matilde, and now he's got Jensen.'

The Christmas stars suspended above the roadway were swinging in the wind. There weren't many people out, little traffic, but still he caught all the red lights.

Thomas Jespersen had an alibi for the day that Lea disappeared, but he could have got someone else to do his dirty work.

He turned the sirens on, pressed the accelerator and blasted across the intersection.

In Wesselsgade, he dumped the car in the middle of the road.

The lights were on in Katja and Thomas Jespersen's flat and the door to the red building was ajar. He ran inside, almost colliding with Gustav coming from the direction of the courtyard.

'Her bike's still outside, chained to the fence,' Gustav shouted.

They ran up the short flight of stairs to the first floor, and Henrik began to pummel the door. 'Police,' he shouted. 'Open up.'

Where were the reinforcements? He could hear the sirens now, getting closer, but not close enough. He put his shoulder to the door, one, two, three times.

'Move,' Gustav said. 'I can open it.' He got out a tool and set to work on the lock.

So that was how the boy had got hold of Dybdal's keys.

He would have to deal with him later.

The lock finally gave. 'Police, make yourself known,' Henrik shouted. He pulled out his gun, keeping Gustav behind him.

In the living room, a large bookshelf was pushed to one side, revealing a door. Inside, a room without windows, a bunk with soiled bedding.

'Fuck,' said Gustav. 'What's that smell?'

There was something on the floor, catching the light. It was a tiny gold stud.

Jensen's earring.

She must have left it on purpose.

God, please, no.

In a boxroom, sparsely furnished, they found an empty cot. In the master bedroom, the cupboards had been flung open, clothes and hangers ripped out and tossed onto the floor.

'What the hell is this?' said Gustav, holding up a soft, flesh-coloured item, like a wide elastic band with a bump on one side.

A bump with a bellybutton.

In slow motion, like frames of a film, it came to Henrik. Katja.

A pregnant nurse with a young child, she had made the unlikeliest of suspects: helpful with their enquiries, steering them exactly where she had wanted to.

She had known about the glove they had found in Palle's lockup because she had put it there herself, or told her husband to do so. As a biddable man of low intelligence, he wouldn't have argued.

He rang Mark. 'Do you have your laptop?'

'Yes, but what—'

'Don't ask questions, just do as I say. Look up the Lea Høgh case, find Katja Jespersen.'

Come on, come on, come on.

'I've got her,' said Mark. 'Married to Thomas, formerly Kim, the guy who testified against Loft.'

'Was her alibi ever checked? For the day that Lea disappeared?'

'I can't see any reference anywhere to that. Wait . . . that's odd, I thought she was expecting a baby, but it says here the couple weren't able to have children.'

'Shit,' said Henrik, staring at Gustav in horror. 'It's Katja.'

'Ah, here it is,' said Mark. 'No, she was never a suspect as far as I can tell. But why are you—'

'She's the Ugly Duckling!' Henrik shouted.

74

The van had finally stopped. Jensen was awake. She had woken up once before, when the van was still moving, and remembered hammering on the door, before something was injected into her arm.

This time, she was staying quiet and still, despite the twinges in her abdomen, sharper now and more insistent.

She wondered why she was still alive. Did they think she might come in useful if it came to bargaining with the police later?

Or had they not had time to kill her?

The doors to the van were open, cold air streaming in.

Out of the corner of her eye, she could just make out Katja, backlit by some kind of projector or security lamp.

Lea was screaming out in pain as Katja bent over her, ready to receive another child that she would be passing off as her own.

A genuine desire to have children, or a wicked scheme to create the victims of future abuse? Perhaps Katja was no longer capable of telling the difference.

Jensen couldn't see Thomas. Behind Katja, there was

some kind of building with a wide, pitched roof. That was where the light was coming from.

She couldn't hear any other sounds. No roads, no cars, no people. The air smelled of manure. It was just her and Lea lying in the back of the van. No sign of Matilde, and the little girl – Lea's daughter – was nowhere to be seen.

Jensen couldn't remember getting into the van. Her last memory was of the door to the dark room in the flat opening as she was talking to Lea, trying to reassure her, saying that everything would be all right. Though she didn't really believe it.

How could everything ever be all right again?

Even if Henrik had received her message, it would be too late now. No one knew where they were.

Katja and Thomas must have had a camera installed in the dark room. They had entered quickly and violently, and Jensen had felt herself sink back into sleep. Presumably, they had given her some kind of sedative.

There was a final, terrifying scream as Lea pushed her baby out in a rush of liquid. Katja wrapped it in a towel, then stepped out of sight. The baby cried faintly.

When the afterbirth came, Katja bent over it, and Jensen heard the cord being cut. Lea had fallen silent. Had she fainted?

Katja didn't seem troubled by that.

'Kill them,' she said over her shoulder. 'Use the knife.'

Thomas came into view. Jensen could no longer pretend to be asleep. 'Don't, Thomas,' she pleaded, her voice slurred. 'You'll never get away with it. Stop it now, stop the running, give yourself up.'

'Shut up,' Katja shouted. 'Do it, Thomas. Now.'

He stood still, hesitating.

Jensen looked around the van for a weapon, anything,

but the floor was empty. She had nothing. Her movements were sluggish, no strength in her arms.

'No,' Thomas said, quietly, his broad shoulders blocking out the light.

'What?' Katja was busy rubbing the baby's chest. 'Quickly,' she said, looking at her watch. 'We've got to get inside, get everything ready. There's just one more hour left.'

'No,' he said more firmly. 'You got what you wanted. We've enough money. We can leave, drive to Germany, like we talked about. Start again. You, me and the children.'

'Yes,' she said. 'Afterwards.'

Still Thomas didn't move.

'Do it, you spineless bastard,' she hissed at him, coming closer.

There was something in her hand. A syringe?

'No,' he said again. 'You promised we were going to stop.'

'Look out, Thomas,' Jensen shouted as Katja's hand moved towards him.

He reached for his neck, fell to his knees, then keeled over.

Jensen braced herself, as Katja crawled into the van, pushing Lea aside, hand lifted, baby screaming.

Using the last of her strength, Jensen kicked, feeling pain ripping through her belly, strong enough to make her cry out.

Katja fell to one side. A few more seconds and she was back on her knees, scrabbling towards Jensen.

She closed her eyes, hoping it would be quick.

She thought of how Henrik would mourn her.

She thought of the baby she hadn't wanted and now wouldn't get a chance to know.

There was a wet sound, a grunt, and then a heavy weight fell on top of her, knocking the air out of her lungs.

Before she fainted, over the shoulder of Katja, in the fading light, Jensen could just make out Lea.

Naked.

Bloodied.

Knife held aloft.

February

75

Henrik had felt it coming all the way across the Great Belt Bridge, had known as soon as he had opened his eyes that morning.

It was the first sunny day of the year, and everything was different.

He hadn't planned to drive this far, had meant to drive straight to the office for the morning briefing where Monsen was going to announce Wiese's successor as department head.

He wasn't excited to find out who his new boss was; they couldn't possibly be any worse than Wiese.

He felt no sense of triumph, no schadenfreude, only revulsion that Wiese – for so long his adversary – had been exposed as a years-long user of Playland, blackmailed by the Ugly Duckling into steering investigations in the wrong direction.

Henrik suspected his colleagues were struggling with it too. No one so much as mentioned Wiese's name now.

He had been offered Wiese's job himself but turned it down, to Monsen's great consternation. 'I thought you'd be pleased,' he had said. 'It's the opportunity you need to move on up the chain. Who knows, maybe when I retire, you'll be ready for the next step.'

'I'm fine as I am,' Henrik had said. 'Not everyone needs to progress.'

He knew that the next step up from detective inspector meant more paperwork and tiresome employee conversations, not to mention endless meetings. There would be less investigative work, more time spent sedentary in the office.

'There is *something* I want, though,' he had told Monsen. 'I want Maja Olsen on my team.'

Monsen had resisted, complaining that Olsen didn't have enough experience.

'But she makes up for it in common sense. Never enough of that to go around,' Henrik had argued.

In the end he had got his way. Monsen was feeling guilty about failing to see through Wiese, placing the two of them in a honeymoon period where Henrik could get anything he wanted.

In a few weeks, Olsen would transfer out of uniform and join them at Teglholmen. She would make a good team with Mark.

Instead of taking his usual route from Frederiksberg to the office, Henrik had pointed his car at the motorway out of Copenhagen and headed for Jutland, picking up speed as he went.

He had stayed away from Jensen, honouring his side of the bargain he had made with God in return for Matilde's safe return.

They were still in touch. Text messages didn't count, he told himself; it was seeing her that was dangerous.

The passing driver who had stopped by the roadside in the middle of nowhere on the island of Lolland, south of

Copenhagen, had thought he was dealing with the after-math of a freak accident when his headlights picked out the bloodied, naked girl, standing by the roadside with a baby in her arms. He had called the emergency services immediately.

The girl had led him to a van parked by an isolated barn, and what he had initially thought were three bodies turned out to be only two: a pregnant woman was found bleeding, unconscious, but alive.

A child of three was asleep in a car seat in the front of the van.

Inside the barn, a makeshift TV studio and a frightened nine-year-old girl.

Matilde's abduction and weeklong imprisonment would scar her for life, but there was hope that she might one day find happiness, like Lea's children, who were still so young.

For Lea herself, the road would be longer, with no guarantee of arrival. Her act of courage, killing her captor, marked the start of her journey.

Henrik would be following them all, from a distance, like he would follow Jensen.

Always.

The thought of her filled him with emotion, adding to the feeling deep inside of him that he couldn't control: lava, bubbling and rising.

The satnav led him to Horsens. The streets of the provincial city were like a re-run of years of arrests made against similar suburban backgrounds, houses staked out, bad news delivered. House fires, burglaries, destruction and death. Lives shattered for ever.

The red-brick bungalow with the name Ravnsbæk on the letterbox was unremarkable, like a thousand other Danish homes.

You couldn't tell that the worst thing had already happened here.

Tone had left her husband to join Henrik's team in Copenhagen as a detective sergeant, only to find herself killed senselessly by a criminal with nothing to lose.

The front garden was neatly kept, the low sunlight slowly melting the frost of the bushes and trees.

Henrik's breath steamed as he walked up the path to the front door, his vision already obscured by a hot mist.

He no more than sensed the shadow of Tone's widower passing behind the kitchen window. His visit was months overdue, to pay his respects, to tell the man how truly sorry he was.

He didn't need to ring the bell; the door was already opening as he fell to his knees and the tears began to spill, running out of him like a flood that would never stop.

76

'Are you ready?' said Margrethe.

'I think so,' said Jensen, glancing one last time round the hospital room at Riget, high above the sun-drenched streets of Copenhagen.

Was anyone ever really ready?

Gustav was almost entirely hidden by the enormous bouquet that had arrived by messenger a few hours ago.

No card.

She assumed they were from Henrik. The nurses had told her that he had been checking on her regularly since her admission.

'And are you sure you don't want to come home with me and Gustav, just for a few days while you get used to things?' Margrethe said. Gustav was back in her good books, the threat of banishment to his father's place in Aalborg lifted after he had provided her with evidence of Google Me's deception.

He still hadn't decided what he was going to do with his life. Plenty of time for that, Margrethe had said. If he wanted to become a journalist, he could still apply to journalism school. In the meantime, he was busy looking after Bodil's cat.

He had visited Jensen every day.

'Yes, I'm sure,' she said. 'Seeing as I have to build a new life, I may as well begin straightaway.'

Ernst Brøgger's call had come completely out of the blue, revealing the reason for Bodil's meeting with him – her solicitor – hours before she was murdered by Thomas on Katja's orders.

Her worldly assets had been destined for the coffers of the Cats Protection charity, but Bodil had changed her will at the last minute, leaving her flat on Peblinge Dossering to Jensen. 'It comes with the cat,' Brøgger had said. 'There should be enough money in her books and valuables to meet the inheritance tax obligation.'

'But I hardly knew her at all,' Jensen had protested. 'If I'd had even the slightest inkling that she was planning something like this, I would have stopped her.'

'Why?'

'I don't deserve it.'

'Much as I like cats, I think you're as worthy a beneficiary as any, and Bodil knew her own mind, as I keep telling you.'

A not insignificant sum set aside for Palle Dybdal was being disputed on the grounds of suspected coercion, after he had been found guilty of stealing from Bodil.

'Chop, chop, I'm illegally parked,' said Margrethe, laden with bags.

Jensen looked around the room one last time before grabbing the handle of her daughter's car seat. It was curiously light.

Her baby was still smaller than average. It had been touch and go for a long time, for both of them, but they were still here, still alive.

'What are you going to call her?' said Gustav.

'I'm not sure yet,' she said. Naming her had seemed like hubris.

On the screens in the neonatal wing, monitoring the heartbeat and oxygenation of the premature babies on the ward, she had simply been known as Baby Jensen.

'You've got to give her a name sometime. Everyone must have a name.'

'I suppose so,' she said, and headed for the door.

As she moved into the corridor, her phone rang. Unknown number.

Something, perhaps hesitation at the thought of bringing her child into the cold brightness of the February day, made her slide her finger to the right.

A male voice, deep, an accent she couldn't place. 'Hello Jensen.'

'Who's this?'

'Did you get the flowers? I asked for pink and white roses, seeing as you had a girl.'

'Excuse me, do we know each other?'

'You could say that,' said the man. 'I'm your father.'

Acknowledgements

Out of the Dark features many real-life places in Copenhagen, including Ørstedsparken, laid out in the late 1800s on the grounds of the city's old fortifications. Peblinge Lake exists, as does Peblinge Dossering, the beautiful tree-lined path running alongside it, but Bodil's yellow apartment building is definitely made up, as are the offices of *Dagbladet* and the Clausens' flat in Kleinsgade.

This book is a work of fiction, inspired by the efforts of the Danish police in finding and bringing to justice perpetrators of child sexual abuse in all its forms. As ever, I would like to thank special consultant in the police Lars Jung and his colleagues for their kindness and generosity through many conversations. Any mistakes are entirely my own. Writing is a solitary profession; a special thanks goes to my wonderful author colleagues for comradery and support, especially Lone Theils, Iben Albinus, Helen Pike and Julie Anderson. Thanks also to my agent Lena Stjernström, publishers Sarah and Kate Beal, copy editors extraordinaire Laura Macfarlane and Catherine Best, and all readers of the Jensen series. Finally, *Out of the Dark*, is dedicated to Nick Aldworth in gratitude for his love and encouragement.